"We shall hear instantly if any demand for ransom comes through. You know the importance of keeping the speaker talking long enough for the source to be traced?"

"Yes. I'm glad to do anything any time if it will help get Julie home s—

But suppose she is away home? Yeadings suggested to himself as he switched on the ignition. Winterton's explanation for the noise upstairs hadn't convinced him for a moment. You had to keep in mind that the man was a fiction writer with a ready imagination.

Could Julie still be in the house but moved elsewhere during the police search? Alternatively, had Julie somehow learned the details of her mother's running away and blamed her father for it? So was her own disappearance deliberate, intended as revenge on him?

As he swung the car to reenter the lane, Yeadings glanced back at the house. All the upstairs windows on this side were closed, but at one he caught the flutter of a white curtain as a watcher moved quickly away.

★

"A solid British procedural..."

—*Library Journal*

CLARE CURZON

DON'T LEAVE ME

W RLDWIDE.

TORONTO • NEW YORK • LONDON
AMSTERDAM • PARIS • SYDNEY • HAMBURG
STOCKHOLM • ATHENS • TOKYO • MILAN
MADRID • WARSAW • BUDAPEST • AUCKLAND

DON'T LEAVE ME

A Worldwide Mystery/September 2003

First published by St. Martin's Press, Incorporated.

ISBN 0-373-26469-0

Printed in U.S.A.

DON'T LEAVE ME

PROLOGUE

THE THREE STONE-BUILT cottages stand in a continuous row. From their cobbled forecourt a long driveway leads up to a country lane. At the rear their unfenced gardens slope gently to the river-bank where between willows you can glimpse a modern boathouse. A modest terrace, it was built originally for workers at Charbridge Mill, now long disused.

Two have been knocked together and gentrified inside with all mod cons. Outwardly they look little changed except for enlarged windows and one front door removed. Daniel Winterton owns them all now, lives in the converted pair, rents out the third.

He has closed down the computer and sits waiting in the comfortable, knocked-through sitting-room, an inner part of him gently seething, the surface in perfect control. A long-case clock chimes the quarter. He has barely moved since it struck eleven.

A car's tyres crunch gently on the drive, the engine note changes from throb to purr. The waiting man gets up and goes through to the kitchen. Headlights shine briefly through the darkened room. He moves close to the open window to listen, hears the engine cut, the driver's door slam and an instant quieter echo.

Who needs to do that—*ease* a car door shut? Nobody up to any good.

A long moment's silence before the garage door clangs. A single set of footfalls, the *click-click* of stiletto heels on stone flags. Her key in the kitchen lock.

He has shot both bolts. He pretends not to hear her call. She must go round to the front. She chooses to go by the long way, skirting their own double property, not past the Harburys' end cottage.

He lets her in when she rings, and she comes in flushed. That look in her eyes: a cat's bowl-of-cream satiety barely fading. But pretending to be put out, pouting. In genuine anger the carmined mouth would pull tight like a drawstring purse.

'You bolted the back door, and you knew I had to get in.'

'You know the rules: drawbridge goes up at eleven.' Spoken amiably, smiling: the perennial half-joke, but he's never acted on it before. 'Anyway, you're here now.'

He kisses her lightly, missing her cheek as she turns her head. She is taller than her husband. He gets her neck, below the ear. The bit vampires go for.

'Good film?' He doesn't wait for an answer. 'I'll put the kettle on.'

'Great. I'm thirsty.'

Bet you are. Dried out. Slut! 'Hot chocolate or Horlicks?'

'Choc, I guess.' She yawns, stretches. 'Can you leave it by my bed? I'll just take a shower.'

'Of course. I'll fill you a thermos.'

At the foot of the stairs she turns, remembers to ask, 'Did you get much done?'

'Finished that sticky chapter. I don't know why the thirteenth always presents a block.'

'Superstitious scruples, perhaps.' With that she flips off

her heels and goes up in her nylons. Mustn't scratch the woodwork.

Is that what he did—slipped his shoes off to quit the car? Or wore sneakers? Does he care that his wife may guess whose car he came home in? No, he'd have prepared some excuse, perhaps say casually, 'Caroline gave me a lift back. The Fiat has a flat. She overtook me slogging it on foot. God, but I'm tired. Think I'll turn in right away.'

Hogging the shower, Caroline sings down, 'Shan't be long.'

No, not long now, Daniel promises himself. *Just a few final details left to fill in.*

'OH BARRY, I DIDN'T HEAR the car,' Peg said, rising from the settee where she'd sat on one folded leg and now had to bend and rub the feeling back in.

He eased off his jacket and draped it over a chair back. 'Had to leave it at work. Bloody thing finally packed up. Magneto, I think. Lady Muck next door overtook me and I thumbed a lift. Have to bike in tomorrow.'

'Didn't she offer for the morning?'

He hesitated. 'Don't want to make a thing of it. Old Weirdo might misunderstand. Have to keep on the right side of our landlord.' The jocular tone was accompanied by a distinct curl of the lip.

'Oh Barry, calling them names. So disrespectful.' A soft rebuke.

He bit back a rush of anger. Peg was forever salaaming to imagined superiors; which meant everyone. He had once found it flattering and quaintly attractive, until he realised that he wasn't the only object of her kowtowing.

Peg had happened along when his spirits were at a low ebb and he'd needed gentle treatment. Now he was saddled with it. A wife you could divorce, but how get rid of a hanger-on? Shove her out the door and she'd be back through the window with her lavender-scented duster and bloody teapot.

He turned on her with a snarl. 'Respect should be earned. Winterton is a pompous little pillock. Anyway, I'm bushed. Going up now.'

He was snappy, and she could understand that: a magneto sounded expensive. She guessed it meant a replacement. And he'd had that wearisome uphill trek from the village before Mrs Winterton would have spotted him on the main road. 'Can I run you a bath, Barry?'

'Nuh. Too knackered. Don't fuss.'

'Shall I make some tea?' She winced, knowing that she'd done it again, before ever he snapped back.

Only this time he didn't, just stood gazing glassily into the distance for a moment and smiling to himself. Then, 'Eh? Nuh.'

He stretched, expanding his narrow chest. Under the shirtsleeves she watched his muscles flex and relax. He turned his lean, pale face on her and she was rewarded with the tail end of his Manilow smile. One lock of the straw-coloured hair dropped over one eye and she longed to stroke it back. 'Mebbe a nightcap.'

'I'll bring it up.'

'Yuh, do that.'

There was an almost empty bottle of Bell's in the sideboard. Enough for two glasses. She didn't need any. She'd pour him the one tonight. That left one over. He'd need a drink when she told him about the baby. Which couldn't be put off forever, but mustn't be brought up tonight because he was tired. It would be fatal just now.

CAROLINE WINTERTON ENJOYED her morning bath most in high summer when she could open the double windows on to the garden, inhale the country scents and feel she was some wild naiad running free in the fields and woods.

Or was it dryad? One haunted trees and the other rivers, as she seemed to remember. Well, a bit of both; amphibious perhaps, but definitely *au naturel.*

Listening for the distant, soft sounds of the weir, she felt the early sun warm her damp flesh through. It would be another gorgeous day and she had in mind just the place to spend the long afternoon—provided no clients upset her plans.

She heard the shower turn off in the next room and Daniel gently humming. Tunelessly. It was agony when he tried to sing. Being tone-deaf, he could make only the words recognisable. But he did know of his defect: had once said, watching a sunset with a colour-blind friend, 'I know what I'm missing in music when I realise what you miss in sight.'

Fortunately he never accompanied her to concerts; which guaranteed one other opportunity apart from her work when she could be free of the closet control freak.

She dressed in a peachy-patterned chiffon blouse and slim, bleached linen skirt; cream sling-back sandals; matching shoulder bag. The full-length bedroom mirrors gave back the reflection of a tall cool blonde, thickly waving hair to her shoulders, shadowed eyes which might be dark blue or slate green.

'All tits, teeth and tight buttocks,' Barry had said last night, enjoying her to the full. Coarse, but acutely satisfying.

She'd need to be careful. He could be addictive. And he wasn't someone she cared to appear with in public, not until she'd worked on him some more. He was too clearly all stud, but his physicality and brashness stimulated her; they made one wonder how far he'd go. Even how far he could get her going.

Spraying her hair at the open window, she heard the metallic rattle of his old bike over the flags behind the far cottage and smiled. Good. It would amuse her to speed past him in the BMW while he pedal-pushed up to his turn-off for the village. Pity it wasn't a wet day with some puddles to splash through. Get that quick flash of temper up. Get everything up.

'Caroline?' Daniel, appearing in the doorway, patting a neatly folded handkerchief into the breast pocket of his best tweed suit, was going to drop something on her. Whatever the day's expected heat, he invariably dressed in his country squire outfit when he was bound for the city. A perverse way of making himself noticed up there.

But this wasn't one of his London days. Or maybe he had warned her in advance and she'd not listened or forgotten. Whichever, it appeared he had a date with his agent.

'Lunching with Geraldine,' he explained himself. 'She rang last night. Terrible row going on in the background, but I managed to grasp that there's some American she wants me to meet. Film chappy. It's worth a try, don't you think?'

Certainly, if it meant big money and prolonged visits to California. 'Terrible row as in fighting or partying?' she asked coolly, not granting him even a tentative compliment on a perhaps-option on a film. He'd already done a couple of scripts for TV, but never anything yet for the big screen.

'Fighting? Partying? To my mind it's much the same.' He gave her his tight smile; switch on, switch off. God, it would really gut him to let out a belly laugh.

'Geraldine's usually a bit lavish, so no need for a meal tonight. I'll make myself a sandwich from something in the fridge.' He was moving off, jingling his car keys.

'Right. Are you going already?'

'There's some research I need to do up at Colindale.'

Caroline considered this. All morning at the British Library newspaper section followed by a prolonged lunch meant a whole day in London, keeping him safely out of her hair and the house. Distance itself being enchantment.

He aimed a peck at her cheek, actually made contact, smirked again, and wished her, 'Cheeribye then,' an expression he knew she hated because it dated him—and therefore herself—so.

'I'll expect you when I see you,' she conceded, allowing him to clear off before she made her own move.

But not before I've seen you, Daniel promised silently. He waved a hand amiably and left.

BARRY MORGAN STOOD ON the pedals until he was out of breath, then sank back to the saddle and plodded desperately. Anything, short of a stroke or heart attack, to ensure Caroline didn't overtake him on the way, snooting past with her patrician nose in the air and a derisory wiggle of the fingers at him from her steering wheel.

And he succeeded in escaping her, receiving instead a hoot of recognition from an overtaking silver Merc which he recognised as her husband's. The front seat headrests prevented him seeing if there was a passenger by the man's side.

This was a break from Winterton's routine. He normally settled to his word processing after breakfast, and rarely made early sorties by car during the week. Barry wondered uneasily what it signified, but the toot of recognition was surely evidence that the man felt no bile towards him.

WITH HER BRIEFCASE DUMPED on the floor beside her, Caroline sat on the edge of her bedroom chair, fuming because the nanny was late. She supposed the girl's excuse would be that she'd stayed on later the evening before. She thought she could get away with it because she hadn't known that Daniel would be replaced this morning by herself.

The delay was eating into business time. Caroline visualised the stack of mail on her desk awaiting answers, Dana, the Girl Friday, licking her lips to get at it herself, enthroned in the big leather chair. Damn Daniel for his selfish decision to take off without warning.

Not that she dare make much of a fuss, since the understanding had been that she only went back to work if the child was otherwise covered.

The thought reminded her of Julie's existence. There was no sound from her anywhere upstairs. In the kitchen a thin trail of soggy cereal led from an upturned bowl and a spillage of milk on the polished hardwood floor, to peter out by the door to Daniel's computer room. Which stood—ajar.

He must have left it so, because at just under three years old Julie couldn't manage the handle.

Oh, my God, her sticky fingers all over his manuscript! But no, she was seated in the office chair staring up at a flickering screen and clasping the operative mouse between both pudgy little paws.

'Your father will skin you alive!' It was out before she could think. Damn! Small children took everything so bloody literally.

Julie's mouth puckered and the blue eyes shut, squeezing out fat tears. She seemed to be holding her breath, so Caroline slapped her smartly to make her suck air in.

The childish threat of tears, putting the adult in the wrong; little manipulator! Where had she learned to do that? She reminded Caroline of that frightful girl in the

William books: 'I'll thcweam and I'll thcweam till I'm thick!'

Loud protests came next, from a wide, square mouth. The child's face had gone from white to crimson. Caroline had to pick her up under one arm, switch off the computer, firmly close the door behind them and return to the kitchen. A smeary stickiness transferred itself to the peachy chiffon blouse as small clinging fingers made rodent inroads into her flesh. Dear God, where was that bloody nanny? Next there'd be a phone call from *her,* calling in sick!

Deposited upright on the kitchen floor, Julie instantly peed into her frilly pyjamas. At least the flow had missed Caroline's skirt.

Daniel had already removed the soggy nappy the child still used overnight. It was the first thing he did when he went in to say, 'Hello, Dolly!' each morning. Or, rather, tried to sing it. Anything to make Julie chuckle.

But she was meant to be potty-trained by day, wasn't she?

Bath her, Caroline decided, despairing of her own top layer of clothes. She carried the still sobbing child upstairs and ran a mix of warmish water on to a collection of plastic ducks, dolphins and farm animals.

Julie became instantly silent and obligingly started removing her pyjamas. With the top half off she peered through the neck hole and complained in a deep, throaty voice, 'Katy gives me bubbles.'

Above the gushing of taps Caroline heard the slam of the front door and the nanny's cheerful, 'Julie, come and see what I've got.'

Caroline let the child go, tempted by bribery. She didn't approve of spoiling the child—she'd spoken to the girl about it—but still Katy went on bringing little presents, buying affection. If she hadn't provided such splendid qualifications Caroline would have started looking for a replacement, hard as good nannies were to get.

'You're late,' she called from her bedroom, sorting a fresh outfit from the wardrobe rails.

Katy came to the door, Julie in her arms. 'Didn't Mr Winterton explain? He gave me an extra half-hour this morning to make up for last night.'

'No, he didn't say anything. Not even that he'd be off early himself. Men! Don't they make you sick?'

Katy grinned, gently pinching Julie's plump arm which then joined the other round her neck. 'Who loves you, Baby?'

'I'm not a baby. I'm almost three now. Three-four-five-six!'

'So who loves you?'

'Katy loves me.'

'Doesn't she just!' And by then they were in the bathroom, with Julie prattling and Katy turning off taps, letting out the excess water and swishing scented foam in.

Caroline binned her discarded clothes, smoothed the new aquamarine suit over her hips and marched downstairs to let herself out.

BARRY OBSERVED FROM the corner of his eye the minute hand pass the hour hand at eleven, and he silently cursed the indecisive couple he was meant to be dealing with. He willed them to make a selection: to say, 'We'd like to look over this one, and maybe that.' Then he could book them in and pass them on to Maisie, who'd be glad to get any bonus that might arise later. *If* the doddering finally gave way to a firm offer to purchase.

'Is that really all you have of the sort we're looking for?' the woman asked for the second time.

'Unless you're willing to consider the next price level.

We find that two hundred and twenty thousand is a market rim. Above it you must expect prices to go up by larger steps.'

'No,' the man said hurriedly. 'Two hundred thousand is our absolute limit. Only we had hoped there'd be something more central, handy for the shops.'

'There's a growing interest in country cottages,' Barry countered. 'With improved bus services, this is a good time to snap up something before there's a run on them and the prices rocket. That's what I've just done myself. Gone for a fabulous riverside house with boathouse and jetty. Got it for a song,' he lied.

'Really? Well, if an estate agent moves outside town, I suppose it must make sense. Let's have another look at the one on the Mardham road. Mind, the country buses need to be as frequent as you say, because we've only the one car.'

While they juggled again with the heavy albums, still murmuring about the inflated house prices in the Thames Valley, Barry was aware of Maisie lifting the receiver to answer a phone enquiry. She said, 'Hello?' three times, shook the phone, grimaced and replaced the handset. 'No one there,' she called across to him and returned to twirling a lock of gingery hair round her finger.

'Miss Barnes, will you look after Mr and Mrs Potter for a moment?'

As she came across to take his place he made for the rear quarters, entered the toilet, sat and tapped out the Delphic Galleries' number on his mobile phone. Caroline, waiting for his return call, answered at once.

'So?' he whispered.

'This is Mrs McQueen,' she gushed. 'I'd like another look at that raaaather attractive place we saw the other day. Pollards Mount, wasn't it?'

'I bet you would. Caroline's mount more like. It's all right; I'm ringing you back from the bog. Nobody can hear. What time?'

'I'll pick you up at twelve forty-five. With a picnic hamper and chilled wine.'

'You know our house rules. I have to use my own car.'

'That rubbish—security precautions in case I mean to kidnap you! I remember; and you have to make me sign in. But if you think I'll show up at your office you're crazy. Drive round and park at the station. I'll pick you up there. And don't keep me waiting.'

'Yes ma'am, no ma'am, three bags full, ma'am,' he told the mobile as she hung up. Getting a bit uppity, that lady. He'd have to do something about it.

He went back to the couple who were making moves towards leaving. 'There's not anything there we really fancy,' said the man, suddenly decisive.

'We'll drop by again,' said the woman falsely.

They wouldn't. If they'd any sense they'd go to a bigger firm in town, see what Marchants had on their computers, modest mortgage seekers like that.

'Sorry, Mr Morgan,' Maisie apologised to him wretchedly.

It didn't matter. Barry was feeling chuffed about the coming picnic. 'A pair of no-hopers,' he consoled her. 'They'd never make the deposit for the places they were looking at. You get to recognise their sort.'

'Cuppa coffee, Mr Morgan? It's gone eleven.'

'Yeah, Maisie, why not? And you can take first lunch break at twelve thirty. Take the spare office key. I've got a second viewing booked for later, so I'll need you back to reopen.'

All eventualities covered, he told himself. All systems very much go. He turned to the office calendar and marked a small red dot on the date, next to the one he'd put on yesterday's, Thursday, July sixteenth.

ONE

A LITTLE OVER EIGHT YEARS later, something occurred to bring the case back into prominence. Mike Yeadings, now a detective superintendent responsible for Serious Crimes, puckered his brows as he worked on recall.

His right hand fondled the pint tankard from which he'd gratefully downed a foaming third. Towards the end of a relentlessly hot day, almost literally stuck at his desk, his feet had outgrown his shoes. He already regretted agreeing to meet the long-winded DI Dawson after work. No matter how pleasant this beer garden, he silently longed for short sleeves and sandals. He could be cooler and more relaxed at home.

He grunted at the man opposite him. 'Winterton. Daniel Winterton, you say. It does sound familiar.'

'Apparently he's a successful fiction writer.'

'Got him,' Yeadings pronounced. 'His wife went missing. It must be at least eight years back. I was waiting to be made up to DI myself, with hopes that the right result might speed the process.'

'But no joy there?'

'It turned out that she'd run off with a lover.' Careerwise it had been disappointing. At first it had seemed to be a possible case of abduction or murder, but then a young man's disappearance on the same day had scotched police suspicion of violence. They had managed to trace the couple as far as the Canaries, then the trail went cold. So no

corpse to meet senior police expectations; just prolonged
heartache for another little family deserted by a philander-
ing woman.

He recalled that Winterton had had a small daughter of
the same age as the Yeadings' own.

'Julie,' he recalled aloud.

Dawson nodded. 'Yeah. Jude, she calls herself. Kids go
for the androgynous these days. Last seen by the cleaner
when she left at eleven this morning. School holidays. It
seems the kid raided the fridge, then took her boat out, a
dinghy with an outboard motor. We found it moored downstream about half a mile away, near a path to the main
road. Her father was working in his study. He never noticed
she'd scarpered. He'd planned they'd go out for lunch later,
but it seems the kiddo had other ideas.'

'History repeating itself,' Yeadings commented absently.
'An unlucky man: first the wife disappears, then the daughter. Took out her boat, eh? So they're still living at the
same place? Gentrified cottages out by the old Charbridge
Mill?'

He remembered their little boat from the first occasion
that he'd met the child. With only negatives to report back
to Winterton, he'd been waiting on the jetty when it came
puttering round the bend in the river, the father red-faced
at the tiller, a knotted handkerchief over his head against
the burning sun. The tiny girl had been perched in the bows
under a makeshift awning, her whitish fair hair tied up in
two bunches. A very pretty little three-year-old with fine
features, quite unlike the puppy-blunt Down's syndrome
face of Yeadings' own Sally.

The thought, as ever, roused a dull, hard pain inside him,
and instantly he condemned himself for the disloyalty of
that moment all those years ago; self-disgust at the remembered comparison.

His Sally was very precious, had a generous heart and her own special kind of beauty. He couldn't say he wouldn't have her different, but he loved her fiercely the way she was. He and Nan were proud of the way she was growing up to face her difficulties.

'She'd be eleven now,' he said for Dawson's benefit, meaning the other child, measured by his own.

'Yeah. Eleven years old, last seen at eleven on the eleventh of August. Odd, that coincidence. To be perfect it should have been November.'

'She'd be less likely to go boating alone in winter.' Yeadings' voice came over distant and chilling. The man from Juveniles was reminded of seniority and the need to show some instant efficiency.

'What I wanted to pick your brains on—'

'My memory.' The superintendent wasn't going to allow any flattery.

'...was whether you thought the mother was likely to have come back and be hanging around aiming to snatch the kiddo. The point is that, before skedaddling, Jude helped herself to more food than even the greediest kid could stomach at a sitting.'

'So you're thinking she took enough to share with someone else, or planned on being away for quite a time?'

'It looks that way.'

'You're already treating it as a Misper?'

'We're acting cautious because of her age. Too many kids lately have ended as nutters' victims. So—a local scour today, and begin the full-scale search at first light tomorrow if she hasn't surfaced. Her father's already jumping on everyone's back, including the Chief Constable's.'

Yeadings recalled Winterton: fortyish, sandy, moustached, dapper and erect, thus looking taller than his actual medium height; lean, but not inconsiderable; a closed, rather unmemorable face. He'd demanded that every stone should be turned, every reported sighting, however wild, be scrupulously followed up in the search for his wife.

It had left him desolate when at first all avenues led to dead ends. In police eyes he was prime suspect for a possible murder because statistics pointed that way, he being her nearest if not dearest. Then proof had come of her flight to Lanzarote and the case had cooled. Some inquiries had continued, seeking confirmation about the woman's whereabouts, her lover and the missing money, but there was less urgency, and no police heartache when the trail died out. By then it was no longer their concern. Adult runaways had every right to freedom of action, provided they weren't guilty of crime. Broken marriages didn't qualify as such: joint bank accounts permitted legal access by either spouse.

Only moderately well-to-do then, and badly hit by the emptying of their shared bank account, Winterton had still been willing to offer a tempting reward for any information leading to discovery of the couple's whereabouts.

It had disturbed the tenacious young Sergeant Yeadings. The husband's offer was unexpected, a bit freaky, as though the wife—Caroline, he remembered now—were a valuable piece of artwork, or as though he was anxious to deal with her possible ransomers; or as if Winterton gambled on the greed of the womanising young man who had gone off with her. In that last assumption, according to local opinion, he might not have been so far off the truth.

But Yeadings knew that if Winterton were obliged to pay up and the wife came back, it wouldn't have been to the same well-heeled lifestyle which the three had enjoyed until then.

As a family man himself Yeadings had been left uneasy— not that any rising CID officer could afford a bleeding-heart tendency over those met in the line of duty. Not becoming involved was an integral lesson in the job. He had come close to crossing the line only because in a wild moment he'd imagined himself in the man's position. Fleetingly, because Nan and this Caroline were never two of a kind. No way would Nan have walked out on him and little Sally.

Winterton could well be overwhelmed by this second loss. It was something Yeadings didn't care to dwell on.

'I don't see,' he said to Dawson, 'that I can be of much use to you. I never met the woman, so I can't speculate on what she might have done. She didn't display any great consideration for the child when she upped and went off with her lover.'

And as far as that concerned him, it must be the end of the matter. A case for Juveniles, hopefully never to qualify for Crimes of Violence.

Later, at home, though, sockless and in sandals, at ease in the garden hammock where he'd replaced Nan scurrying indoors to answer the cooker's buzzing, Yeadings was left to rebuild the missing-wife case in his mind.

There had been albums of family snapshots, mostly taken in the garden, on the river, or on holidays in brilliant sunshine. Little Julie was there in many of them, right from babyhood, shawled in Winterton's arms as they left the nursing home after the birth. But most often she was the single subject, and Caroline too usually appeared alone; which made Winterton the photographer.

He recalled clearly the enlarged photograph Winterton had offered him, removing it with trembling fingers from a silver frame on his writing desk. Caroline was beautiful, a willowy blonde with high, Slav cheekbones and wonderful teeth. She had been caught from above by the camera, about to climb the river-bank from the mooring, one arm raised to brush away willow wands that trailed towards the shaded water. Her smile was something special. If directed

at me, Yeadings had thought then—wow, better *not* think
of it.

If he had to sum her up in one word it would be 'fetch-
ing'. Which was why, once they started probing, quite a
list had grown of those who'd been fetched, including her
own doctor (from whose practice she had suddenly and
discreetly transferred a few months earlier, presumably to
save him from accusations of unprofessional conduct)
through various clients and artists whom she met as manager of the art gallery, to this latest toy boy they'd un-
earthed from right next door: her husband's tenant and,
according to Yeadings' boss then, the long-retired DI Calthrop, her 'bit of rough'.

As the picture emerged it had seemed that the eclectic
lady had played a very wide field, possibly looking for what
she had not found at home. Where Winterton seemed col-
ourless these others were the reverse. How, Yeadings had
asked himself at the time, had such a woman ever come to
marry the man?

He remembered asking Nan and she had chortled at the
question, then turned deadly serious as she considered the
implications. '*How* and *why* are very short words,' she'd
said, 'and they take a lifetime to answer in full. Why did I
marry you, for instance?'

'Momentary madness?'

'Well, of course. But there must have been something
else, don't you think? Sex, naturally; the kind of loneliness
that a busy career gives rise to; availability; your persis-
tence; an intuitive knowledge that we were right together,
complementary but both sharing the same standards and
ambitions; fondness. All of that, and also things I'm only
beginning to understand after all these years that we've
shared.

'But I know a virtue of yours that I couldn't have accepted any man without; and that's kindness. Just simple kindness. That could be one thing a dull man might offer too. Something such a woman could feel safe with, so that she could afford her adventures and still get away with everything she wanted.'

'Am *I* dull?' he'd asked, appalled.

'Heavens, no; any more than I'm promiscuous. We're talking types, not us.'

Anyway, however complaisant the husband, Caroline Winterton hadn't chosen to come home and be forgiven, so Winterton had never parted with his reward money. She had either settled finally for her toy boy or travelled on to pastures new. The kind man—if that's what Winterton was—had been left with a small motherless child to devote his loving care to. Until now.

At the sound of children's voices Yeadings removed his gaze from gently swaying leaves above him. Sally made her way down the sloping path from the house, pushing her little brother on his tricycle with total concentration. Yeadings watched their unsteady progress as Luke, feet short of the pedals and still not co-ordinating eyes and steering, made wild zigzags into the grass verge to either side. The little girl heaved him back and sorted him straight. This was his Sally, at the missing child's present age, with her younger brother.

That was something Dawson had neglected to mention and he to ask: what other children were there? In the years after his first loss, had Winterton divorced the runaway, married a second time and provided siblings for his little daughter? If not, who did she talk to, run to when she was unhappy? What had happened to that nice nanny who'd helped both her and her father through the bad times?

DI Dawson would surely know. Grumbling silently at himself for being unable to let a question rest unanswered,

Yeadings rolled out of the hammock and padded in through the patio doors to reach for the telephone. Nan, watching for the number he pressed out, sighed. Couldn't the man ever forget his blessed work for even half an hour?

The nanny—Katy Anson, he learned from Dawson—had married, and was now Katy Bisset, with two little ones of her own. Dawson hadn't needed to scout it out because George Bisset was himself in the Thames Valley force, an Area uniformed PC and a fellow member of the local darts team which Dawson seldom got enough time for. After a tournament he'd once joined others for supper at the Bissets' semi and been well received by Katy. Nice girl, devilish good cook.

And no, Winterton had never remarried, Caroline not being assumed deceased, and he never having tried for a divorce on the grounds of desertion. There was no gossip locally about the man. Either he was unusually discreet or had given up on the idea of women. A tad pathetic really.

So it would be her schoolmates that young Julie spent most of her leisure time with?

Have to go into that tomorrow, Dawson agreed. Interview the headmistress and staff, get a list of close friends from them and the child's father. Probably wouldn't be the easiest thing to contact the children, since school had broken up a couple of weeks back and everyone could be off on vacation. Still, the kid could yet turn up unharmed.

Dawson's tone changed from grumble to apology. Look, he was sorry to have set up a hare for Yeadings. No need as yet to think the case would be passed on to Serious Crimes. He'd never meant more than to ask casually if the Superintendent recalled anything special from the previous case, et cetera.

An appeal to coppers' gossip, Yeadings acknowledged. It had its values, something he never underestimated. Many

a missing link had been provided from words unthinkingly
dropped in the canteen by some beat or patrol man not
involved in a case.

At least now he'd had one question answered. Katy the
ex-nanny was kept busy enough these days without maintaining a close connection with the Wintertons. Not, he admitted to himself, wandering back to the dappled shade of
the apple trees, that knowing that was ever likely to be of
any use to him. Instead his mind slipped into past tense,
into himself as an ambitious younger copper; easy enough,
since it was so much the same kind of day.

'SERGEANT,' OLD CALTHROP had addressed him, with grim
conviction, 'we'll be looking for a body here.'

Yeadings knew why: because the DI didn't like the look
of Daniel Winterton, who, despite the modestly converted
cottage, had kept a couple of decent cars in his double
garage, and whose accent was clearly the outcome of a
privately funded education. And quite another reason was
that the DI was due for retirement in no more than three
weeks, and was suddenly determined to go out on a high
trumpet note.

A murder classification meant he could draw on anything
up to fifty extra men and women from over the force, provided that his super accepted his assessment. He took Yeadings along as a supposed ally when he went to put his case.

'*Possible* murder,' their super had cautiously allowed.
'Get all other options eliminated fast and then we'll see. I
don't want a lot of yahoo and expense if the lady's simply
gone home to mother.' He glanced enquiringly at Yeadings
who kept his mouth tight shut and his gaze on the ceiling.

'There isn't a mother,' Calthrop enjoyed telling him.
'And we've drawn blanks with the woman's special cronies.'

'I'll see what uniformed branch can do to expedite matters. House-to-house enquiries and so on.'

'There aren't any neighbours either, except a young couple renting the adjoining cottage.' Calthrop spoke with evident satisfaction.

Next morning Yeadings had taken a young WPC along when he went to question the nanny and child. Winterton sat in on the interview, sunk in an armchair, virtually catatonic but occasionally stirring to agree with some statement from Katy.

It was Katy who had seemingly been the last to see Caroline Winterton before she left. She had been supervising little Julie's morning bath before taking her out for the day and hadn't noticed whether Mrs Winterton had luggage with her as she went downstairs. There had been none waiting in the hall. She couldn't say about the car. It was possible any packing and loading might have been done between Mr Winterton's departure and her own arrival.

'Did Mummy have a big bag, a suitcase, with her, lovey?' the policewoman knelt to ask, but Julie hid her face against Katy's knee. All that could be got out of her was a wretched whisper, 'I weed in my 'jamas.'

Katy was gently rubbing the child's back. 'Never mind. We popped them in the washing machine and watched the bubbles go round, didn't we? Accidents do happen. We can't stop them every time.'

'Mummy squashed me.'

Yeadings assumed she'd been holding the child close to say goodbye. So maybe the mother was emotional, preparing not to see her baby for some time? He turned to the nanny. 'Can you give me a rundown on everything that happened here yesterday morning?'

'Well, to begin with, I was later than usual. Twenty minutes actually, due to the bus times, though Mr Winter-

ton had given me the half-hour off. Because I'd stayed a
bit later the evening before.'

'Why would that be?'

'Well, Mrs Winterton was out and he wouldn't risk cooking his supper while Julie was running loose in the kitchen.'

'I'm always scared she'll reach up and burn herself,'
Winterton said. 'I was frying liver, you see, and it spits.'
He sank back into silence.

'What time was that?' Yeadings asked.

Katy took over again. 'Sevenish, I suppose. Julie goes to
bed between seven thirty and seven forty-five as a rule. Her
daddy, or sometimes her mummy, will read her a story and
then draw the curtains.'

He didn't miss the 'sometimes'. It seemed Julie was
Daddy's girl. That could be some compensation for the
child if he was left as the single parent.

Yeadings turned back a couple of pages in his notebook
to Winterton's statement about Caroline's return at eleven
fifteen that night. She had not struck him as unduly excited.
She had supposedly been to see a film with an old school-
friend (though later this Helen Masters had denied the fact).
On arriving home Caroline had said she was tired and gone
for a shower before turning in.

The interview came clearly back to Yeadings' memory.
'I made her a thermos of hot chocolate,' Winterton had
broken in suddenly, as though it had happened ages ago.
'She was thirsty, and she often likes to have something by
her if she wakes in the night.'

Thoroughly domesticated, Yeadings had noted; but then
Winterton was a book-writing house-husband while his
wife went out earning. It was hardly the same situation as
with himself and Nan. More often than not when the job
overran so much that Nan had already gone to bed, his

supper was waiting in the fridge for him to reheat and he'd have to creep upstairs to kiss Sally as she slept.

'Could I see the bedroom?'

It turned out to be Caroline's room exclusively, large and lavishly furnished, the colours pastel, the bed and drapes softly swagged. The husband's was next to it, with the communicating door at present wide open.

Through there the style was simpler, almost austere, a man's room with a single bed under a tailored cover. Again Yeadings found himself thinking: not our lifestyle at all. He wondered about Winterton, whether after the child's arrival sex had taken a back seat.

Caroline's walk-in wardrobes, their mirror doors opened, appeared as full of empty hangers as clothes. 'There's a lot missing,' Katy whispered. She had accompanied him upstairs, leaving Winterton to take care of Julie below.

'She had heaps of wonderful clothes. It does look as if—'

Calthrop would point out that the husband could have removed them. He'd had time enough before the police visit. They would need to get a SOCO looking for snagged threads in the boot of his Mercedes. Caroline's car was gone, of course, not sighted since she'd driven to work on the Friday. A pale blue BMW, its licence number had been notified throughout Thames Valley, but no sightings had so far been reported.

'Do you know what luggage she had?'

Katy shook her head. 'I'm not sure, but I know where the bags ought to be. I went up in the loft once to bring a grip down for Mrs Winterton. She had a number of cases up there.'

'Let's have a look then, shall we? Is there a ladder?'

Katy fetched the pole used to spring the trap open, and they watched an aluminum ladder begin automatically to descend in two stages.

'That's crafty,' Yeadings appreciated. 'Something like that appeals to the couch potato in me.'

'Mr Winterton fixed it up. He's clever like that, very gadgety. It's pressure-triggered, like the light in a fridge. He showed me once how it works.'

Yeadings, already halfway up into the roomy loft, could see the little motor for himself. A set of ceiling lights had also come on, worked from the same sensor. He checked by pressing the stud which the ladder's removal had released, and the place was instantly plunged into darkness. He let go and the lights came back on.

The fully floored room was tidily stacked with unneeded items of upholstered furniture, four white-painted wooden chests, and matching shelves along one wall which were filled with paperback books arranged alphabetically by author.

On his way to the luggage Yeadings opened each of the chests in turn. Three held an assortment of household china, curtains and bric-a-brac. The fourth was crammed with electrical components, several old-fashioned table lamps, ceiling roses, spare fuses, light bulbs, extension cables and fitments. But no body, despite being capacious enough to take a good-sized man when folded.

Katy had climbed through the trap and now stood beside him. 'The cases are over there. I'm not sure how many there were, but I'm pretty sure some are missing now.'

She went closer. 'Yes, there was a matching set of three, a sort of honey colour with maroon braid straps. They've gone.'

'Would they all fit in the boot of the BMW?'

'I should think so. Mr Winterton would know for certain because he carried them out to her car last time Mrs Winterton went off to an auction up north.'

Yeadings' ears pricked up. 'When would that have been?'

'Back before Easter. I'm not sure of the date. He could tell you.'

'Then I'd better go down and ask him.'

He stood below in the corridor and waited for the ladder to disappear, but it didn't. 'How do you make the thing go back?'

'There's a button on the far side.'

Yeadings found and pushed it. Accompanied by the whirring of the invisible motor the contraption started to slide up into the roof space. He had to assume that when it was again in position the lights would be extinguished, it being the sort of thing you must take on trust, again as with fridges. As a comfortingly non-hi-tech finish, Katy was obliged to shut the trap with the pole she'd used to open it.

'I've just been checking on the luggage in your loft, and I'm impressed,' Yeadings told Winterton when he regained the lounge. 'You're a talented electrician. Was that your original line of work?'

Winterton seemed momentarily to shake off his lethargy. 'No. As a young man I spent a couple of years training to become an architect, but decided I couldn't stand the accountancy and law involved. I wanted to get to grips with the houses themselves, being more a handy sort of person, so I dropped out. Without a proper job, I turned to mapping out some ideas for a story I'd had in my mind for a while, and actually got it published. Then the writing bug really bit me.

'My early books didn't make much at first, but then I wrote one that went down well in the States, and my name caught on with the public. Which justified my staying home and working from here. I did all the alterations to the cottages as a sort of hobby, with help from a plasterer. I enjoy DIY. It gives me a breather from the written word.'

'Have you done any renovations lately?'

'Not indoors. But I've made a start on a rockery for—for Caro. Not sure now that I'll ever finish, though the site's been prepared and some of the stones are delivered.'

'I'd like to see it. I'm a bit of a gardener myself.'

It didn't deceive the man. He gave the detective a bruised stare. 'Of course, Sergeant. But I haven't buried my wife there. You'd better come and check.'

Yeadings glanced away. 'I'm sorry, sir. We have to cover all possibilities. So while we're on the subject can you show me the cellar?'

'There isn't any cellar.' Winterton's tone was bitterly distant. 'There was one when we first came but I had it blocked off. It was under the enlarged kitchen, and the floor there's been covered with ceramic tiles for a matter of years. We'll go out by the back way and you can see for yourself.'

'Thank you, sir.'

He was quite right. There had been no recent disturbance to the sealed floors anywhere in the downstairs rooms, and this included all cupboard space.

The mechanically dug site for the rockery was something else. It was extensive and the soil freshly turned.

DI Calthrop, Yeadings knew, would relish having every inch of it excavated, by sweating, spade-wielding coppers.

TWO

TOMORROW, DS YEADINGS had hoped, someone would phone in a sighting of Caroline Winterton. Then they might determine whether the case was an abduction or a desertion. Or indeed she might turn up in person, or send a message. Cases of domestic strife were becoming too common, time-consumers that the Serious Crimes squad didn't need to have gumming up the works. Meanwhile he re-routed Winterton's anxious call to his superior, enjoying a relaxed Saturday at home.

Informed that the man's wife had failed to return on the previous night, DI Calthrop had grimmer hopes: that with the required passing of twenty-four hours some sinister find would signal the all-important start of a murder hunt.

With this promising possibility in mind he turned up in person and sketched out allocations for the next two days: plans which eventually included assigning DC Ward, a foxy-faced but naïve young transfer to CID, to interview the Harburys in Winterton's rented cottage next door.

Ward, reminded by a distant peal of church bells that it was Sunday and everyone else's rest day, arrived on the doorstep at a little before ten thirty. He found only the woman there, a slim brunette with doelike dark eyes and delicate facial bones. She informed him for his notes that she was called Peg. No, not Margaret. Peg was actually her baptismal name. Her parents had insisted, despite a bossy young curate with a passion for the saints.

She told him that Barry didn't care for the name much either. He said it sounded like something used to hang up the washing or secure the tent guys. He had a sense of humour, Barry. Every syllable of which opinion DC Ward transmitted into his private version of Pitman shorthand. He had her spell out the man's name, however, which he rendered in longhand.

'That would be your husband?'

'Er, yes.' She was busy pouring boiling water into the teapot during the admission. Ward observed her unease and wrote down 'partner' with a query.

'Well, actually Harbury is my surname. Barry's is Morgan. I signed the rental agreement with Mr Winterton, you see, so it's my name we're known by. He never asked if we were actually married.' Her face was flushed, and not from steam from the kettle.

Ward made the alteration to his notes. 'Right. Barry Morgan, then.' He had already decided that this lady was a sweet innocent, her over-chattiness due to nerves. Her hands were shaking. She had red-rimmed eyes and an occasional sniff which he put down to heavy pollen from pink lilies on the window-sill, which was also exciting his hay fever. He determined to be tactful with her: no call immediately to suggest linking the next-door people with suspicions of desertion or foul play.

'We're making a few general inquiries about people in this neighbourhood,' he assured her, 'and it's possible you could help us.'

'But I don't know any neighbours. I mean, we've only lived here about eight months and it's a good quarter-mile to the next house. You'd do better to ask the Wintertons next door. They've lived here for years.'

He nodded. She had been out for most of yesterday, he

knew, and so had missed the preliminary police visit to Winterton.

'We'll be getting round to them for sure. Still, since you know them, let's start there. What sort of people are the Wintertons? Do you find them easy to get on with, or…?'

'They're really nice. He writes novels, and Mrs Winterton works at an art gallery in Aylesbury. They have a dear little girl. She's nearly three, and she has a nanny who comes in every day. Except weekends, usually.'

'Do you see a lot of them?'

That seemed to stump her. 'We rent from them. Living right close, we try not to be a nuisance. I mean, they're not the sort of folks who'd want you to pop in, so we're careful. And we were lucky to get this place. It was cheap because not everybody likes living so far out, but Barry thought we should snap it up as soon as it came on the agency's books for letting.'

'What agency would that be?'

'Wright's Homefinders, in the village. Barry's the manager there.'

'I see. Do you work there too?'

'No, I went in first looking for a flat. And to sell Mother's house after she died. That's when we met. But I'd be useless in an office. I'll show you what I do.'

She let him take over the tea tray and follow her through into the living-room. There was a flat cardboard box lying on the lid of the old-fashioned music centre and she brought it across to open for him. Wrapped in tissue paper inside were three silk blouses in pastel colours, each with rows of pin-tucking and fine machine-stitched embroidery.

'I work from home and do sewing for a couple of shops. These were ones I did for my City and Guilds certificate. Yesterday I took them as samples to a possible new client who imports cotton from Egypt.' She folded the tissue paper tenderly back round the blouses, and now there was no tremor in her hands. DC Ward congratulated himself on having won her confidence.

Despite spending most of every day in the cottage she had little enough to tell him about the neighbouring family, who appeared to have over-impressed her. Even the child's nanny qualified for the same unstinting admiration. 'If ever I had a little girl,' she said wistfully, 'I'd want to be just like Katy is with Julie.'

Katy the nanny, not Caroline the mother, he noted. That seemed to underline DS Yeadings' first impression of the set-up *chez* Winterton. 'And Mr Winterton—how does he get on with his wife and the little girl?'

'I've never met anyone like him,' she said. 'He's wonderful. He can cook, and he'll do anything for them. You should see him playing with little Julie in the garden. He's so patient and gentle. They're a picture together.' This was again what Yeadings' notes had implied. Ward surmised that DI Calthrop's thirst for murder wouldn't get much mileage here.

'Mrs Winterton's away from home at the moment,' he ventured. 'Did you happen to see her leave on Friday morning?'

Peg had done. She'd been at the bedroom window fixing her hair before going for the bus, when Mrs Winterton ran out to her car.

'Ran?'

'Yes. She was in a hurry. A bit later than usual, but her husband had brought the car round to the front for her before he left. He's thoughtful that way.'

'A very smart lady, Mrs Winterton, I believe. Did you happen to notice what she was wearing?'

'Yes. A lovely silk suit. A sort of turquoise. No; more like aquamarine.'

That was interesting: the husband had stated she was in a pinky top and a white skirt. So either he was as blind as women accused most husbands of being, or else she had changed her clothes before leaving. Or for some obscure reason the man had chosen to lie.

'Had she any luggage with her?'

'Not that I—' Peg Harbury stopped in mid-sentence and fixed enormous, shocked eyes on him. 'Saw,' she added lamely. 'Oh, you don't think, do you…?'

All her confidence had drained away in an instant. Ward wanted to put an arm round her and murmur, 'There, there.' Instead he closed his notebook and slipped the rubber band tidily over it.

'There seems to be some difficulty locating her car,' he said in half explanation. Better that this poor girl should be bothered over a car than a neighbour. 'I don't suppose we need trouble you again,' he continued, with regret. 'Unless your—er, husband—can help us.'

'How could he?' She spoke with a defensive abruptness.

'There's a chance he noticed something out of the ordinary.'

She stared obstinately back at him. 'He couldn't have done. He wasn't here. Friday he went off really early. On his bike.'

DETECTIVE SERGEANT YEADINGS, as faithful amanuensis, accompanied his ponderous DI to the Delphic Galleries on the Monday. Why the name appeared on the elegant fascia in the plural he never discovered, for it wasn't extensive. The first, Grecian part of the title was due to the owners being a pair of brothers of Athenian extraction (now in their late seventies, and one in the early stages of Parkinson's disease). These details, in no way relevant to the enquiry, were volunteered by Dana, the young woman assistant who suddenly found herself elevated to stand in for Caroline Winterton.

Witnesses, Yeadings often found, either clammed up or suffered from a form of verbal diarrhoea which demanded a deal of sometimes unsavoury searching through. This Dana was whippet thin, and slightly out of control. Speed? Yeadings wondered, trying to size up her pupils behind the froggy glasses. Or was it merely excitement at the heady thought of being in charge, with the added zest of learning of some possible scandal featuring her boss?

Calthrop, content to lurch about squinting incredulously at the paintings and statuary on show, left the questioning to him: the normal 'when', 'where', 'how', 'why' and 'who' of the early days of a disappearance. Yeadings noted down that Caroline Winterton had arrived late at work on Friday, her last day there, and Dana, having a duplicate key, had let herself in to open up and see to the mail. Which hadn't pleased her ladyship one bit when eventually she did put in an appearance.

'It wasn't just a strip she tore off me,' the girl said. 'It was a bloody great chunk. Anyone would think I wanted to read her private love letters.'

'So was there something personal for her in the mail that morning?' Yeadings asked mildly.

Dana thought back, stroking one crossed leg absently and earning a tight-lipped scowl from Calthrop who saw short skirts as an invitation to abuse. 'Yerss, you could say so.'

Yeadings waited, confident that she was in imparting mode.

'Depends, I suppose, on what you mean by personal. There was a note from some London clinic about a sched-uled booking in a few weeks' time. With a list of what to take with her and so on. Then there was a handwritten note apologising for a hold-up in supplying information she'd requested. It ended 'Lurv you, D'.

D for Daniel? No, her husband wouldn't need to write to her, especially by post.

'Have you any idea what that might refer to?'

'It could be anything. Maybe to do with provenance on some artwork she intended bidding for. Or a fill-in on some client's cashflow situation. But I hadn't come across any D before. There was nothing on file.'

'So your seeing one of those items had annoyed her? Which, do you suppose?'

'I wouldn't know. It could have been general bad temper. She can be very high and mighty. Anyway, I hadn't got through opening all the post. And she was spoiling for a fight when she came in, mad at whatever had delayed her in getting here. She snarled for coffee, and if I hadn't been needed to make it she'd probably have torn me limb from limb.'

'The art world sounds much more exciting than I'd imagined,' Yeadings commented, turning to a new page in his notebook.

'Oh, like you wouldn't believe,' Dana assured him, and she was off again on a string of gossip.

Calthrop grunted and barked a few questions of his own to bring her to heel. Eventually they had covered all Caroline's movements until she left for lunch at about twelve thirty, warning that she might not be back before four. The galleries always stayed open over lunchtime because it was often then that business customers found time to drop in. If Caroline went out Dana ate her sandwiches at her desk as and when she found a free moment.

Since Dana couldn't recall the hospital's name from the letter and was equally unhelpful about where her boss might have intended lunching, it seemed that the detectives had all they were likely to get. For the moment.

'Did you get a look at the post that came for Mrs Winterton at her home on Friday?' Calthrop demanded of Yeadings when they were again in the car.

'It hadn't arrived before she left. I was told it seldom gets delivered before nine out in the sticks. We'd have to get the husband's permission to examine anything that's arrived since, and I get the feeling he'd respect her privacy until it's beyond doubt that she's met with foul play.'

'So what do you make of the two items the girl mentioned?'

'As she said, the note from D might refer to gallery business. As for the hospital appointment, I'd like to know why she'd used her business address for that. Could it be that she was keeping some health problem dark from her husband?'

'Keeping what problem dark, though? You'd better take a trip to London and find out. Her health may well have a bearing on where she is now.'

Confidential medical information, Yeadings gloomily reflected, was as hard to get hold of as statements of private accounts from a bank. Even harder, in fact. It was no surprise that the DI had landed him with that chore.

When he reached the CID office he rang back to the gallery but there was no reply. A second attempt also drew a blank. Either Dana was too busy with customers to answer or she had abandoned her workplace. He decided there was nothing for it but to go back in person and dig the girl out. Since neither item of personal mail had come to light in the gallery's office he would have to work further on Dana's memory to get the address of the hospital Caroline was to attend. But if Dana had decided to play hookey in the boss's absence, he could waste his morning chasing her up.

The blank he'd drawn was explained as he entered the premises. The mouse was making the most of the cat's absence. He found the girl with a half-eaten Chinese take-away and with a mobile phone glued to her ear, sprawled on a chaise longue under a Modigliani-type portrait of a kneeling nude.

'Hang on, Dot,' she commanded as his shadow fell over her. 'My dishy copper's back.'

Whatever the reaction to this from the other end of the line, she let out a wild shriek of laughter. 'Wait and see then.'

Despite her instruction to her crony she snapped shut the aerial, rose and smoothed her diminutive skirt.

'I've been trying for hours to reach you on the gallery number,' Yeadings complained.

'I was busy on the mobile,' she explained unnecessarily, dropping it on the desk. 'Actually it's Caroline's. Funny she didn't take it with her. I suppose she wanted to be sure she wouldn't be disturbed.' She raised her eyebrows in a suggestive manner.

This was the first hint of a real lead she'd given him, and he seized on it at once. 'Disturbed from what?'

Calthrop's absence made all the difference. Dana was warming to the situation. 'Aw, come on. You know what I mean. She had that randy look about her. You can't tell me she was going for a business lunch in some stuffy local restaurant.'

'So you think she was meeting someone she was per-sonally involved with?'

'That's a very proper way to describe it. I'd say she'd gone off for some red-hot nooky. Especially saying she might not be back before four. It didn't surprise me that she never turned up at all and left me to lock up. That wasn't the first time I'd been dropped in it that way.'

She was grinning at him saucily, begging to be invited to spill more.

'You're suddenly much more forthcoming.'

'Do you think I'd grass up my boss with old Sourpuss standing by? The first thing he'd do when she got back would be tell her what a dead loss I was.'

If she ever gets back, Yeadings thought. For the first time it really struck him that Calthrop's hopes of skulduggery might be fulfilled. Caroline Winterton could herself be the dead loss.

If she had merely run off with some man she fancied to replace her husband, why would she abandon a useful standby like her mobile phone? Admittedly she might prefer to be free of it temporarily, but not forever. It was always possible to leave the thing turned off. Had something untoward happened to her during what she'd intended as a brief adventure? Was she actually a victim of abduction?

He pressed the girl for names of Caroline's male friends and art world associates, but her boss had been canny enough to keep any private life separate from business. If she did give clients a come-on, any resulting intimacy was out of hours or off the premises, out of Dana's sight.

Hoping for better results from the other item of personal mail, he suggested, 'Let's try a little experiment. Sit down where you opened the post. Now stare at this blank piece of paper. Imagine it's about the hospital appointment. What colour was the paper, and the print on the heading?'

'Dark blue print,' she said instantly. 'Nice quality cream paper. Not a National Health form.'

'So the hospital's a private one?'

'It would have to be for Caroline. Couldn't share an open ward with hoi polloi.'

'Close your eyes. Can you see any of the print? The hospital's name?'

'Nope. Just South Kensington. It sort of jumped out at me because that's where we take the tube to for the V & A museum. Is that any help?'

'You're a poppet,' he told her.

She gave him a shrewd glance. 'She's done a runner, hasn't she? She's upped and left her husband.'

'Had you any idea that she might?'

Dana thought about it. 'Not really. Unless she'd got a better offer. Money-wise, I mean. Money was really big with Caroline.'

'I'd like you to check that there isn't any missing here.'

'What, petty cash? Our customers don't pay with *money*. It's all plastic, cheques or promissory notes.'

No, Yeadings agreed: the place he should be asking at was the bank, and the only person they might listen to there was the husband. Same thing if he contacted the missing woman's doctor.

He thanked Dana again and left, returning to the CID office from where he phoned through to Winterton.

'Have you any news?' the man asked anxiously when he identified himself. Yeadings suppressed the hospital item.

'I'm afraid not. It's early days yet, Mr Winterton. Just another question, sir, if I may. Does your wife have a separate bank account?'

'Yes, of course. It's with Barclays, the same as our joint account. We hold credit cards from them as well. Do you want the numbers?'

'It could help, sir. If she applies for cash or makes purchases it could indicate where she is.'

'I should have thought of that. I'll fetch the file, if you'll hold on.'

After a short wait he was back with the information. 'Is there anything else I can do to help, Sergeant?'

'At this early point the bank is unlikely to divulge her personal details, but perhaps you would check that no withdrawals have been made from your joint account?'

'I'll need to go in myself. They don't like to give out information over the phone.'

'If you would, sir; and you can ring me back on the number I left with you. In my absence DC Ward will take a message.'

This left Yeadings to drive the thirty-odd miles to London and root around nursing homes in the locality of South Kensington. He hit the right one on his second shot, the Tolwardine, externally a discreet hotel, and inside run with the efficient sense of purpose of a luxury liner. At reception armed with a bunch of roses, he asked to see his sister, Mrs Caroline Winterton.

The name appeared familiar. There was some consulting of a display screen and then of a daybook from under the desk. 'I'm sorry, sir, but Mrs Winterton is not a patient here at present.'

Yeadings looked shattered. 'Have I mixed up the dates then? I was sure she told me it was today.'

The receptionist smiled at the big man standing helpless and bewildered, the roses drooping from their cellophane cone.

He adopted an air of puzzled concern. 'Maybe it wasn't this month. August, then? I should have listened properly. I guess I was just knocked all of a heap when she told me.'

A gentle pattering on the keyboard and the receptionist smiled. 'You're just a little early, sir. We are expecting her a week tomorrow. Mr Barling's patient.'

Mr. That meant only one thing. 'I've a horror of surgery,' Yeadings confided in a near-whisper.

'There's no need, really, sir. Mr Barling is probably the best plastic surgeon in the country. Just a short while and you'll see her looking more lovely than ever.'

Yeadings made off before the girl could regret such release of confidential data.

'D,' he repeated to himself as he drove back, determined to get a result regarding Caroline's second item of private mail. 'David (there are millions of them), Dirk, Dorian, Dashwood (that's daft), Drake, Douglas, Darren, even Dagobert for heaven's sake!' No, the odds would be on one of the less exotic, unless of course he had a pet name, special for her, like Doggy-eyes, Duck-feet or Demon Lover.

Then again, it might be a woman who had written the note regretting that she hadn't come up with the required information, and the final 'Lurv you' could be girlish jokiness. He scowled at the traffic snarl ahead, scrolling through his mind's screen: Doris, Doreen, Dorinda, Deirdre, Delia, Délice, Delphine, Dulcie, Dympna.

Garaging the car, he still hadn't come up with anything that clicked. Instead, as he kissed Nan perfunctorily while stepping clear of Sally's articulated caterpillar whose string was wrapped around the legs of a kitchen chair, he demanded, 'Barling, plastic surgeon. What can you tell me about him?'

'A well-timed entrance, Mr Plod,' Nan commented, waving towards the coffee-maker, which was working up to its ultimate burble. 'Sit down and cease worrying. I like your face just the way it is.'

A solemn Yeadings considered this. 'Honestly?'

'I'm particularly sent by your furry eyebrows, like black caterpillars, but then you know that or you wouldn't use them at me the sexy way you do.'

He performed a few demonic expressions in quick succession, sank on to a chair and pulled her, unresisting, on to his knees. 'I've been up to town this afternoon.'

'Harley Street?' she guessed.

'Is that where the great man lives?'

'It's where he has his consulting rooms. I believe he's much in demand. Does a lot of cosmetic jobs privately and gets called in for really sticky burn and crash cases. He's very highly thought of in the profession. I hope you're not thinking of running him in.'

'Even worse. I'm hoping to get confidential information on an operation he's scheduled to perform in a week or so.'

'Where?'

Yeadings told her, supplying the name of the patient.

'And you calmly expect me to use my connections to find out just what?'

'The sort of op it's likely to be, how serious and so on.'

Nan removed herself from his lap and poured their coffees while she considered this. 'I don't know anyone at the Tolwardine.'

'But you know somebody who does.'

'Quite possibly. But it's highly unprofessional to gossip about one's patients.'

'Don't tell me it's not done.'

'It's almost as common as coppers' tittle-tattle, but that's not the question. I'd need to know how far it will go, and what harm it could do.'

'I'll trade confidence for confidence,' Yeadings offered, 'if you'll play. Look, I've a possible missing person, abduction or worse; a Caroline Winterton, due to have this surgery. The details may be irrelevant to whatever has happened, but again it might indicate her state of mind when she disappeared. It's unlikely the hospital information would ever become public knowledge, but it could help me find her. So will you wade in?'

'Winterton,' Nan said. 'Of course; I read about it in this evening's paper. It said she has a little girl of nearly three.'

'Sally's age, yes. I don't think she realises yet that her mummy's gone.'

'So get her back quickly,' Nan said sharply, already on her way to the phone.

He could almost hear the starchy swish of uniform skirts, an echo of the one-time Theatre Sister Nan Randall of the Westminster Hospital. Seven years back, when he'd been a young DC in the Met, he would slip out to snatch a furtive lunch with her between committal hearings in the Horseferry Road Court.

They had been great days, and these were even greater. It was the best decision he'd ever taken, marrying Nan and transferring out to the Thames Valley. Settling down and having Sally, poor little scrap. All that excitement and hope building, and then the agonising truth that she would never be quite like other children—and was therefore even more precious because of it. Which had somehow made all other children extra wonderful too, as Nan also felt.

She came back po-faced and he had to ask her, 'Well?'

'It will take a little while, but somebody knows somebody who has a great friend—'

'…who danced with the Prince of Wales.'

'Even better. Who happens to be Barling's consulting-room secretary. So you may get your answer before bedtime.'

Yeadings eyed her proudly and relaxed. Then something else caught up with him. 'I don't suppose Barling's first name is Dougal?'

'No,' Nan answered serenely. 'It's Brian. When less famous he also used to answer to "Brain".' She smiled seraphically. 'I knew him quite well at one time.'

THREE

'DUNCAN; DENNIS; so also Denise,' Yeadings muttered into the windscreen, queueing at traffic lights next morning on his way to work.

The handwritten note would probably prove to be totally irrelevant, but the yawning possibilities of the initial letter tantalised him like a single blank left in his daily crossword puzzle. Even as he drifted off last night the spectre had continued to haunt him into the brink of sleep: *Donald,* connecting with Disney; and he'd faded out on the image of a monster cartoon duck with a pen in its beak scratching some illegible message on a Thames Valley duty roster.

But at least he'd had one question answered over break-fast. Nan, lifting the kitchen phone in one hand as she mopped fruit juice spilt from Sally's beaker, had grinned at him as the brief conversation ended.

'A cosmetic nose job,' she said. 'Apparently your lady thought her hooter was too long. So either vanity will bring her back next week to strive for perfection, or the hypo-thetical lover can't face up to the early scars and she'll opt out of having it done.'

'Or else she won't be capable of turning up,' Yeadings said heavily, 'for one of two very nasty reasons.'

The more he considered it, the more likely it seemed that a woman planning to run off with a lover would previously have had corrected any imperfections she fancied her face suffered from. Or else she'd have felt secure enough on the beauty front, and not have bothered to make the appointment. As a mere man he might be wrong on that, because women weren't entirely logical creatures, thank God. Here was something else he'd have to put to Nan later.

As soon as he was in his office he rang home and asked her.

'I follow your reasoning,' she said. 'But how do you know what order she made up her mind in? Suppose she'd had to wait months and months after booking that appointment for the op? Barling's a very busy man, and even if it's a private job it's hardly an emergency one. Then, supposing she'd just recently decided to decamp with Romeo, she could have forgotten she'd made the date, or simply not troubled to cancel.'

Yeadings groaned quietly.

Nan sighed. 'So now you want me to find out *when* the appointment was made, presumably. Would there be any more details I could get settled at the same time?'

'Nan, I'm sorry, but she hasn't turned up yet and there have been no reported sightings. It's now a formal Misper inquiry and Calthrop's determined to have a body. I'm just off with the SOCOs to look round the marital home.'

He took young Ward along and they had been there a bare half-hour when Calthrop's Nissan drew up outside. 'Well?' the DI demanded, wanting instant results.

'There's nothing to show she returned here after leaving Friday morning,' Yeadings reported. 'We've found the clothes she changed from. The nanny explained the child might have made a mess of the blouse, so Mrs Winterton probably changed after her husband had left. By then Katy was bathing Julie and didn't actually see her go. However, the woman next door, Ms Harbury, did see her from the window and is sure she wore an aquamarine suit. Just as Dana told us at the gallery.'

'It's the woman we're interested in, not her bloody wardrobe,' Calthrop grumbled. 'Is everyone satisfied she's not stashed in the house? Attics? Cellars?'

'*Satisfied,* Mr Winterton is not; but at least he didn't stand in our way. We've been as tactful as possible. The attics have been searched. There was a cellar once but it's been sealed off for years.' He recognised the sudden glint in the DI's eye and put in quickly, 'I'd like you to see for yourself, Guv.'

They went through together and even Calthrop couldn't deny that the solid wood or ceramic-tiled floors showed no sign of interference. Which next obliged DS Yeadings to draw attention to the partly completed rockery. He was aware that as they surveyed the heap of newly turned earth and carefully spaced stones with small alpines sparsely tucked between, they were in full view of the study windows where Winterton was supposedly at work.

Calthrop was humming and rocking suggestively on his heels. Yeadings knew he was jumping to conclusions again. 'The rockery won't have gone away,' he pointed out, 'when we've exhausted all other lines of enquiry.'

'By which time he could have moved the body elsewhere. We haven't the manpower to leave someone indefinitely standing guard over it.'

'I'll get the SOCOs to photograph it the way it is,' Yeadings insisted, 'and ensure Winterton doesn't know. But Guv, if we start digging it up straight off we're going to earn ourselves a bad press. There's a lot of public sympathy going for the poor devil at present. The super will come down on us like a load of bricks—a whole rockery, even— if the tabloids start screaming about brutal police measures.'

Calthrop scowled, muttering something about the 'bloody

bleeding-heart industry', but Yeadings knew that the mention of Superintendent Gardner had shifted the balance.

From the corner of his eyes he saw a man's figure in the window of the study, facing in their direction. 'We're being watched,' he warned the DI. 'Let's look satisfied and trot off to admire the rest of the layout, like a couple of amateur gardeners.'

To strengthen the impression he retrieved his pipe from a trouser pocket, sniffed it, tamped down the half-smoked tobacco with one thumb and regarded the unclouded sky before lighting up. Then he sauntered away, the DI in his wake, past a bed of scented stocks, to stand in delight before a huge clump of agapanthus, midnight blue.

'Now that's really something,' he told Calthrop, waving his pipe expansively towards the flowers. 'Someday, not fifty years hence, I'll have a shot at growing those.'

The DI snorted. 'Bloody play-acting. I'm going down to see what they've found at the boathouse.' With which he trudged off.

And next thing, Yeadings told himself, we'll be dragging the river and have frogmen in. At least he can order that while still pretending he's considering an accident.

Which, of course, might well be the case, although if Caroline Winterton had taken out the boat someone else had certainly returned it. There was just a chance that after lunch she had come back either to the house or its grounds, but he felt in his bones that the first find would be made by uniformed branch, searching for the restaurant Caroline Winterton had gone to on the day she disappeared.

He turned back to the house and was met at the back door by Daniel Winterton looking, if possible, more drained and hollow-featured than before. 'Sergeant, can you spare me a moment?'

'Certainly, sir.' He made to knock out his pipe against the outer wall but the man put out a hand in protest.

'I'm a smoker myself. I know how it helps when you need to think.'

They went through to his study, where Yeadings observed that the screen of the man's computer remained dark. There were no papers on his desk, only an ashtray full of crumpled cigarette butts.

Now that they were seated Winterton was reluctant to begin. Eventually, however, he cleared his throat, stared at his clasped hands on the desk and said, 'This morning…'

'Yes, sir?'

'I find this difficult, Sergeant.' He made an obvious effort, then plunged in.

'Earlier this morning, remembering what you'd said about cheques and credit cards, I went—to see my bank manager. Our bank, that is, Caroline's and mine.'

'Was he helpful, sir?'

'He was—very understanding. Of course, he'd heard that my wife was missing, so he was prepared to meet my requests. Except over Caroline's private accounts. Banks do have to observe a certain discretion between husbands and wives. It seems. I could see his point, but it was—hardly reassuring. Especially in view…'

'Sir, can I get you something? Water? Brandy?'

'No, I'm all right. I'm sorry. It's been quite a shock.' He took a firm grip on the edge of his desk and brought his eyes up to meet Yeadings'.

'She's almost emptied our joint deposit account,' he said hollowly. 'They hadn't the details because she didn't do it through our usual branch, but I asked for the final balance and they gave it to me.'

'Under the circumstances we can probably request the details for you, sir.'

'Never mind that. But do you see what it means? She drew the money out *herself.* She's alive, safe somewhere. But, but…'

Yeadings looked swiftly round the room, then dived through to the dining-room and reached for the old-fashioned tantalus. He slopped brandy into a tumbler and brought it back. The man took it with shaking hands. But he wouldn't drink until he had got the odious words out.

'She meant to do it. Sergeant, my wife has left me. Deliberately. Abandoned little Julie. I don't know what to do.'

Winterton had no neighbours except the Harburys next door. Yeadings offered to fetch someone but Winterton refused. 'Katy will be bringing Julie back later. She's taken her to a toddlers' group. I'll be quite all right once my daughter's home.'

'Perhaps Katy would stay over. Just for tonight.'

'Sergeant, she's little more than a girl herself, for all she's so competent. I can't prop myself up on her. No, everything must go on as normal. I don't want my daughter upset needlessly. We don't know yet, do we, how this will settle itself in the end.'

Meaning he hoped his wife would come back? Yeadings doubted it somehow, but he made all the right encouraging noises. Not until Winterton's colour began to return did the DS feel it safe to leave him.

'I'll be reporting to DI Calthrop, sir, and then we'll all clear off. If anything fresh comes in we'll let you know at once.'

Winterton saw him to the door. On the point of leaving, Yeadings looked back. 'One little question, sir. Beyond the list of acquaintances you have given us, do you know of any other friend of your wife's whose name begins with D?'

'I can't say that I do. D, no. Only my own, Daniel. And

there's Dana, at the gallery. But certainly I'll give it some thought. May I ask why you're interested?'

Yeadings explained about the handwritten note in Caroline's mail on Friday.

'May I see it? Perhaps I could recognise the writing.'

'Unfortunately we don't have it, sir. She must have taken it away in her handbag. We know of it because her assistant opened the mail first, since your wife arrived late at work.'

'I never knew that. Did you find out what delayed her? Maybe she met someone on the way?'

'She was late leaving the house, sir.'

'Oh, I see.' He didn't sound as if he did. And it wasn't Yeadings' business to remind him he'd been partly the reason she wasn't on time.

'Well, think about that D person, sir, and let us know what comes to mind.'

He said he would. At any rate, Yeadings consoled himself, it left him with a more positive subject to ponder than his own desolation.

DC Ward had just been sent by Calthrop to check on Winterton's movements in London. Now, with the knowledge of Caroline's withdrawal of the money, it looked like wasted effort. Nevertheless, Yeadings didn't begrudge the DC a day let loose on a longer leash. A positive alibi for the husband should finally calm the DI's fervour for a manhunt. Until he insisted on an alternative murder suspect.

In the CID office Yeadings went through the list of outstanding queries before the case, barely begun, should be closed. The woman was of age, of sound mind as far as anyone knew, and not a known criminal. If she wished to leave home she had every legal right to do so. The police had enough on their plates without disputing the non-fulfilment of marriage vows.

Details of her car's make, colour and licence plates had

been notified throughout the Thames Valley and neighbouring counties. There was little point now in extending this further, but he'd let the local search continue. If Winterton intended employing a private investigator to trace his wife, any outcome could be of use to him.

Uniformed branch were called off inquiries in the Aylesbury area. They had visited every restaurant, hotel, teashop and pub without discovering where Caroline had spent her lunch hour. Either she had left the area at once or she had visited a private house for her midday meal.

Persuaded to co-operate—under Calthrop's insistence that it would turn into a murder case—the bank manager dived into the system and brought up Heathrow Terminal Three as the branch at which she had made the money withdrawal. But it couldn't be assumed that she had left on a long-haul flight, since her name was not present on any Terminal Three passenger lists.

'And the BMW hasn't turned up there,' Calthrop reminded them. 'We've tried all the terminals' car parks. If she drove there, *somebody* must have driven it away afterwards.'

'Unless it has been garaged elsewhere and she took a taxi to the airport,' Yeadings pointed out. 'It's a valuable car. She may have sold it on, or intends to pick it up at some later date. Which could imply she'll be coming back.'

'To live happily ever after,' the DI retorted with heavy sarcasm. 'I'll not be satisfied she's alive until we've gone through the CCTV videos at Heathrow and picked her out.'

The quality of the tapes could have been better, but she was identified at the airport Barclays Bank at approximately the time the withdrawal was made. The long blonde hair was unmistakable and the distinctive leather vanity case on her arm was identical with the one Katy had described as missing. She had partly hidden the aquamarine suit under a loose-fitting off-white coat and her eyes were obscured by shades, but even Calthrop was forced to admit that at the time given, fifteen twenty-seven hours, Caroline Winterton had still been very much alive.

'I want that bloody car,' Calthrop growled. 'Are we still looking for it?'

'Throughout Thames Valley,' Yeadings told him.

'Spread it nationwide. I don't know how that bugger's done it, but I know he has. He could have arranged to meet her later, done her in and torched the car.'

Ward's eyes met Yeadings' with an acknowledgement that the Old Man had gone right over the edge on this one.

'Sir, Winterton's covered. He was with his agent in London like he said, until three fifteen. Then he went back to Colindale to do some more work and pick up his notes. Caught the seventeen twenty-seven train from Marylebone to Chalfont and Latimer where a witness saw him get off about six o'clock and pick up his car, which had stood there all day. He'd have got home in good time to relieve the nanny when she went off at half-past six.'

Calthrop sat rubbing his chin and muttering to himself. Yeadings picked up the words 'known enemies'.

'If she has met with foul play, it can't have been her husband, sir,' he said, satisfied that Winterton's new rockery stood a good chance now of being left undisturbed.

Calthrop still wasn't convinced. 'He could have employed someone else to do his dirty work. And don't overlook that there's always X with reasons of his own.'

'Right, sir,' Yeadings patiently allowed, and padded off to extend the search for Caroline's car.

It was two days later and other cases had accumulated when the BMW was reported in a two a.m. head-on crash on the M25 in Hertfordshire. It had bounced off a Volvo while overtaking on the wrong side, broken through the barrier, overturned and crashed into an articulated lorry travelling in the opposite direction. The car was a write-off.

Of the two occupants, male and female, the woman driver had been DOA and the man was comatose in Intensive Care with concussion, multiple injuries and internal bleeding.

'I knew she was dead,' Calthrop crowed. 'I could feel it in me water. Only bloody difference is that she did herself in.'

Hertfordshire police described the dead woman as being aged between thirty and thirty-five, five feet nine inches tall, blond and thin. It fell to Yeadings to drive a shocked but tightly controlled Winterton to identify her body.

He sat slumped in the passenger seat, only once breaking silence to mutter, 'Caroline isn't dead. I just know it. She can't be. I don't understand. I just don't.'

At the morgue he had to steel himself to go in. He stood stunned as the sheet was drawn back from the dead face.

'No,' he managed to gasp. 'She's nothing like my—like Caroline. I've never seen this woman before. Who is she?'

Relief was only one of the emotions that shook him on the way home. His hands were constantly kneading each other in his lap. Yeadings, accustomed to many forms of grief, spoke only occasionally, but the man made no reply. At last, as they pulled into the driveway of his home, Winterton shook his head. 'Thank God,' he said fervently, 'it wasn't Caro. But poor girl. Poor girl, whoever she was. I wouldn't have had this happen for all the world.'

'It was no fault of yours, sir. You mustn't feel responsible.'

'But it was Caroline's car—'

'Stolen, and driven under the influence of drugs. A blood

sample taken at the hospital showed the woman was incapable of driving even at low speed.'

'They said that the body they had was thin. Caroline is slim, willowy. That girl was—emaciated. She must have starved herself. But she's someone's daughter, Sergeant. Perhaps even somebody's wife.'

Identification was made later through the dead woman's medical record. Both her arms had shown her to be a long-time drug user and she was registered to receive methadone. She and the younger man with her had been members of a squat in Slough with a record for joyriding with cars stolen from the airport car parks.

But that day wasn't to end without any positive information regarding Caroline's disappearance. Yeadings had driven Winterton home to find little Julie shut away in the living-room watching television while Katy comforted a hysterical Peg Harbury in the kitchen.

For days she had cowered at home, suppressing her fears and shame until at last it became too much to bear. Barry had been gone since the Friday of Caroline's disappearance, when he had ridden off on his bicycle. When he failed to return that evening she had believed he was punishing her for not giving him the money to buy a second-hand motorbike. She hadn't wanted to upset him, but the money from her mother's house was in a building society account without instant access; and anyway, motorbikes were such dangerous things. She'd been afraid he would injure himself.

The estate agency had rung that Saturday to ask where he was, and she had made up some story to cover for him. But then he'd stayed away all weekend—and when they rang again on Monday she'd lied, saying he was ill and wanted Maisie to take over in his place.

Yes, she had known Mrs Winterton was away, but she

hadn't connected it. She hadn't listened to the local news service, or been into the village shopping, because she'd felt too sick to eat much.

Then suddenly it was so awful being without Barry that she just couldn't stand being alone any more. She'd run round to next door and poured out her troubles to the nice nanny.

So now she knew about Mrs Winterton too—and could hardly believe what Katy had suggested. Barry wouldn't have done that—run away with the lady from next door. Peg had thought he was happy enough in the cottage with her. No, there must be some other explanation.

But all the time that the words tumbled out and the tears fell it was obvious that she was becoming less and less sure.

Calthrop went off like a thunderclap when he heard. DC Ward's entrails had unmentionable—but publicised, none-theless—futures promised them. Stuff the blockhead for breaking it gently to her about the Winterton woman. Spades were bloody spades and had to be referred to as such. He'd better steel himself for a career of school-crossing duties when they stuck him back in uniform.

He had at least recorded Barry's surname correctly. Upon a thorough search of passenger lists at Heathrow it was discovered that a Barry Morgan and a Caroline Winterton had taken a BA flight from Terminal One to Lanzarote on the Friday evening of the disappearances.

But from then on they were untraceable.

Yeadings was sufficiently interested in what had suddenly become an inactive case to wonder how long the couple had been close and where they had arranged their meetings. He was still pondering this when the new manager of the estate agency rang through to give some revealing information.

Barry Morgan's assistant had mentioned a Mrs McQueen who had always asked for Barry himself and was interested in a large property known as Pollards Mount. It appeared overpriced and so had stayed for a long time on the books. The lady's particulars, if indeed there had been a file kept, were missing, so the manager had gone out himself to view the house and consider a revaluation. As a result of what he found there he suggested the police also take a look.

It fell to DS Yeadings to inspect what the man had described. The house was unlocked and in the large conservatory were found a number of cushions, a rug, the remains of a picnic, two empty champagne bottles and a well-equipped hamper.

Caught in the uncut fringe of one of the silk cushions was a small length of fine gold chain, perhaps torn from the safety clasp of a bracelet or necklace.

Running through the list of clothes and jewellery Caroline was thought to have taken away, Yeadings considered it might have significance. Especially since caught in the links was a fine thread of aquamarine silk.

Only one factor had left him uneasy: that was a small reddish-black stain on the same cushion. He had moistened his finger and rubbed at it. The stain smudged and became recognisably blood.

So small a quantity did not necessarily imply violence. It seemed more likely that in love-play Caroline had torn her skin on the damaged chain.

There was not really sufficient evidence there to merit mention in a report, but at that time Yeadings had been a stickler for following the book, so he logged it. By the time it reached Calthrop's desk the DI had other interests. A double shotgun killing had been reported at Wendover, providing him with a real murder case to make his spectacular exit on.

FOUR

NAN YEADINGS GROPED around the bed and felt the empty space cool on the far side. No light showed under the adjoining bathroom door. She rolled on to one elbow and squinted through tousled hair at the illuminated dial of the bedside clock.

It showed either a minute or two past three a.m. or a quarter past midnight. She really must swap the thing for a digital alarm. Without her new reading glasses the two hands blurred into equal length.

She decided it had to be the later time because they'd both come up after eleven thirty and she had the heavy feeling of having slept for some considerable while. So what was Mike up to? Or, more properly, what had he gone downstairs to? If the phone had rung, surely it would have woken her?

She swung her legs out and plunged her toes into bedroom slippers, prepared to apply remedies for her husband's wakefulness, whether of physical or mental origin. Standing to listen on the landing she could detect no movement in the house.

At the children's doors she peeped in. Each room showed a little pool of light from a plastic mushroom on which squatted Tweedles Dum and Dee, for Sally, and for Luke a bespectacled caterpillar reading from *Alice in Wonderland*. Both children slept soundly, Luke emitting a soft popping sound as regular breaths escaped his pursed lips. Mike wasn't there; she must follow him down.

He had shut the kitchen door on himself so that light shouldn't spill out and disturb anyone. On opening it she blinked as her eyes adjusted. 'What is it?' she demanded. 'I didn't think I'd overdone the cheese and garlic.'

'Oh, Nan. Sorry I disturbed you. No, I'm fine. Just having a wee think.'

She drew out a chair opposite to where he sat hunched at the table. 'How long have you been here?'

He consulted the kitchen clock. 'Half an hour and something. Had a catnap, then woke up with something on my mind and I couldn't get off again.'

'Would a milky drink help?'

He gave her a mock hangdog look. 'How about the calories?'

She yawned behind one hand. 'I just abdicated as obesity counsellor. In fact I think I'll join you.'

He watched her at the fridge and hotplate. Already her matter-of-factness was re-establishing the present. When she brought their mugs over and settled opposite him he was ready to share what had been on his mind.

'Do you remember a case of mine some eight years ago, when a married woman ran off with her toy boy lover from next door?'

She frowned. 'Should I? You'd have been a DS then, under that awful oaf Calthrop.'

'You helped me by checking on a surgery booking the woman had made with your one-time admirer Barling. Remember now?'

'It's coming back. She left her little girl behind, of the same age as Sally. Has the mother turned up again?'

'That's what I'd like to know, because this time it's the child who's gone missing. I'd much prefer to think Caroline

Winterton has reappeared and abducted the child. Any alternative must be more alarming.'

'But we've had no child molester loose locally for some time, surely?'

'There has to be a first, to restart a sequence. But it's the family aspect that's bothering me.'

She frowned, not sure she followed his thought. 'Lightning striking the same place twice?'

'Something of the kind. It resurrects old Calthrop's suspicions of the man, among other possibilities.'

'Is it your case?'

'Not yet, but if Uniform and Juveniles don't locate the child straight off, it could come our way by morning.'

'And you're pretty certain they'll drop it on you, because you've already met the family.'

'I've a nasty feeling about it.'

She looked at him wryly, this self-confessed inheritor of his old Welsh granny's sixth sense. 'Don't worry, love,' she comforted, leaning across and gently ruffling his stiff, dark hair. 'The Wise Woman endowed you with the right genes to get it all sorted. Bring your drink and come back to bed. It's tomorrow already, and we'll both have plenty to do later.'

DOWNSTREAM FROM THE derelict water-mill, lights still shone from the ground-floor windows of Long Gable. The name dated from several years back, when the last tenants had vacated the end cottage and the original three were finally made into one.

Tonight Daniel Winterton, exhausted by tracking up and down the living-room in anguish, had collapsed into his favourite wing chair and at last succumbed to the comfort of a good single malt.

Through the archway the long-case clock in the hall

struck four, and after it the house's emptiness was mocked
by its dragging tick and a soft purr as the kitchen refrig-
erator cut in. What should have been comfortable and domestic now sounded dauntingly hollow, because upstairs in
the white-painted bedroom the poppy-patterned duvet lay
flat, the matching pillow unrumpled. Even Gruntle Thread-
Bear sat abandoned on the window seat. If she had felt able
to leave me, Winterton thought, would Julie have gone off
without that long-time comforter?

All she'd taken was food for a picnic. And it had been
understood that they would go out for lunch together. She
couldn't have forgotten. She had been listening when he
rang the Barley Mow at nine and put the order in: her
favourite roast duck followed by lemon pancakes with raspberry purée and cream.

So what had happened later to change her mind? There
had been no phone calls. Nobody had rung at the front door
or he would have heard. But, engrossed in his writing, he
could have missed anyone outside waving to her through a
window.

Was that what had happened—a school friend inviting
Julie out, or inviting herself in? And then Julie impetuously
deciding an impromptu outing would be more fun, punishing him at the same time for neglecting her and leaving her
to her own devices? Was that how she had seen it: that
temporarily he had abandoned her, not she him? He'd truly
believed she'd understood how important it was that he
wrote when the ideas were flowing.

But in that case surely she would have left a note. And
who could have persuaded her to rebel? She had sense
enough not to go off with a stranger. He'd explained it to
her often enough: the dangers of it. Not explicitly, because
she was only a child, innocent of adult evil. But she knew
there were people who would hurt children.

So what did she understand by hurt? A bee sting, a cut knee, a finger caught in the car door, a bilious attack through overeating at a party; little else. And what did a child understand by the word 'stranger'? If she'd seen someone three or four times in the village; if it was someone her daddy had casually spoken to from the window of his car, would she consider them familiar, safe?

The thought sickened him. Even dwelling on the emptiness of the house had been more bearable than speculating where she might be now. Groaning, he heaved himself to his feet and stumbled blindly towards the stairs, past his own bedroom. Outside the closed door of her room he stood a moment, motionless. Then he pushed on the panels, went in and fell on his knees by the bed, burying face and hands in the bright poppy pattern.

As SUPERINTENDENT YEADINGS had feared, he was summoned early that morning to Kidlington for a parley with the ACC (Crime). They had little enough progress to discuss, since yesterday's local inquiries had yielded no sightings of the missing child. While the uniformed branch continued a fingertip search of the area between river and road, and house-to-house questioning in the village, it was passed to Yeadings' team to search out the whys and wherefores of family and school background.

He returned in time for the close of the general briefing given by DI Angus Mott, and from his position near the door was able to assess the listeners' reactions. There were some who still seemed to regard the assignment lightly, with a 'Kids? The little bleeders will try anything!' attitude, but most were family men capable of imagining their own youngsters suddenly vanishing without trace. The women officers were uniformly grim-eyed, one or two perhaps tending towards the men-are-our-natural-enemy posture.

Angus Mott and DS Beaumont separated themselves from the crowd of uniforms as it was dismissed, and joined him in his office. 'Where's Z?' Yeadings demanded.

'In court,' the DI told him. 'Grant James is up again on that handling charge. His brief suddenly found the papers he'd conveniently lost last week.'

'We'll need her. If it drags on you'd better ask Uniform for a WPC on loan, however thin on the ground they are. Meanwhile—'

He was dialling on his outside line and broke off to issue orders to someone at the other end. 'Well, let me know the minute court rises. It's essential I have a word with him about releasing a police witness early. She's required on a Serious Crimes inquiry involving a minor.'

He replaced the receiver in time to catch Beaumont's muttered aside about sexual inequality.

'Equal,' he insisted, 'but different. Nature has supplied Z with more of the normal female attributes than it has to any of us three. Something you shouldn't be complaining about. Now, Angus, let's hear what *you* have to offer.'

'Right.' Mott spun a chair and sat, long legs crossed at the ankle and stretched towards Yeadings' desk. 'Besides the father, there's Julie's schoolmates and teachers to work outwards from. Summer holidays, so a lot of them will have scattered. I'm putting Beaumont on charting their whereabouts until we can share that out between us. The man Winterton, I'll take myself. From what I've picked up it seems there were serious doubts about him when his wife disappeared some years back.'

Yeadings, fixing a filter paper in the coffee-maker, darted him a quick glance. He hadn't imagined the hint of censure in his DI's voice.

'You've read Calthrop's report, then.' It wasn't a question.

'It seemed relevant. The name Winterton rang a bell with some of the older men.'

'I was his DS then,' Yeadings said quietly, 'but it was almost Calthrop's last case so I barely featured when they ran the titles. There was a shotgun murder over at Wendover to cause a diversion just as the Winterton case sorted itself. The DI had meant it to be his exit to trumpets. It nearly broke his heart we couldn't pin a domestic murder on the man.'

Angus grunted uncomfortably. 'I didn't read the whole thing through.'

'Make up for it then, and if you think anything's too sketchy you can always ask me.'

'What did you make of Winterton, then, sir?' Beaumont put in hurriedly.

'He was under pressure,' Yeadings offered. 'I liked the man, but it would be a mistake to hang on to the same impression all this time later. Circumstances alter folk. I'd like to know how he's got along as a single parent, what his present relationship is with his daughter, how each faced up to her mother's deserting them. In fact, I think I'll come along when you interview him, Angus. With a watching brief.'

'Right, sir. If Z shows up—'

'There's someone I'd like her to have a word with first, woman to woman. PC Bisset's wife, Katy. Arrange that, will you?'

'Katy Bisset. Right, sir.' The DI could pick nothing off the boss's lack of expression. It was left to him to ask, 'So where does she figure in all this?'

'She used to be the child's nanny and they seemed fond of each other. She has a family of her own now, but I think it's unlikely she would cut herself off completely. Katy Anson, she was called before. You'd have found the name in Calthrop's report.' He glanced across at the coffee-maker, which was now starting to burble companionably. He had generously set it up for the three of them before Mott's gaffe, but now he changed his mind.

'Well, scatter then, and get on with it. I'll be down by your car in ten minutes, Angus.'

'Shit,' said Mott under his breath as they reached the corridor outside. 'He certainly got out of bed on the wrong side this morning.'

'Nuh, you walked right into it.'

'And you didn't? You should know by now how he picks up on equal rights.'

'At least I didn't try bluffing,' said Beaumont waspishly. 'You're the reason we have to poison ourselves at the drinks machine. Anyway, I doubt he got out of bed at all this morning. He looks as if he sat up all night.'

DS ROSEMARY ZYCZYNSKI had returned from forty-eight hours' leave too late the previous night to have caught the news of a missing child. As she tossed her travel bag into her sitting-room she saw the red light flashing on her answerphone.

The first message informed her that she was required in court early next morning for a repeat attempt at Grant James's committal hearing. The second offered a check-up at the local dermatology unit for eleven forty-five a.m. With luck she could just about fit both in and turn up for duty after lunch.

She tried twice that morning to contact DI Mott on his mobile phone but it was switched off. She assumed he'd be in conference with the boss, and left a message for him with the duty sergeant.

In court the James handling case was first on the list and as arresting officer she was called early on. The defence barrister was a supercilious, youngish man she'd had a verbal tussle with before, but she held her ground, gave an unvarnished account of James's arrest and was unfazed by the expected sarcasm. The bench released her without any application being made to recall her later. It allowed her barely twenty minutes to cover the fifteen miles to Mardham hospital for her medical appointment.

The first unusual thing there was finding a parking space opposite. Previously, cars had always stretched nose to tail along the kerb, and the difficulty of getting in would only be matched by the near impossibility of ever getting out. A twenty-seven-point turn scenario, she reminded herself.

Today was different. The cars, vans, pick-up trucks were relatively sparse. The reason, she discovered on crossing the road, was that the hospital's main gates were padlocked.

Detective Sergeant Rosemary Zyczynski reached in her shoulder bag for her outpatient's card and checked that date and place were as printed on it. Only the hour of the appointment had been inserted later, by hand. Now it looked as though she should have been sent elsewhere. Had some office-bound clerk forgotten to overstamp the discontinued heading?

A pick-up truck was manoeuvring in a rutted opening forty yards along, sending up a cloud of sandy dust. As it lurched on to the road it left revealed a new noticeboard: *To All Departments*. A door in the temporary wooden structure behind it stood ajar.

Inside she found a familiar rising corridor strangely changed. Connecting a makeshift wartime collection of buildings long made permanent through lack of funds, it had run irregularly uphill with offshoots leading to wards and treatment rooms on two levels, those on the left being some six feet higher than the others.

Now on either side she passed double doors gaping on

to long rooms empty but for an occasional jumble of un-
serviceable iron beds, broken cabinets and disconnected tu-
bular piping. Her steps echoed hollowly. Wind blew in
from some unseen source to disturb little piles of sweepings
decorated with fluff and drifted leaves.

She made for where the outpatients' reception had once
been and found a little centre of electric light and clicking
keyboards amid the dim, ghost-town emptiness. 'Right,'
said the receptionist on duty. 'Dermatology. That's up the
hill. New red block past the building site and car park.'

'Thank you.'

'You'd do better to drive round and miss the mechanical
diggers. We're rebuilding, see? Surprised you hadn't heard.
It was all explained in the local paper.'

Zyczynski barely got her words for the sound of metallic
fabric ripping as some gigantic mechanical hand ripped fit-
tings from nearby corridor walls.

Too busy with dead bodies to get round to reading the
small-town news, she accused herself. She'd missed even
a whisper of the demolition.

The receptionist muttered and blew fine dust off her computer screen. 'Can't wait to be moved on,' she complained
in a dreary litany.

The DS retraced her steps and drove round as recom-
mended. The entire new development was on the side of a
steep hill behind the original buildings and would eventually be split-level. The new block just completed must be
an architect's prize entry, resplendent inside with comfortable seating, shiny vinyl flooring and potted palms.

As for reception, it and the male consultant were pleas-
antly brisk. After a minimal wait she was ushered into his
small, modern office. He removed his spooky magnifying
glasses to give her a casual nod. 'Ah yes. The assault damage you suffered has healed nicely. Minimal scarring, even-

tually none. Policewoman, eh? I suppose it's a hazard of the course.

'Those other two little spots, though. Rodent carcinoma. Lucky you came in with the lacerations or we mightn't have noticed them for some time. I'll do them right away.'

'Today? Now?' She was startled by the promptness.

'Just a minor job. Sounds nasty. Rodent—sort of ratty.' He made a little pouncing movement with his gloved paws and snapped his teeth at her.

'Carcinoma sounds worse.'

'Not one of the real baddies, I promise. And quite tiny as yet. But you just don't want them to get bigger.'

No, she didn't, so she spent another quarter of an hour in a second waiting-room until a nurse took her off to a vacant treatment cubicle. There she stretched out on a paper-swathed couch, the consultant breezed in, there was a jab of local anaesthetic, another pause while part of her face beside the nose went numb, then a lot of prodding and scratching around in the neighbourhood of her left eye and it was all over but for the bleeding.

In mid-afternoon, when Yeadings' team reassembled for a progress debriefing, Zyczynski turned up with a plaster and gauze from the bridge of her nose to a slightly bloody eyebrow, which meant enduring Beaumont's corny cracks about a wooden leg and a parrot on her shoulder.

Even DI Mott demanded, 'What have you done to yourself?'

She put in a disclaimer. 'It wasn't me. And you should see how I left the surgeon.'

'Right,' said Yeadings, suppressing the frivolity, 'if you're up to reading with one eye, Sergeant Zyczynski, I've a report here on the Winterton child's disappearance.'

It was the first she'd heard of it, and Yeadings' failure to respond with jokey sympathy was warning enough. She raised her free eyebrow at the DI, who nodded. 'This could be a big one,' he said. 'She went missing at midday yesterday. Eleven years old.'

Zyczynski took the sheaf of papers and skimmed quickly through, then reread while the others appeared to be ending their session. A starred paragraph immediately relating to herself referred to questioning the ex-nanny, Katy Bisset. Her address was attached.

'I'll get right on to it,' she offered.

Yeadings was rising from his desk and stretching. 'I'm going that way. I'll drive you. It'll give me a chance to fill in more background.'

'Thank you, sir.'

In his Rover, with the windows lowered to relieve the stored heat, he regarded her searchingly. 'Are you sure you're fit enough to be back?'

'Definitely, Boss. It was a very minor job. So minor that I didn't know anything was wrong until I had those scratches checked on.'

'You didn't by any chance have a Harley Street man called Barling for the surgery?'

'No. Just a local dermatologist my GP knew of. Why, sir?'

'I suspected a coincidence for a moment. It's a long story, Z, going back to my own days as a DS, but I think I'll tell you. We'll need to consider every bit of background we can get on this one. There could be echoes of something that happened eight years ago.' And so, while he drove, he told her.

Just as Yeadings—against received training—had felt a personal slant on the child's disappearance, seeing her in parallel with his own daughter, Z was transported back to her own childhood. Orphaned at age ten, old enough to understand desertion through death and too young to know how to handle grief, she'd been unwisely passed to an aunt with a closet paedophile husband, and she silently prayed that the missing Julie wouldn't be subjected to any of the horrors that she'd suffered.

Yeadings' thoughts had passed on to something else. 'I went out to the house with Angus this morning,' he said. 'I was curious to see the father again, to know what difference the years between had wrought on him.'

He drove in silence a while. He hadn't observed any dramatic physical change in Winterton after all that time wifeless. So how had he coped alone—by having casual recourse to sexual substitutes, or by remaining rigidly celibate and possibly embittered?

Above all, how had he managed as the single parent of a growing youngster? At three Julie had appeared a perfectly normal, healthy, intelligent little girl. Now suddenly all that promising future was under threat. Or—hopefully—just interrupted, because if they found the child, *when* they found the child, she would be restored to him. *He'd* be restored, except for that older injury of the wife's desertion.

Winterton hadn't answered to their ringing at the front door, so Mott and he had begun to walk round the side of the house. The sound of their feet on gravel had brought a man almost running from the direction of the garage. Morning light struck the naked face. Alarm, despair, hope chased each other across it, then left him looking almost blank. What emotion remained wasn't clear to Yeadings then. He thought he recognised a stiff mask that time had grafted on. But under it…?

'He struck me,' Yeadings decided now, 'as a man of enormous patience.'

Mott had noted down their conversation as soon as they regained the car. A forensic psychologist would need to study and assess it, then try matching it to an insubstantial figure whose profile would emerge as they closed in on whoever was behind the child's disappearance.

The father—a victim?—as their first suspect. Yeadings felt his own face set grimly. Dear God, what hidden nest of vipers was he expected to force into the daylight?

'Is there any news?' the man had demanded tersely. On Mott's negative he had recovered at once. 'Superintendent,' he said in a tightly controlled voice, turning to Yeadings, 'I had hoped you'd be in charge of the case.'

So he remembered the one-time detective sergeant, recognised him now and knew that time had brought promotion.

'You have my sympathy, Mr Winterton. It's an anxious time. Let's hope for a speedy solution.'

'I want her back unharmed.'

'We all do, sir.'

'It wasn't deliberate on her part. I know that. She wouldn't just walk out. Something has happened to Julie. Some unknown person—'

'Can we go indoors, sir? Inspector Mott will need to ask you some questions.'

And then he had left it to Angus, who knew the drill and wasn't affected by having any child of his own.

The man could tell them nothing new. He'd been writing until the clock alarm went off, the one he always set to remind him of meal times. If he didn't he was inclined to work on. And he hadn't meant to shut himself off during Julie's school holidays, only there was a tricky part he'd got to. He needed to get it down while it was fresh in his mind.

'So when did you last see your daughter?' Mott asked.

'Yesterday morning. When she brought me my coffee at eleven. She had lemonade. I broke off for ten minutes with her, then resumed. She said the cleaning lady had just left, so she was going to put on some music in the sitting-room. When I went to fetch her there was a CD still in the slot and she'd left it switched on.'

'What had she chosen?' Yeadings interrupted.

He had to think back. 'I think it was orchestral. Yes, Tchaikovsky. His string serenade. I remember hearing it distantly. It's one of her favourites.'

It struck both policemen as an unusual choice for a modern eleven-year-old. Mott took over again. 'She's not a pop fan then?'

'Well, yes, she's got quite a collection of modern discs. But she's learning the violin, so she likes the classics too.'

Classic strings. Not the heaviest stuff there was, Yeadings considered, but it could have covered any sounds of conversation with another person in the house.

'The outer doors of the house—' Mott began.

'Were open. It was so hot. I've been leaving them that way recently while Julie's been all day at school, and I never thought... It's so quiet out here. We seldom get tramps or visitors on foot, and I'd hear any car that drove up.'

They had learned little more, but before leaving Yeadings had asked to look through the music available.

If Julie had intended to swamp any other sounds she could have picked on a dozen discs in preference. But that didn't mean she'd stayed indoors to listen. The Tchaikovsky could have been sufficient cover for flitting. He hoped that when Z contacted Katy Bisset they'd get a lead on just how open or deceptive the missing child had been.

FIVE

YEADINGS AND Z FOUND Katy Bisset in her back garden among tall raspberry canes. Her two small sons were with her, their mouths and hands stained bright red. 'Here,' she told them, offering the bowl of fruit, 'don't eat any more, but I need you to pick off all the green spidery bits while I make these friends some tea.

'Come through, Superintendent.' She smiled at Z and waved them towards open patio doors. They entered a large square room furnished with soft pale sofas and chairs, and free of any scattering of toys. For the second time that day Yeadings marvelled at modern children. Katy caught him peering over the back of the sofa before sitting. 'Where's the toy box?' he covered himself.

'Oh, they have their own playroom. These are the grown-ups' quarters. The boys have to be sanitised to be let in here. Would you prefer coffee or tea? Or maybe something cold?'

When she brought in a tray with long glasses of chilled fruit juice she admitted, 'I'd wondered if I should come and see you, Mr Yeadings. It's about Julie Winterton, isn't it? I just can't believe it.'

'I'm hoping you can tell us something useful about her. Do you still keep in touch?'

'Not as well as I'd like, but we've stayed friends. She joins us sometimes when we're going somewhere special, and twice lately she's stayed overnight. She's a responsible little person and helps me with the boys when we go on trips. They adore her. We phone each other up every few weeks.

'For a while after she'd started school I used to collect her in the afternoons, cook her tea and oversee her bath at bedtime. Mr Winterton got her up and took her to school in the mornings. I stayed on until she was able to look after herself, which she picked up quite quickly. She's an independent little soul. Well, she's had to be, not having a mother. I gave up going there after I married and young Billy was on his way. She was seven by then.'

Z leaned forward. 'So she walks to and from school on her own now?'

'No. Her father still runs her there in the car and picks her up again, unless she's going out to tea with one of her friends. He's very protective. It helps that he works from home, to his own timetable.

'I would cover for him on the school run, but my boys are at a primary school in the opposite direction and the hours are the same. Julie started there but changed after we found she was being bullied.'

'How was that?' Z asked.

'She was different from her classmates, more accustomed to adults, and they began to taunt her about the runaway mother. Children can be very cruel, even at an early age. So Mr Winterton sent her to a private school, girls only. And there it seemed there were more broken homes than whole, so she was accepted as one of their kind. Only now she'll have to change schools again, because they don't take pupils over twelve. She's nearly a year ahead of her class and doesn't want to repeat the same final-year syllabus.'

'How does she feel about the move?'

'Quite excited. A little apprehensive. Just as you might expect, really. None of her friends were exactly close, but she quite likes three other girls who're making the same change, so I think she'll be all right.'

'How about grandparents?' Yeadings asked.

'Sadly she hasn't any. Mr Winterton's mother died when he was at university, and his father was much older. He died before Julie was born. Mrs Winterton's parents were both killed in a light plane crash in Italy when Julie was a baby.'

'And there was no one else?'

'Only Clive, Caroline's younger brother. No, I've got it wrong; it's Clifford. I don't remember his surname, if I ever knew it. They didn't keep in touch and she didn't seem to think much of him. ''A boring old fart'' was what she once called him. I think he worked in hospital management. I can't imagine he had much in common with his sister. Does it matter after all this time?'

'Probably not.'

'So how do you feel about the idea that Julie might have deliberately gone off, either alone or with someone she knew?' Z pursued.

Katy frowned and shook her head. 'I want to say it's impossible, but—I can't explain. You see, besides her father I'm still the closest to her, but I know there's always been a part of her I can't quite get through to. It's as though it went away when her mother did. She's not withdrawn, but she's not wholly—approachable.'

'Do you mean she's a loner?' Yeadings leaned forward to regard her evenly.

'Not exactly. But she could get to be that way. To some extent all children have a private life of the imagination, and Julie enjoys her own company. She has some special ways of doing things, and a secret place she'll hole up in if she feels out of sorts. But I never knew her to go off alone outside the garden.'

Yeadings straightened. 'Where would that be, her secret place?'

'Well, not so secret really. She wasn't entirely hidden. There's an old apple tree down near the river-bank. When she's had enough of us she'll get up there and make herself small until she's ready to face the world again. I used just to leave her to it. She always came back happier.'

'And Mr Winterton? What can you tell us about him?'

Katy had only praise for the man. He worked hard at his writing but still did everything in the house, apart from a cleaner who came in twice weekly and cooked on Friday to stock the freezer.

'He thought up treats for Julie, even if they were more suitable for an older child. He was kind and the two of them were close.'

'No women in his life?' Z queried.

'Not that I know of. I don't think he sees any need for female company. There just isn't room in his life. He very seldom goes out for an evening, and when he does I cover as Julie's minder, if George is at home for our boys.'

'So it looks,' Yeadings mused in the car, 'as if what you see is what you get with Daniel Winterton. And yet I wonder.'

When he had dropped Z off to pick up her car he went straight home and found Nan on the terrace patching Sally's dungarees. He burrowed in the freezer and filled two bowls with tutti-frutti ice cream, then carried them out, ready to tap her mind for ideas.

'Nan, you buy a lot of fiction. Have you ever read anything by Daniel Winterton?'

She put down her sewing and removed her thimble, making room for his tray on the table. 'No, I've not even picked one up to riffle through. The covers put me off. They look like men's books. Macho adventure and technical cliff-hangers.'

'I don't know. I guess I'll have to read one myself—the equivalent of confronting a suspect at his workplace. The trouble is, it'll be a durn sight more time-consuming.'

'You said "suspect." Is that really what he is?'

'Has to be at this stage. Everyone comes under suspicion—father, friends, teachers, milkman, postman, delivery lads if there are any. Until first reports are in we can't even begin to start eliminating.'

IN HER LANDLADY'S KITCHEN Z surveyed her bare half of the fridge and saw it had to be a toast and canned soup make-do for the lunch she'd missed. Tonight she and Max could go out for a meal.

While she opened a tin and sliced the wholemeal loaf her mind was still on the interview with Katy. The image of Julie she'd been left with recalled her own childhood, security abruptly shattered by the death of her parents, and the struggle to adapt to a harshly alien world. She too had needed a refuge where she could be secretly wretched and hide her cherished gizmos which no one else knew of. Stowed away in an old suitcase she still had Oliver, the hug-worn velvet owl her mother had made her as a toddler, her father's bent tie-pin rescued from returned effects after the car crash, the *Jungle Book* she had been reading when her aunt came to take her away, the china nameplate with *Rosemary* hand-painted on which was screwed to her bed-room door at the only place that had been a real home.

She hadn't seen herself as lonely. Other things perhaps, but not that. The child, Julie, might be the same, compensating for what she'd lost with imagined friends in a private world among cherished treasures.

An old apple tree down by the river-bank, Katy had said.

Z wondered if anyone had thought to search up among its branches; whether any clue might be there to what had been in Julie's mind.

By the time Z had cleared her dishes away she knew she must go and look for herself. The Boss might not be happy about Winterton being disturbed a second time in one day, but positive leads were lacking and it seemed to her a possible one to follow up.

As she turned her Ford Escort into the stony track to Long Gable she saw Winterton's Range Rover coming up to meet her, but he reversed a few yards into a passing point to allow her to draw level. She showed her ID card through the open window and he read it all through.

'Sergeant Zyczynski,' he said anxiously, 'is there any news?'

'I'm sorry, no. I just hoped to take a look at the riverbank and boathouse, if that's all right. I thought Julie might have left something there which could help.'

'Your people have searched it already, and I've had a good look around myself. But by all means see if you can turn any clue up. There might be something a woman would find significant and a man could overlook.' He paused. 'I'm obliged to keep an appointment with my GP, or I'd come with you. I didn't want to leave the phone but the answering machine's left on, in case a message should come through. I'm carrying my mobile phone too.'

He certainly looked sick enough to need a doctor, especially when he mentioned a message. She assumed he was dreading a call from kidnappers. Or perhaps he thought a runaway Julie would ring him, finding herself in unexpected difficulties?

'It shouldn't take me long,' Z assured him.

'Take as long as you need.' He lifted a hand and nodded her on.

She manoeuvred the Escort past him and continued down
to the house. Its long frontage reflected golden sunshine
and was still cottagey in character, with all the country-
calendar essentials of blue-painted trellises and heavy-
headed pink and yellow roses hanging about the windows.
Not a scene suited to tragedy. And somehow that made it
all worse. She had to remind herself that this was just a
case like any other; she had no cause to feel personally
involved.

On the rear slope to the river there were three twisted
apple trees, the only remnants of a small orchard. Allowed
to grow wild, they even had a few dozen young fruit rip-
ening among the spotted leaves but, except for one, their
contorted branches were criss-crossed by a network of brit-
tle twigs allowing no access for the smallest child.

The third and largest showed whitish scars where seca-
teurs had been used to keep a way clear. Z enlarged the
space with her Swiss Army knife to make room for her
upper body. Then, with her feet braced on a creaking lower
branch, she reached up to explore with her fingertips.

Just above the level of her head her hand encountered a
space where the ancient trunk had split, leaving a vertical
recess some four inches wide. There was something hard
and regular in shape lodged in there which she had some
difficulty in pulling out.

It was cylindrical, metallic and rusted. Just enough red
paint remained for it to be recognisable as a toy postbox.
The central panel at the front was hinged and a slot in the
top revealed its original function as a child's money box.

Z regained ground level to examine it properly. When
shaken it produced a muffled rattle. Katy's recollection had
led her to Julie's secret treasure chest, but the odds were
on whatever it contained being quite irrelevant to the present mystery.

Z opened the tin. There were a number of small pebbles carefully wrapped in tissues grown creased and grubbily stained, and a larger object double-wrapped in paper and an outer plastic bag once intended for the freezer. Inside, Z found a beautifully cut sapphire set in heavy Victorian gold with a small ring from which to hang it as a pendant.

So what was an eleven-year-old child doing with a quite valuable piece of jewellery? And how long had it been hidden away here in secret?

Surely it had been her mother's. Perhaps her father had given it to the child for a keepsake after Caroline's disappearance. Or had she come across it herself and treasured it as a secret link?

Z thought the second explanation was more likely. If Winterton had meant Julie to have it, wouldn't he have kept it for her somewhere safer? More likely the child, only three at the time, had seen it left behind in her mother's room and admired it. The other pebbles were all chosen for their shape and colour. At that age she would hardly have been aware of a difference in value. Except that she had wrapped it more carefully.

Then again, why should Caroline have taken other things of value away with her, but not this? From what Z had picked up about the missing woman, she would hardly have made a farewell present of the gem to her daughter.

Perhaps the paper which wrapped it would supply an answer. There appeared to be writing on it in a tightly formed hand which had to be an adult's.

The sheet was torn across, the top half of a page from a pad of duke-sized correspondence paper. Despite the protective plastic bag the thickish texture had combined with possibly years of handling and atmospheric penetration to affect the ink. There was no address in the upper right-hand corner and she had difficulty in making out the date. The year could be 1993 or 1995. The figures before it were smudged and would require enhancement. It was unlikely to prove worth the cost of expert examination. Z returned with it to the car and spread the paper on her knee.

M— —r Jul— wasn't hard to decipher as the letter's opening. There were blobs of mould disfiguring the words.

Going by either year it would probably have required an adult to read out the screwed-up writing. The word 'sorry' appeared in the next sentence, and what could be 'mother' after two intervening words which Z assumed to be 'that your' or 'about your'; which must eliminate Caroline herself as the writer.

Since it must have been either her father or Katy who had read the letter out to the child, it was to one of them that Z must now go for further enlightenment. In any case, the sapphire pendant had to be handed over to Winterton together with the other finds.

Again she wondered how urgent must be his medical appointment, to make him leave when hoping for some contact by phone over Julie's whereabouts. Perhaps he'd intended a quick visit to pick up a prescription. In which case she would stay parked for a further half-hour in the hope of tackling him on his return.

Seated on a garden bench facing the driveway she was conscious of now being in shadow as the insistent sound of the phone awoke her from a doze. By her watch, Winterton had been gone some forty minutes. Z went across to the sitting-room window and peered into the darker room. She could make out the oval table where the answerphone's green light suddenly changed to red and started blinking, tantalisingly near but inaccessible. It seemed even more desirable now to stay until Winterton's return.

He came some twelve minutes later, the Range Rover

bouncing down the gravel lane towards her waiting on the seat. Winterton left the car hurriedly and almost ran across.

'No,' she said quickly, 'there's no new development. I just wanted to have a word. And to show you something.'

His expression slid from instant anxiety to patient forbearance. Already he was expecting to be let down.

'Come in,' he insisted, thrusting his key into the door and waving her through. He made straight for the answering machine, muttered, 'Excuse me,' and pressed the button. Z made no pretence of walking tactfully away.

It was a reporter brashly pushing for an interview. He would be visiting next morning at nine thirty. The breath hissed out of Winterton as he dialled 1471 to get reconnected, then he angrily clamped the receiver back in place. 'Number withheld. Damn them, why can't they leave me alone? They've been all over the place since the police withdrew. I thought I'd got shot of the last of them. What if Julie's been snatched? Kidnappers could be watching the place. There's been too much publicity already.'

Z perched on the edge of an armchair. 'Usually,' she suggested, 'a kidnapper gets in first with a warning not to contact the police. I don't believe you'll be getting a ransom demand. I think my boss would tell you the same. Will you let me make you some tea? Or coffee?'

'I'm sorry. I should have... Let's go through to the kitchen. You said you've something to show me, ask me. What, then?'

'I went to see if Katy Bisset could help. She told me about Julie's apple tree bolt-hole.'

'The Retreat. That's what she calls it. We each allow the other the right now and again to go off and "huff." It's a sort of joke between us.'

'So you've never taken a look at it yourself?'

'Oh no. That would violate— Do you mean there's...?'

Z produced the toy postbox from her shoulder bag. 'I found this.' She emptied it over the kitchen table, moving the stones apart with the tip of one finger.

Winterton was staring at the polished blue one in its pendant setting, but he made no move to touch it.

'Do you recognise anything there?'

'The last present I gave Caroline. To celebrate our wedding anniversary. It's antique.'

'The sapphire? Didn't you wonder where it was?'

'I assumed it had gone with all her other bits and pieces.'

'Julie had wrapped it in some paper. It looks like part of a letter. I wondered if you could tell me who it was from.'

He appeared puzzled, but also he darted her a glance that warned, *Why should I?*

She allowed him a moment while the kettle came up to the boil and, as it clicked off, he stretched out a hand to flatten the folded paper and pore over it.

'I haven't the remotest idea.'

'It couldn't be your wife's writing?'

'It's nothing like it. Caroline's hand is looser, with flourishes on the initials. Look at this capital J. It's positively cramped. To the best of my memory I've never seen this writing before. Can you make out what it says?'

'Unfortunately it was written with a fountain pen in blue-black ink, so over the years it's smudged. I've been trying to work it out and it seems to be a sort of invitation. The words 'come and stay' are clearer than most just here.' She pointed. 'It's a pity the rest of the sheet's missing or we might have a signature.'

'It's addressed to Julie. But how would she have got hold of it? Why didn't she ever mention it to me?'

'I doubt if she knew what it was, apart from something to wrap the pendant in. Going by the date she would hardly have been able to read it, even if it was typewritten. Whoever sent it had meant you or Katy to read it out to her.'

'If it had come by post, that would have been me.'

'And you still can't remember?'

'It doesn't mean a thing to me.'

'After your wife disappeared there must have been offers of help, invitations…'

Winterton slumped on to a chair, the teapot still unfilled. 'You're right. There must have been. But for the life of me I can't recall…'

Z took over the tea-making and fetched milk from the fridge. She was almost certain that Winterton's puzzlement was genuine. In time some useful memory might surface in his mind. And even if nothing did, could an offer of assistance from someone unmemorable so many years ago really matter?

SIX

THAT AFTERNOON, after his visit with Z to see Katy Bisset, Superintendent Yeadings decided against waiting to harvest others' efforts. As the sole direct contact with the earlier Winterton disappearance he could do better than passively ride a desk. He would go back over the original case and check on everyone involved.

Winterton and the ex-nanny he'd already caught up with and could reinterview at any time. The runaway wife's present whereabouts were unknown, also Barry Morgan's. Which left the Harbury woman who had rented the end cottage. Once tracked down, she might offer some lead to her ex-lover and through him, to Caroline. A seamstress working from home, with a modest lifestyle, she hadn't sounded the sort who would stray very far from her roots.

Yet, as PC Ward's notes had implied, it wasn't her way to disturb calm waters and throw up a wake behind her. Her name didn't even appear on the current register of voters or in the local telephone directory.

She had only leased the cottage, so there was no trace through real estate ownership, and the village agency where Barry Morgan had worked had been closed down four years back, removing any record there of the earlier sale of her late mother's house.

Again it was necessary to disturb Daniel Winterton, to discover which bank the woman had used. Yeadings put a call through to a markedly tetchy Winterton and was told that the author was no preserver of rent books or small slips of paper. What data he ever chose to keep was filed in his computer. All references to the third cottage's tenants were long deleted. He was also annoyed that the police request concerned only dead issues.

Yeadings silently acknowledged that he had a point there, but insisted that the most urgent inquiries were being made elsewhere.

He then turned again to PC Ward's slipshod interview with the Harbury woman concerning Caroline's departure, and picked up on the three silk blouses with machine embroidery and pin tucks (whatever those were).

With overtime already stretched for the neighbourhood search, no uniformed men could be spared for what admittedly sounded a trivial pursuit. So Yeadings did as the advertisement said and let his fingers do the walking through the Yellow Pages.

His resultant list of stores and boutiques which he guessed likely to sell women's separates covered an area Peg Harbury might have reached by public transport. He rang them to inquire whether anyone could recall a supplier from eight years back and learned what mushroom growths boutiques were and how rapid was staff turnover even in long-established firms. When after a frustrating fifty minutes he had still drawn a blank, it occurred to him to seek advice from Nan.

He rang home and caught her about to leave the house for an afternoon walk to pick up Sally from a friend's house. Luke, already strapped in his buggy, loudly protested at the delay, kicking vigorously and audibly at the metal foot rest.

'Where I would go for an embroidered blouse?' Nan repeated. 'Frankly that's not my style, but if the obvious shops can't help, buy a women's magazine and look through the small ads in the back.'

Any excuse to remove pants seat from chair base was welcome, even for so unmacho a task. Yeadings went briskly in search of ammunition from newsagents' lower shelves and bore his booty back in a bulging but anonymous plastic carrier.

He spent the next twenty minutes running a finger down columns in the final pages and resisting the temptation to stray into more glitzy and fascinating areas.

'Expert machine embroidery,' the advertisement ran, and it appeared in two of the publications. The address both gave was 'Singer and Bernina Repairs Service' with a daytime telephone number following the Slough code. Without great hopes of success Yeadings rang through, getting an engaged signal at first but hitting the target on the second attempt.

'Yeah,' a youngish male voice told him when he asked for the embroiderer. 'But we doan do nothun like that ourselves.' There was the hint of a snigger. 'We jess take messages, like, for the lady upstairs. Giss yer nummer and she'll ring you back.'

'Her name wouldn't be Harbury by any chance?'

'Nuh, mate. Clough.'

'Right.' Having gone so far on a no-hoper it would be feeble not to pursue to the bitter end. Maybe there was some unofficial guild for women doing this type of work from home. This Clough person just might have heard of Peg Harbury. As a last resort Yeadings gave his office number and retired to fire up his coffee-maker.

Perhaps there was a lull in the repair of sewing machines, because less than ten minutes passed before the external phone on his desk buzzed. 'Yeadings,' he offered.

'This is Mrs Clough, Expert Machine Embroidery,' a soft

voice answered. 'I understand you rang a few minutes back. How can I help you?'

The superintendent explained himself, apologising for not being a customer.

'The police?' It seemed to disturb her. There was a slight pause, then almost breathlessly she enquired, 'Why do you need to speak to Miss Harbury?'

The name meant something to her. Yeadings' sagging spine stiffened. He sat bolt upright like a dressage contender. 'It concerns a woman's disappearance some eight years back. We're asking for help in our enquiries.'

A longer pause, then, 'I see. You mean Mrs Winterton. I never thought I'd hear of her again. You see, I was Peg Harbury then, Superintendent. What do you need to know?'

'As much as you can tell me, Mrs Clough.'

He managed to disguise his revived hopes, to sound total Plod. 'I should like to come and see you. Today if possible.'

She was reluctant.

He visualised her in an upstairs bedsitter overflowing with swatches of cloth, an ironing board and half-finished pieces of sewing. She sounded the sort who might be embarrassed at being discovered among clutter.

'Perhaps we could meet somewhere. Since you're in Slough, how about the cafeteria in Allders?'

It evidently cured her misgivings. She agreed to meet him at five p.m. Yeadings swallowed a scalding mugful of coffee, switched off the rest of the brew, checked he had his car keys and thundered downstairs to drive over to Slough.

SHE WAS THERE BEFORE HIM, seated at a corner table. Which was why he failed to notice the large basket down beside her feet. A slight woman in a patterned green sundress, she held up a hand as he stood in the doorway surveying the room.

He went across to her. 'Mrs Clough? You recognised me.'

'Yes, er—Superintendent. We've never met, but I saw you from my window when you used to visit Mr Winterton.'

'You have a good memory. That could be a great help to us. It's just over eight years since Mrs Winterton disappeared. How well do you recall the circumstances?'

'Too well, I'm afraid.' She moved her handbag from the chair opposite and waited while he sat, then resumed frankly.

'I'd made a fool of myself, believed I really mattered to Barry Morgan. But it seems I was only a stopgap for him. I think he imagined I'd inherited more from Mother than I had. Some of us have to learn the hard way.

'Yes, I remember well, Mr Yeadings, everything that happened that awful weekend is burned into my mind.'

She surprised him, one of those viola-soft faces with a voice to match, but by now she seemed to have picked up some worldly wisdom. She was watching him with a little smile and he felt she knew what he was thinking.

'And I made much the same mistake a second time, so I'm divorced now and quite glad to be on my own.'

Should he say he was sorry? Yeadings *hrrm*ped and considered the empty cup in front of her. 'Can I get you something? A snack, perhaps? I'm going for a very late lunch myself.'

'A Danish would be nice, thank you. And perhaps a glass of milk.'

'Full cream or…'

'Please.'

He joined the short queue, last orders before closing,

helped himself to her requirements plus a plate of lasagne and bore the tray back, over-conscious of his own Goliath proportions among the mainly female shoppers at the toy-town tables.

Mrs Clough cut the Danish into six dainty pieces and made it last while he tackled the hot pasta. 'So what in particular do you want me to remember?' she asked finally.

'As much as you can about Barry Morgan. You see, I doubt he would have stayed until now with Mrs Winterton, but if we could locate him he might tell us where she was when they split up. As it is, we know nothing of what happened after they flew to Lanzarote. Once it was known she was alive and well the police interest was over.'

'He went on to Morocco,' the woman said calmly, as if it were an everyday matter.

'You knew all along?'

'Not until the hue and cry had died down. It would be about five or six weeks later. Nobody seemed to care any more where they were. I thought hard about whether to tell Mr Winterton I'd had a postcard, but I decided against it. Barry never mentioned Caroline, and her husband seemed better off without her.'

'Weren't you surprised to hear from Morgan?'

'At first. Then I realised he would want me to know, to crow over me. And I did feel jealous. Not about Caroline by then, but I'd have loved to be there living it up with him. Daft, isn't it? I still would have taken him back then, begged him to give *me* a second chance.'

'Do you still have the postcard?'

'No, but I remember exactly what he wrote. "Crossed to Agadir by cabin cruiser. Marvellous fun here. Don't sell my golf clubs. B."'

'You're sure it came from Morocco?'

'The card was franked in Marrakesh.'

'I see.' He smiled faintly. 'And did you—sell his golf clubs?'

Her smile was a little twisted. 'No. Eventually my husband went off with them. He'd left me twice before, but that showed it was serious.'

She would be all right, Yeadings thought. There was humour in her eyes, even if of the black variety. He wondered if she managed to support herself adequately, with something put by for the inevitable rainy days.

She was gazing into the distance now. 'You know what they say about unlucky in love? Well, I took it to heart, and a couple of months back I thought I'd try it out, see if I'd be lucky elsewhere. Not at cards, but the lottery. And I was, straight off. Quite a number of other people were that week, but I won just under half a million. So I shan't starve. I might even train to do something that's more in demand than this awful needlework. It's served its purpose and I want to move on. We both do. Beryl and I.'

He flashed her a quick glance at the last words. She hadn't struck him as a lesbian.

'Beryl,' she repeated and bent below the table, fiddling with the catch on a large basket by her feet.

Never, Yeadings vowed. Not a *cat* called Beryl?

But it was: a large marmalade female.

'Beryl, because of her eyes.'

He saw what she meant. They were huge and an amazing emerald green; but what shook him was that again this woman seemed to have guessed what he was thinking.

'What were you intending to train in?' he asked.

'As a marriage guidance counsellor,' she said flatly. 'I think I have plenty of the experience it takes.'

She could have been laughing at him. All he knew was that she'd come a long way. It took a hard time to bring out the latent potential in some folk.

She nudged the cat aside with her ankle, lifted a bowl from under its head and poured in about a third of the milk. Then, flicking back a jangling chain bracelet, she finished off the rest.

'Well, I wish you every success in the new life, er, both of you.'

'We're a threesome,' she said. 'I have a young son. By Barry Morgan, but I'd rather he never knew. As for Beryl, I don't normally cart her around with me everywhere. It's just that we have a vet's appointment in twenty minutes, so I'm afraid I have to be brief.

'That postcard was the last I heard of Barry. And there's nothing more I can tell you about him except that originally he came from Newtown in Wales, and there may still be some of his family there.'

From Wales, and called Morgan, Yeadings thought with mixed feelings. That'll be like looking for a pebble on the beach.

'It could be worse,' she said rising and picking up the cat basket. 'He might have been called Evans.

'Look, we have to leave now. They're wanting to close the store.'

SETTLED AGAIN IN HIS OFFICE, Yeadings reached for the internal telephone and asked to be connected with CID at Newtown, Gwent. Within a few minutes he was put through to a solid Welsh voice which identified itself as DS Davies and drily agreed there'd surely be some folks answering to the surname of Morgan on his patch. As it happened, they were holding one at present on a charge of unlawful entry, and a pair of the scallywags were already doing a stretch for fraud.

Yeadings gave what information he had on Barry Mor-

gan and was prepared for the long-drawn triphthong, 'No,'
of a disclaimer.

'He's a new one to us. Doesn't mean he's not related to
somebody here though. We'll have an ask around.'

Yeadings disconnected, asked for Newtown, Powys, and
repeated the process with much the same result. So far as
he recalled, that exhausted the unimaginative place name
as far as Wales was concerned. He supposed he should be
grateful that Peg Harbury-Clough had recalled that he'd
hailed from the Principality.

With that Yeadings had to be content for the moment.
He took a stroll along the corridor and looked in on the
Julie incident room. The office manager had a phone tucked
under his chin and was scribbling on a pad. Chalked down
a blackboard were the names of personnel actively allocated to the inquiry. Most were ticked as being absent from
the building. Four computer operators were steadily enter-
ing data from witness statements. Nobody looked particularly inspired.

He went next door to get up to date on the analysis
display.

Along one wall ran a time chart of the incident and investigation, the later stages mainly blank. Below this were
pinned several reports highlighted in one of three colours
to indicate witness reliability or independent confirmation.
There was nothing yet from schoolmates or teachers of the
missing child. Z and Beaumont would tackle that. And
nothing on any car to match tyre tracks found in the soft
verge by the path Julie would have taken from the river.
That was the point at which tracker dogs had lost the trail.

He returned to his office. He would hang on here in the
hope that one of the team might come in with something
positive. Nan was familiar with how the early stages of a

Misper went. She would leave his dinner in the fridge and not wait up.

Although there was still a complete blank on sightings of Julie, tomorrow—as soon as newspapers hit the streets—the claims would flow in from cranks and attention-seekers in worldwide time zones: Julie would have been seen in Montreal, Timbuktu and Tonga.

Eventually Sergeant Tebbit came through from the Incident Room with a phoned note from DS Zyczynski. 'Don't hold your breath, sir. It's ancient news, I'm afraid. She's on her way in, since I said you're still here.'

Meaning he wished Yeadings wasn't hanging uselessly around getting in his way? Not more than Yeadings regretted it himself. Ruddy office-wallah, never knew the live scent of the hunt, held back from tooth-and-claw action by red tape, as Yeadings was by seniority. Still, give the man his due, Tebbit ran his office well. Horses for courses, and all that. Or hacks for harness rooms.

Yeadings scowled at the wad of unrelated papers in his in-tray, recharged the coffee-maker and stood jingling keys in his pocket as he stared out of the window at night-shift cars manoeuvring into the marked spaces below. DS Beaumont, stiffly extricating himself from his Vauxhall Astra, glanced up, almost waved a hand, then changed it to a shrug.

That was a negative, Yeadings decided. He'd been over to the Norfolk Broads after a holidaying bank manager's family which included one of Julie's schoolfriends. That left just two she might have confided her plans to. If any plans there had been; if she wasn't simply overtaken by events.

Events or someone's plain evil-mindedness.

Beaumont reported direct to the Incident Room before

sliding in through Yeadings' open door. 'Nothing, then?' the Boss greeted him.

'Not a lot. The mother was co-operative, but the step-father didn't want the little darling questioned. The kid—'

'Yes?'

'Mousy-looking little thing, but she had the measure of them both. Expressed a poor opinion of Julie Winterton, though the pair of them hadn't shared secrets. She supposed Julie would be playing her dad up. I'd say it's fifty-fifty whether she had a true picture of the kid or if it was what she'd like to do herself. And she might have invented that opinion for home consumption rather than my ears. I got the impression the holiday was already off to a bad start. She'd wanted to go to Ibiza.'

'Had she discussed holidays with Julie, got any notion what the other little girl hankered after?'

'I asked that. She went sour on it, said Julie never wanted to do anything cool. She was "a bit soggy really".'

'Which runs counter to her previous supposition.'

'I guess.'

The both looked up as Z appeared in the doorway. 'Sir? I rang in direct but you were out. So I reported in to Sergeant Tebbit.'

'I got your message. I'd gone chasing a bit of ancient history, hoping to trace Morgan for a link to Caroline Winterton's present whereabouts.'

The other two waited expectantly.

'Coffee?' Yeadings offered, waving for Beaumont to pull out three mugs from the cupboard behind him.

'A link to Caroline,' Z echoed. 'Could you trace Morgan?'

'Set it in motion,' he told her and explained the Newtown connection. 'It appears Morgan sailed across to Morocco after Lanzarote, sent a jaunty postcard from Marrakesh to his old flame Ms Harbury, now Mrs Clough, divorced, of Slough. No mention in it of Caroline. I think that wherever Morgan is now there's little chance he's still in touch with her. They both seemed to get through partners at interplanetary speed. Still, it's worth trying.'

'Meanwhile we're circulating her photograph locally,' Beaumont considered. 'She was a striking woman. If she'd come back, planning to snatch her daughter, someone should have spotted her.'

'Unless she used a third party for the pick-up.'

'It would have to be someone Julie knew and trusted. Remember the makings of a picnic she took with her. And she doesn't sound the sort who'd entertain strangers.'

'So who fits the bill? Any ideas?'

Z looked uncertain. 'There's a doubtful lead I want to follow up: an unknown from way back who wrote to Julie after her mother's disappearance. I found this scrap of a letter she'd wrapped some treasures in to hide in her secret cache. I've included a photocopy with my full report.' She produced the stained and barely legible original.

'Ancient history,' Beaumont complained, reading it over the seated Yeadings' shoulder.

'That's why I didn't log it as significant.'

'But it's as much as we have to work on so far,' Yeadings said ruefully. 'We can try getting this enhanced. What do you make of it, Z?'

'No signature, no address; dated December 93 or 95. I thought it might have been enclosed with a Christmas present and Winterton never got to see it. It mentions ''your mother,'' and seems to be some sort of invitation. I showed it to Daniel Winterton but he didn't recognise the writing.'

'Possibly because whoever wrote it was connected with the other parent,' Yeadings suggested. 'I'm not familiar with the handwriting of my wife's lot, for instance. She'll read me out the bits that could interest me and I never handle the letters myself.'

'We know both of Mrs Winterton's parents are dead,' Z explained. 'But this morning Katy mentioned a younger brother Clifford, surname unknown. She thought he was some kind of NHS administrator. Was he interviewed when she disappeared, sir?'

'Listed, probably,' Yeadings recalled. 'But as soon as we knew she'd gone off with Morgan the case was dropped. I doubt if there was time to put out feelers beyond any locals. Leave it to me, Z. I'll chase up his details. I seem to be blessed with all the dead ends.'

Approaching footsteps in the corridor stopped abruptly as Mott's tall figure filled the open doorway. 'You're just in time for the dregs,' Yeadings told him, indicating the coffee machine. 'Take a seat and look through this note Z's found. Tell us what you make of it.'

The DI folded himself on to the vacated chair as Z went across to pour. He frowned over the barely legible words. 'I don't make much,' he admitted shortly. 'Where does it fit in?'

Yeadings left it to Z to explain how she found it and what she supposed it meant. Mott nodded. 'Could be,' he languidly agreed, 'but where does it get us?'

'Still up the creek,' Yeadings said mildly. 'Which brings us to the dinghy. I assume that's what you've come about?'

The DI nodded. 'Forensics phoned in. They'll fax the full details when they're printed out. The SOCOs had provided a whole lot of fibres and mud samples scraped off the boat, including cotton thread from Julie Winterton's dress. I've checked with her father and it seems she'd changed from the T-shirt and shorts she got up in that morning. When she brought in his coffee she was wearing the dress as described in the handouts. What he hadn't thought to mention before was that the dress was new. She'd chosen to christen it because they were going out for a hotel lunch and she wanted to look presentable.'

'How much thread was there?' Z asked sharply. 'Was the dress torn enough to indicate some kind of struggle?'

'A single two-inch thread of spun cotton voile showing three colours of dye from the print pattern. They've compared it with a similar dress obtained from the same store.

'The thread was snagged on the rough front edge of the dinghy's rear seat. It does indicate that Julie used the boat that morning and at some point was probably at the tiller herself. Winterton is going to package up the clothes he always wore when sailing. I explained we'd need them in order to eliminate him.'

'Hang on,' interrupted Beaumont. 'Why *eliminate* him? We've only his word for it that he stayed at his word processor. Why couldn't he have told Julie he'd changed his mind—they'd have a picnic instead? That would account for the raided fridge. Then they both went off in the dinghy, moored it where it was found and—'

'—she disappeared into the sunset? Only it was midday. You're suggesting he's done away with his own daughter?' Mott shrugged. 'Well, most murders are domestic after all, so why not?' he conceded finally.

'That implies a degree of cold-bloodedness I wouldn't have expected of him,' Yeadings commented. 'Admittedly I could be deceived, and I'll allow the man is ingenious, possibly devious. But downright evil? I wouldn't say so.'

'It's a possibility to consider,' Mott cautioned.

'So we'll bear it in mind. Anything else from Forensics?'

'No.' Mott looked round at the others. 'But I had a call from Reading University Geology Department about some pebbles. I don't know where they connect. I never sent them in.'

'You weren't around at the time,' Z explained. 'They were part of Julie's treasures. I found them today along with the note and wondered why she'd kept them. Sergeant Tebbit had them delivered to Reading. The geologists are certainly quick reactors. What did they say?'

'They're ordinary stream-bed examples, water-washed and valueless except as textbook samples.'

Z nodded. 'I was afraid so. Julie collected them for local interest, perhaps towards some playschool game.'

'I think we can safely forget them,' Yeadings decided. 'Right, Angus, I'll let you get on with the fibre matching. I suppose that means you'll need to check other people's wardrobes as well as Winterton's. You'd better list the possibles.' He began searching through the pile of papers on his desk, muttering darkly.

'Hold on,' he ordered Beaumont, thrusting a handful at him. 'These aren't mine. See they get to the right people. Illegal hare coursing! That's not Serious Crimes' concern yet, however fanatical the Animal Rights nutters.'

'Maybe they're aiming to recruit you,' Beaumont suggested blandly, then caught the glower Yeadings directed at him. 'Er, *sir!*'

'On your way, Sergeant. We've a missing child to find. Go home now and be in for eight a.m. tomorrow. Z, you're excused. I want you to chase up the other two schoolmates first thing, then report in ASAP.'

SEVEN

DRIVING HOME, Z FELT despondent. Before putting the car in gear she had inspected her face in the driving mirror, rooted in the glove compartment for her pot of cream cover-up and blotted out the two tiny red eyes staring from beside her nose.

She told herself they didn't bother her. The *things* had been removed. These were just healing scars.

But if they had come, why shouldn't others? Not that her face was so wonderful—though she liked the way men sometimes smiled at her with their eyes—but *inside,* that would worry her.

Not a real baddy, the surgeon had said; but carcinoma, just the same.

She wished she could creep into her flat and have a sneaky little weep on her own. But there'd be no real privacy. She'd have to avoid her landlady, Beattie, by stealing upstairs without her shoes.

Max Harris might be there too. Recently returned from a visit to Yemen, he was staying over with her. Dear old Max; but she didn't need company right now. And much as she relished the break from celibacy, there was a real drawback: the sleeping part of sleeping together.

Overnight Max got by with catnaps, in the intervals often requiring sustenance or entertainment. Z, who was accustomed to a solid eight-hour knockout, found that kind of shared bed quite wearing. However low he turned the TV, the raucous or scary overnight programmes got through to her. Or else she was aware of him downstairs, rattling ice cubes from the fridge or tossing a stir-fry in a sizzling wok.

Only last night she had been conscious of him rising at four thirty to make a mug of decaf, followed by a half-hour's reading by shaded torchlight beside her. She had kept her eyelids obstinately sealed, hoping that a pretence of sleep might persuade the real thing back.

At the end of his wakeful stint Max had reached for a leather bookmark to keep his place, extinguished the torch, sneezed five times, waited, ascertained that the barrage was completed, calmly lay down and was asleep within thirty seconds.

Z had stayed tensely awake until a little after six.

This didn't guarantee alert performance of police duties. Nor romantic dreams of a lifetime with her lover.

When they shared Max's roomy Pimlico apartment it was different. He accorded her a room to herself, and she was free of any duty roster, so sleeping late didn't matter. But, she decided, in the cramped quarters of her lodgings at Beattie's, cohabiting was definitely out. Tonight she would have to warn him.

She persuaded herself that meanwhile, she'd no choice but to see Katy Bisset again, this time regarding the finds from Julie's apple tree. She turned off from her homeward direction and followed the route of the morning.

When Z rang, their door was opened by George Bisset in cricket gear with grass stains down the right side of his white trousers. From this she gathered he was prized as a bowler.

'I thought your game was darts,' she greeted him.

He had a slow, boyish smile. 'That's for winter, Sergeant. Can't waste good evening sunshine indoors. Is it me you're wanting or Katy?'

'Katy, if she can spare a few minutes. I'm surprised you haven't been out in the search squads.' She began to follow him into the kitchen when he turned back.

'It wasn't my choice. The CC decreed the match mustn't be scratched. He traded our side for a dozen volunteers sent over from Bicester. Have they come up with anything yet?'

She shook her head. At least he'd inquired after the case and not given the cricket score first. But then he was a dad. Fatherhood knocked a sense of proportion into some men.

Katy looked up from lifting a half-leg of lamb from the oven and fanned her face with a padded glove. 'You've judged your entry just right, Sergeant. George, set another place, love, and fish out a bottle of red.'

'I'm on the job,' Z said shortly, 'but thanks all the same.'

'Well, you can talk with a fork in your hand, surely? Anyway, I'm too hungry myself to answer more questions for the moment.'

PC Bisset promptly conjured up the place setting and wine, then took over stirring the gravy as Katy removed the meat to a serving dish and set it on the table. Delicious herbal smells reminded Z that she'd missed out on a proper lunch. 'In that case can I help?'

'Strain the peas and carrots? Colander to your right. Good-oh, the roast spuds are ready. Hope you like them crisp. Plain home cooking. It's just stuffed baked apples and sorbet for afters.'

Something about the brisk approach rang a faint bell in Z's head. She paused by the cork Yogi Bear noticeboard and, sure enough, drawing-pinned to the top was a sheet of paper signed by Katy and headed with the Scouts' logo. She might have guessed that the one-time wonderful nanny would still be carrying the torch, as Akela, or whatever.

'Sorry I've not changed,' George Bisset apologised, 'but

the match started late so I'm only just back. I guess you've done a day's hard graft and you think I'm swinging it.'

'Needs must when the CC drives. I could do with a bit of diverting myself.' She helped herself to vegetables and decided not to spoil the meal with serious talk. It was left to Katy to raise the subject as she set out the dessert.

'Has nothing turned up yet?' she asked. Her voice had changed, hesitant and vulnerable.

Z felt for her. 'There's something you can maybe throw a light on. I looked where you told me and found Julie's treasure stash. It goes back a long way, but Mr Winterton can't explain it any more than I can.' She told them about the collection of pebbles with the sapphire pendant wrapped in an almost indecipherable note. She offered the crumpled paper to Bisset, who passed it across to his wife.

Katy frowned over the cramped writing. 'It's part of a letter to Julie.'

'But look at the date. I'm sure she wouldn't be old enough then to read joined-up writing. So who opened it and read it to her? You or her father?'

'I've never seen it before. You say Mr Winterton can't explain it?'

'Maybe Caroline herself…?'

'Unlikely. Down here it mentions "your mother", and then some kind of invitation. Is it jumping too far to assume that since it came shortly after Caroline disappeared, it was from a sympathetic adult who wanted to help out?'

Bisset took it back and scowled in turn at the writing. 'No envelope, I suppose? Or the rest of the page?'

'Maybe,' Katy suggested, 'Julie took it directly from the postman and no one else saw it. As a three-year-old she could recognise her own first name if it was clearly enough written on the envelope. And people often take greater care over addresses, knowing most postmen are half blind. It could even have been in block capitals.'

'But the message inside wasn't. So surely she'd show it to her father, to find out what it was about.'

Katy shook her head. 'Not necessarily, especially if she'd lifted it from the mail herself. That would be like admitting to what she'd consider naughty. It's more likely she'd treat it as grown-up rubbish, and not think twice about using it for wrapping paper. I wonder what she did with the rest of the page?'

'Threw it away,' Z realised suddenly, 'because it was too bulky. Half the sheet was enough to wrap the pendant. Any more and it wouldn't have fit into the tin.'

'What tin's that?'

'It started life as a money box. Shaped like a red Royal Mail postbox. But, having been up in the apple tree all these years, it's pretty rusted.'

'About so big?' Katy demanded, measuring with her fingers.

'Yes. Do you remember it?'

'Yes, I do. I bought it for her as a stocking filler. It was that Christmas, the first one after Caroline disappeared. Come to think of it, I never saw Julie with it; not once I'd stuffed it in with her tangerine and the usual glitzy kitsch on Christmas Eve.'

'Which confirms the letter's date,' Bisset said. 'Not that it can matter after all this time. The mystery is what the child was doing with a valuable piece of jewellery.'

'It was her mother's,' Z explained. 'Mr Winterton couldn't imagine why Caroline didn't take it with the rest of her stuff.'

'So it was left behind and somehow Julie found it, a memento of the mother who'd vanished together with a whole chunk of her young life. It was real treasure, to be hidden away—'

Katy's voice broke and Z filled in the space for her.

'In her new money box, which was special, too because it came from you. I think it could be one of those Christmas notes from a family friend or relative who only pops up once a year. Thus handwriting that was unfamiliar to Daniel Winterton, if he's telling the truth—and I don't see why he shouldn't. It came from someone who doesn't know much about children's reading ability, or else assumed her father would open it for her.'

'And it didn't need an envelope. It could have been slipped in with a present,' Bisset concluded enthusiastically. 'If there had been an envelope, why didn't she wrap the pendant in that? She wouldn't have needed to use part of the letter.'

He groaned, recharging their glasses. 'Brilliant deduction! Only, what the blazes is the use of knowing all that? This was eight years ago. It's now that the kid's gone AWOL.'

His basic logic deflated the two women. The euphoria of juggling with the puzzle gave way to hollow reality. It brought the reminder that, slender as Z's findings were, as yet there was little else.

The missing child's past Christmases were suddenly pathetic. Katy sat hunched and despondent among the used dishes. Z felt obliged to seize on some positive aspect.

'At least we know there was once someone who made an offer to have the child, even if only for a holiday. And presumably the note went unanswered, since Winterton was ignorant of it. I wonder how the writer took that? Not that he or she would be likely to wait eight years to snatch Julie.'

He or she: who could that be? Surely more than a casual

acquaintance, and not anyone whose writing was familiar to Winterton. Someone connected with Caroline, then?

'Katy, you told us there weren't any grandparents.'

'That's right. Just the younger brother, Clifford.'

'Yes. Mr Yeadings is going to check on him.'

Z felt suddenly exhausted, and it wasn't just physical tiredness. She couldn't see why she had ever thought her find important. And any light the secret cache shed on Julie was only what she could have learned from observing any three-year-old only child. She had no first-hand experience of children, as these two had; wasn't likely ever to have, because just lately she'd known why she was reluctant to marry Max. It wasn't just the domesticity trap, but reluctance to have children. He would certainly want them, but for herself there was a mental block: she wasn't sure she could risk it for them. Her own fearful childhood made the idea pitiable, and experience of police work hadn't made the world look any safer for innocents.

The Bissets were watching her, waiting for more. 'I can't make up my mind about Winterton,' she admitted. 'He's under terrible pressure, of course. People seem to like him, but how much of that is sympathy for an apparent victim? Katy, you say yourself that he was patient with Julie as a three-year-old, but at eleven she's reaching an independent age, one an over-protective man might have difficulty coping with. Suppose she openly defied him over something, worked his temper up, even blamed him for her mother's deserting them. Facing her on his own, might he eventually have lost his cool, lashed out? I don't see him meaning to harm the child, but maybe accidentally...?'

'You'd know if he had done. He couldn't have hidden it. He'd be out of his mind.'

'Which he almost is.'

'With grief, though. Not guilt.'

'It's not easy to see the difference.'

Katy leaned her elbows on the table. 'Look, if you think it could help, I'll go and see him. Maybe he'll open up to me and we'll have something to work on. All the time he's still in the frame as a suspect you could be missing out on following up someone else.'

Z nodded. 'I'd be grateful. Anything that could eliminate him. Or prove positive. I seem to be thinking in circles, but it was good to talk with you. Thanks anyway,' she said. 'And especially for the meal. It was great.' She tried not to make it sound flat, but knew she left the other two as disheartened as she was.

'Maybe tomorrow…' Bisset offered, showing her out.

'Something will turn up,' Katy promised, with only a slight quaver.

So, apart from the unattributed note from the apple tree cache, what had today's efforts yielded? Z asked herself.

Nul point. The thought wasn't invigorating. She considered wryly the remaining friends of Julie's she had to question, who would change to the same secondary school in September.

What right had the Boss to assume she could automatically deal with children because she was female? Maybe he found it easy, Yeadings the father figure switched to cuddly bear mode. But then he couldn't see Z's ten-year-old self that kept intruding from the past. This was the wraith Rosemary Zyczynski had to deny, the child victim of abuse still able to scare the daylight out of her when she thought what might be happening now to young Julie Winterton.

Work was the best way of keeping the ghost at bay.

Tomorrow, Z promised silently as she started the car. Tomorrow I'll give it everything I've got.

WITH THE TEAM DISPERSED, Yeadings had sat on, added to his shorthand notes, read them through and highlighted one sentence in bright yellow. His personal ray of sunshine perhaps. According to Katy Bisset, Caroline Winterton had a younger brother, Clifford, surname unknown. In this search, if no stone was to be left unturned, however long settled into the mud, this was another bit of history for him to go after.

Hidden deep among all this bumf there must be a reference to Caroline's maiden surname. Dinosaur as he undoubtedly was in his instinctive aversion to the white heat of modern technology, he must pad along to the Incident Room and pull the info out of a computer.

Dubiously, a WPC cleared her screen for him and surrendered her chair. Yeadings was aware of her watching uneasily from the corner of her eye as he took over and keyed in his request. 'Why don't you snatch a coffee?' he murmured. 'I heard they had fresh doughnuts in the canteen.'

He registered the flare of her nostrils and guessed she was probably on a self-imposed diet. Well, let her fight her conscience out of his sight. And he would operate out of hers.

He found the right data menu and typed in Caroline's name. The screen filled with information, but he didn't have far to scroll. It was in the second line of her ID. Before marrying Daniel Winterton she had been Caroline Anne Hook.

Yeadings sat back, smugly satisfied with his technical accomplishment. Canteen coffee was beyond endurance, but maybe he would join the WPC in a doughnut, by way of self-reward, and to reassure her that he hadn't crashed her program.

HE RETURNED HOME TO FIND Nan still up but half dozing in front of the TV. There was salmon mayonnaise in the fridge for him and he washed it down with chilled Montrachet.

'What was your day like?' he asked, knowing she'd accept it as his personal confession of having achieved nothing of much value.

'Pleasant enough. Luke found the heat a bit much, so I put him down for a nap before lunch and he went out like a light. Sally couldn't make sense of some holiday task from school, but we sorted it and then she pottered around in the border with a trowel and went to bed happy.'

'That's their day. I asked about yours.'

'The usual—in a negligee, stretched out on a sofa scoffing chocolates and sherry to smooch music. What else?'

'I don't know why I ask. Like the chorus doesn't quite say, "A policeman's wife is not a happy one."'

'Mike, it's a great life, really. I just wish you could share more of it with us. I'd tell you if I got itchy feet.'

He reached over a large hand and picked up hers, stared at the gold band on her fourth finger. It had started off chased and faceted. Now it was worn smoothly round. He squeezed her hand gently.

'I'm a lucky beggar, Nan. I promise I'll take some time off when this case is finished and we'll go away together. You can pick the place.'

NEXT MORNING, WHEN HE looked into the Incident Room, Sergeant Tebbit was totting up figures. Costings. The budget was going sky high, he said, with nothing to show for it. Only Day Three, and already there was grumbling from above over enhanced working rates for the uniformed branch: all that overtime on house-to-house and fingertip searching. (Even then, some of it had been unpaid, because it was a child they were looking for and all the family men had volunteered.)

So let the upper brass do the worrying over money, Yeadings allowed. In his opinion it was far too soon to start hanging that albatross on working shoulders. For himself, he had other matters to look to. Like chasing up Clifford Hook.

Since Katy Bisset, who had her feet on the ground, was familiar with the family, he'd try her again for info on Caroline's brother. He hunted in his notebook for her number and rang from his office.

One of her boys answered in a piping treble, offering to go and get Mum. When Katy picked up and he put his question to her she thought for a moment. 'What I know about Mr Hook? Well, only what I told you yesterday. He was asked to dinner at the Wintertons' once or twice to even out numbers at table. That was before Caroline went away. Afterwards I don't think he ever came to the house, unless it was evenings when I'd gone off duty. Left on his own Mr Winterton gave up entertaining.'

Yeadings decided she couldn't be much help. She'd thought Hook was a bachelor, had seen him as a rather awkward uncle who didn't know how to talk to small children. He had little in common with his brother-in-law, but there was no open hostility. They had been polite to each other. Which wasn't really the case with Caroline. She looked down on him, called him Old Dumbo, and it hadn't been a term of affection. Clifford, however, seemed impervious to her scorn, thought the world of his older sister and would have done anything for her.

Had Hook struck Katy as unstable?

'Lord, no,' she told him. 'Rather nice really, in a bumbly sort of way. Easily embarrassed, though, and too ready to apologise when it wasn't necessary.'

This didn't make him sound dangerous. He could, however, have written the note to Julie all those years back. Which still didn't make him a pressing subject for looking into.

Mott having delivered an updated briefing to the augmented team, Beaumont went to chase up developments from Forensics' findings. Both had returned to Yeadings' office by the time Zyczynski reported in just after eleven.

'So what did you get from the other two schoolmates?' Mott demanded.

'Only background. I caught one family just a day before they were off to Italy. The others will stay put until the end of the month.

'It seems Julie never carried money on her, apart from anything needed at school. That would be cash for lunch tickets and something for the charity box. They confirmed she never walked or took a bus home. Mostly her father picked her up, otherwise she'd go with either of the friends' mothers who sometimes asked her back to tea. Invitations were made and accepted well in advance. The third friend—the one Beaumont has checked on—never invited her home. Parents too snooty, was the opinion offered.'

'Did Julie return the hospitality?'

'Regularly. Both girls enjoyed their separate invitations to the Wintertons'. He'd lay on a special cream tea or a picnic with salmon sandwiches and soft drinks, take them out in the punt or the dinghy. Then videos in Julie's room until it was time to take them home.

'Rosie Marlowe's mother is a divorcée, owns horses, and the girls would ride at her house. Fran Benson's parents are both members of an orchestra, on tour a lot, so the granny sometimes took over entertaining the girls. Not riveting fun, it seems. I think Fran enjoys playing the old lady up.'

'Julie too?' Yeadings interrupted sharply. 'If she was a bit of a joker...'

'No. Fran complained she wasn't much fun, took everything too seriously. But it seems she rubbed along with Julie for lack of an alternative, and because she enjoyed the outings to Long Gable.'

'And neither child could suggest what plans Julie had made for the holidays? Or if she had a secret friend her father didn't know about?'

'Apart from saying she was good at her schoolwork and music, neither claimed to know anything of Julie's likes or dislikes, let alone being bothered whether anything was on her mind. She comes over as an unusually self-contained child. And polite—both families remarked how very correct she always was.'

'Which makes it even more unlikely that she'd willingly go off with a stranger, especially when she knew her father had booked her favourite hotel for lunch.'

'But still she raided the fridge for a picnic,' Beaumont insisted.

Yeadings grunted. 'We've assumed she was to enjoy part of that herself. Suppose we're wrong and she collected the food for someone else she felt needed it?'

They all considered the new slant. 'But a *stranger?*' Z queried.

'We all know that the word has an elastic definition,' Yeadings reminded them. 'She took a generous amount of food, so maybe she was thinking in terms of hunger. I think we need to know what Winterton's attitude to beggars was; whether he habitually handed food out to anyone who came to the door. Z, you mentioned a charity box in connection with school. Did the children organise that themselves, and who were the recipients?'

'Cot Box,' she answered instantly. 'It's been running for

cats' ages. Every Monday the girls take in some cash—it's supposed to come from their pocket money, but mostly the parents fork out once again—and the kids put it in the collecting box after morning assembly. Originally the money went to support a cot in the children's ward of the local cottage hospital. More recently it's been spent on clothes or special requirements for needy local children who go there for treatment.'

'So she's been raised to a tradition of giving.' Yeadings considered it, chin on chest.

'She's eleven,' Z reminded him, 'and by all accounts a serious child. I still think she'd have too much sense to go off with a total stranger. But if it was someone who had come to the house before and had already received help from her father, then…'

'…Rather than disturb him when he was working…' Beaumont provided.

'…she just might have put some foodstuffs together.' Yeadings nodded. 'Are we agreed on that?'

'Maybe so far,' Z conceded, 'but I don't see why she would then leave the house, take out the dinghy and sail downriver.'

'We don't know that she did that willingly. This person—call him X—could have forced that on her once he'd got her safely out of Winterton's hearing. Having won the child's trust he could have asked the way to somewhere and she'd innocently go a little way to show him.'

'Him or her,' Beaumont pointed out.

'As you say,' Yeadings said heavily. 'Either's possible. And it freezes the blood to think with what purpose in mind.'

There was a silence during which faint sounds of altercation came up through the open window, cut off by the roaring of a car engine with a deal of irately applied welly.

'I've offered you the worst possible scenario,' Yeadings summed it up. 'Give me others.'

Z came up with an alternative. 'If it had been Caroline who'd returned to get her, she could have said she had a surprise for Daddy but it was in the car some distance off.'

'But wouldn't Julie be terribly excited, want to run straight to Daddy and tell him who was there?'

'Maybe she couldn't,' Beaumont said grimly. 'Caroline Winterton wasn't a famously good mother. If she'd let Julie glimpse her down by the river and waved, the girl might have gone close to make certain who it was. Then Caroline could have used force to spirit the child away. If she'd finally run out of funds she'd know she had a strong bargaining counter in Julie.'

'So why hasn't she been in touch with her husband since, making demands?'

'Because,' Beaumont supplied with all the spleen of a hard-done-by husband, 'she's enjoying making him sweat it out. She'll wait until the poor devil's so demented that he'll give in to whatever she cares to ask for.'

'Hook,' Yeadings threw into the silence created by Beaumont's outburst. 'No, nothing to do with fishing. Hook was Caroline Winterton's maiden name. Also presumably it's her brother's. Clifford Hook is employed somewhere by the National Health Service in hospital management. I want him traced.'

'Shouldn't be difficult,' Mott remarked without noticeable enthusiasm. 'Beaumont, you can follow that up. Now.'

'A doddle.' The DS rose, stretched and left to set up a phone search from the CID office. Less than half an hour later he came back grinning.

'Now here's a turn-up for the books. Our Mr Clifford Hook isn't just any old doctor-harasser. He's lording it over a team of shrinks. At Craythorpe Park High Security Psychiatric Hospital. All among the nutters, would you believe?'

EIGHT

CLIFFORD HOOK RAN A TREMBLING hand over his thudding brow. It came away moist. He was getting nowhere with the report. He shouldn't have brought the work home, had never meant to. But recently he had ended up doing a lot of things contrary to his first intentions. It was as though some robotic part of him lumbered on in defiance of what he'd already decided, pursuing what he'd ruled out.

He knew he should do as the Medical Director advised: delegate more to others, then sit back and take things gently. It was easy to say, even sounded good sense when suggested, but in the extra, empty time acquired he'd be left staring at the same problems. More than problems; recurrent crises—almost a state of permanent disaster—and with no more room for free choice than a drowning man had of staying afloat.

Too leaden for even the idea of surfacing, he could no longer identify the initial problem on which all the others had accumulated. There was money, of course, and how to stretch funds. And time—never enough of that. When personalities were added in, it became beyond his ability to face the magnitude of expectations. A plan, so simple-seeming on paper, became crazily complex when people were added in.

He knew that sooner or later he was obliged to get things sorted, get *himself* sorted. But how to start?

Seek professional help? All sorts of people did these days; there was no shame in it.

The truth, though, was that the idea of analysis scared him; the thought of what might emerge: his wounds bared, as shaming as he would feel physical nakedness with spectators staring. And the horror of admitting that sometimes his actions were out of kilter, then submitting himself to another's control.

But the alternative—letting ever more pressure accumulate unchecked—threatened a repeat of what had happened once before. The mistakes went back so far, involving people who were no longer around. Instantly fear griped at his guts and, huddled in pain, he knew he would vomit.

He came back unsteadily from the bathroom, his mouth bitter despite the gulped water. Sweat had sprung out all over his body and now he shivered in the after-chill.

There was Scotch in the kitchen's top cupboard but he didn't trust himself to get on the stool to reach the bottle down. And that, of course, was why he'd stowed it up there. So that it wasn't easily to hand. Because he mustn't break out again. He'd even boasted to himself that he was safe from it now.

He could hardly believe in his brief period of imagined strength, when the pressures hadn't crushed him. He'd been eagerly looking forward, confident in his ability to plan and see the project through against whatever opposition. Because, safe in an undemanding post before, he'd been lulled into a belief that his theories of reform were unquestionable. And of course Halliday had been around then, needing a deputy to take off some of the load—and the heat—from him. But Halliday had won his knighthood, retired from the action, and had taken to the full-time ivory tower of writing his much lauded book: Sir Godfrey Halliday, now the (mainly theoretical) international authority on modernist management of high security hospitals.

But for himself there was no way out from soldiering on, unless to go over the edge and join the inmates. It had all been too demanding; interminable.

There had been a time when he'd known he was right. The arguments were irrefutable. But, modest in his expectations, he wasn't prepared to be thrust into the front line and constantly under fire; not him, plain Clifford Hook— then an unexceptional family man who had worked to routine and only occasionally put in extra hours.

Not that hospital management at any level was a sinecure. There were built-in difficulties, logistical and financial, and you couldn't avoid making enemies because demands came from all sides and ran counter to each other. It was a question of adjusting and maintaining balance. And now he was at risk of losing his own.

While his home world seemed secure he had been able to stand the strictures and hostilities. Olive was there and the baby on its way. They had an assured future. They were his security.

But that was when everything had started rushing downhill. Being overworked—holding the warring factions apart while forced to cut staff and cut costs, treacherously challenged over agreed rebuilding plans—he hadn't noticed close dangers. Grappling with the big issues, he'd been undermined by others under his own roof.

If only he had—

The shrill of the doorbell sliced suddenly through him. He felt a leap of his heart and warm blood pounding in his head. It left a metallic taste on his tongue.

No, he resolved; I'll not answer. I'll stay quiet and they'll go away.

But the robot self was already lumbering to its feet, responding to alarms. Perhaps it had been inevitable, he thought, fumbling with the lock on the outer door. Anyone waiting by the porch could have seen him inside the room. It was as though walls had become transparent. They would have gone on and on ringing.

He opened on the chain, and against the bright sunlight glimpsed a tall, heavy man in a light summer suit. He was a stranger, and any unknown appearing unannounced within the hospital precinct must bring with him some threat.

'Yes?' Hook said thickly.

The man was showing him something, a card in a worn leather wallet. 'Thames Valley Police,' he announced, but Hook had missed what he said, concentrating on the action.

'No,' he said desperately, 'I don't give to charity on the doorstep.' He held tightly to the door's frame to still his tremor. Then the word 'police' came fully through to him, meaning more than an appeal for their Widows and Orphans Fund. The tightness in his chest made it almost impossible to breathe.

Yeadings grasped the other's confusion, uncertain at first whether he suffered from a drinking problem or some mental imbalance. Through the door's crack he saw a stocky man, rather overweight, in a crumpled suit too heavy for summer weather. He had a large, square head that deserved a more impressive body, but as it was the short legs made him appear top-heavy; little more than five feet five or six in height. Thin, fair hair receding from a broad forehead left exposed lardy-pale, shiny skin above straight brows; washed-out, fugitive grey eyes behind thick-lensed spectacles; fleshy nose; a wide mouth pursed at the corners, and a puckered chin. He was frowning and his gaze flickered as he waited for his visitor to remove himself.

But now Yeadings was explaining: he would appreciate

a few words on a serious matter under investigation. It concerned the disappearance from home of a young girl. Perhaps Mr Hook had been informed of it, seen it on the TV
news?

'N-no. No, I'm sorry. I'm afraid I can't be of any help
to you.'

'I believe you can, Mr Hook. At least with some background information. About your sister's daughter, Julie
Winterton.'

'My late sister,' he muttered automatically.

His immobility halted Yeadings a second, then he gave
a reassuring smile. 'Perhaps I could come in? It's rather
public out here.'

Hook moved back, then remembered the chain and shakily removed it.

He would be little more than forty, Yeadings thought,
but he shuffled like a much older man, or someone with
Alzheimer's. Perhaps he had sat for a long while without
moving.

'I—I'm not feeling well,' Hook faltered. 'Could you
come at some other time?' But he continued leading the
way into the study and stood waiting for Yeadings to take
a seat facing him.

'This shouldn't take long. Just a question or two,' the
policeman excused himself, taking a surreptitious glance
round the scrupulously tidy room. It was the man himself
who was the shambles. He had not even picked up on the
question about Julie—though it could be that he hadn't
properly heard it, or else knew nothing of what had happened.

'I wondered if you had seen this before.' Yeadings
reached in his breast pocket for the photocopied scrap of
paper.

Hook took it across to his desk, automatically switched

on a lamp and frowned over the writing. His hands were shaking as he looked up, appalled. 'Where did you get this? What is it?'

Two reasonable questions, Yeadings thought, considering the almost illegible state of the note. But surely they'd come in the wrong order—unless the man had some idea of the note's origin.

'You recognise it, then?' he suggested quietly.

Hook sat down dumbly, his hands hanging loosely between his knees. The paper had fallen to the carpet.

'My—dear—Julie,' Yeadings prompted.

The man looked up vaguely, staring sightlessly through him.

'She's dead,' he said like an automaton.

Yeadings felt a rush of nausea. Whatever he'd expected, it wasn't this, an immediate confession. 'Tell me,' he said flatly.

'What does it say? I couldn't read it.' Again the man seemed not to have heard his question. So go along with him, Yeadings decided.

'It seems to be an invitation to Julie to come and stay. We believe it was sent almost eight years ago, a few months after your sister disappeared.'

'She did mention it,' Hook murmured to himself. 'But I couldn't tell for sure if she'd actually sent it.'

He couldn't be talking about Julie. She wasn't old enough then to write; and if they'd assumed the correct date, then Caroline would have been gone. He meant another 'she': the note's writer.

'Whose handwriting is this, Mr Hook?' Yeadings waited while the man slowly came back to present reality, faced pain and eventually let the words out.

'My wife's.'

Yeadings shifted his weight on the chair. 'I'd like to speak to her. Is she in?'

'She's dead. I told you.'

'Your *wife* is dead?' Not the child, then? Thank God for that much! But did this disturbed man know anything that could help in finding her?

'I'm sorry, Mr Hook. The note was written a long time back. We didn't know you'd been widowed since.'

'My wife—Olive—killed herself. I thought everyone knew.'

Silently Yeadings cursed his over-eagerness to meet the man once he'd pulled his name out of the computer. He should have checked with Winterton first, but he hadn't wanted to trouble him again so soon. Somewhere in police files there would be a reference to Mrs Hook's death, checking whether it had been natural or a suicide, or whether anyone else had been involved.

Hook was explaining, wretchedly. 'She hadn't been well, but she covered it up. I thought it was over, the depression. It was more than a year after she'd lost the baby.'

More grief, Yeadings accepted. They were an unlucky family. Or a complicated one. He took his time, barely formulating questions but waiting on the man's mood, supplying the silences to be filled, until the story should suppurate out by itself.

Then it was his duty to probe a little further, to secure dates, because sequences mattered. They accounted for so much.

Olive Hook had lost her baby after ten weeks of its fragile little life. 'Her' baby. Yeadings noticed how the husband never spoke of it as theirs. A detached man, he would have seen the birth of children as something to be left to the women. One couldn't imagine him present at labour, holding his wife's hand, urging her to pant or to push. The baby had never lived long enough for him to bond with it. So, Olive's baby. And she could have felt herself isolated in mourning its death.

Maybe that was a harsh assumption, but Yeadings had this feeling about the man. Unable to empathise, he was falling apart. It seemed doubtful he would have close friends. The superintendent had met his kind before, in job-obsessed, over-worked junior policemen whose home life got crowded out and finally broke up.

So, Hook: an introverted, negative man who appeared unsure, spoke little, seldom smiled, was probably humourless. Afraid of emotion, how had he reacted to his sister's disappearance all those years before? The police had never approached him for help because the case had so rapidly drawn to a close.

'And soon after your baby died your sister disappeared,' Yeadings prompted. 'It left little Julie motherless, so perhaps your wife…'

'Olive couldn't think of anything else. She kept on about it, phoning my brother-in-law three or four times a day, until he came round to see me and said she'd have to be— legally restrained. He resented any interference. He was going to bring up his daughter himself, with the nanny's help. I tried explaining to Olive he'd likely remarry and then Julie would have a mother again.'

Slotting in new for old, just like that. How insensitive the man was. Enough to drive a grieving woman demented.

'That was an awful winter,' Hook said. 'I had this new post coming up. There was a lot of preparation involved, and it meant being away quite a bit. She took against the idea of moving, although it had meant upgrading, and we'd get a big house in the hospital grounds. She said she didn't want to give up her job.' He sounded mildly indignant. 'She'd only just started, and it was nothing important. Driving a minibus for local schoolchildren. She had been quite a good driver once, but then she had a couple of accidents, the second one a really bad crash. Four of the children were injured and sent to A & E. The police—the police found three times the permitted alcohol level in her blood. I hadn't known she'd started drinking like that.'

'So she lost her job anyway.'

'I thought I might lose my chance of the new one too, but by then I had strong backers and they overlooked it. The new project was being pushed by the government— they wanted results overnight. All the old Special Hospitals were in an appalling state, indistinguishable from prisons; they were condemned. The programme was strictly a choice between reform or closure. There weren't a lot of suitably qualified managers who were considered fit to force through the changes. You must have read all about this in the press.'

'Yes, I remember.'

For a moment, speaking of his work, he had come more alive, but now tension came back. His mouth was so tight that the lips disappeared into a single straight line. The story had reached a part he preferred to forget.

He had really tried to make Olive get a grip on herself. Tried everything, even bracing himself with a couple of stiff Scotches before getting home of an evening, to cope with the state he'd find her in. But joining her hadn't beaten the problem. She simply got worse, foul-mouthing and physically attacking him as his job grew more demanding.

If he admitted the truth, it must be that in the end her death had been a release.

To Yeadings, considering the dead woman, the sequence explained itself. A lonely marriage, the lost baby, a turning to other children in her school-run with the minibus.

Then—which came next, the crash or the rejection of her hopes to take over Julie?

'When was the minibus accident?' he asked quietly.

'Eh? Oh, in February. The roads were icy and they said she was going too fast.'

That would be the February after she'd written the Christmas note to three-year-old Julie, probably enclosing it with a present. She'd waited and waited for a reply which never came. And, despairing, she'd found no comfort or release, except in drink.

Time to change the subject. 'Have you any idea where your sister may be now?' Yeadings asked.

Hook lifted his heavy head from his hands and stared at the policeman blindly. 'Caroline? She's dead. Winterton killed her.'

He was clinging to that idea. At the beginning, before he'd seemed truly focused, he'd referred to his 'late' sister.

'Why do you think that?' Yeadings pursued.

'I just know,' the man insisted.

'Do you have any proof that Caroline is dead?'

Hook turned his head away. One hand reached out for the top sheet of paper on his desk and he appeared to absently read it, as though Yeadings wasn't there.

'We had proof she flew out to Lanzarote with her next-door neighbour, Barry Morgan.'

'Morgan,' Hook repeated tightly. He seemed on the point of saying more but clamped his jaws firmly shut. Against what emotion—disbelief, or was it anger?

'So you haven't been in touch with her since she disappeared?'

'How could I?'

'Nor with Julie? Nor Daniel Winterton?'

Hook blinked several times but said nothing, staying slumped, half turned from his desk. Yeadings recognised

the stubbornness of a naturally weak man and knew he'd
get nothing more at present. In any case he had already
asked questions for which he would have preferred a witness present. All he could do now was take his leave.

Hook didn't stir as he let himself out.

Yeadings sat in his car watching a group of patients
packing up after hoeing the flower-beds, and he remembered being sent as a young Met DC to interview a doctor
at the Maudsley Clinic. The receptionist had been busy but
friendly, waving him through. 'He's in the table tennis
room with a patient.'

So he had gone in, sat and watched until the game was
through and then accosted the doctor.

But he'd picked the patient instead. The man he was to
interview was the gangling, uncoordinated one, an inter-
nationally famous psychiatrist.

Clifford Hook was no doctor of anything, simply a civil
servant responsible for the management of a secure hospital
for the mentally ill and sexual offenders. Long exposure to
the inmates must be a sentence in itself, however, and it
could leave its mark. Surely it was obvious to others that
the man himself was almost over the edge?

It was possible that Daniel Winterton could add some
details of personal history on Hook. Since the poor devil
was stuck at home expecting a kidnapper's phone call,
Yeadings decided he must visit him.

Lights were already on in Long Gable. The farther trees
and shrubbery were turning into grey silhouettes, the cosy
house an idyllic picture against a primrose-yellow horizon
reflected in the river. When Yeadings knocked at the open
front door Winterton came hurrying down from upstairs,
his hair slightly ruffled as if he had been lying down.

'Superintendent, have you…?'

'There's no news, I'm afraid. Urgent inquiries are being pursued in several directions.'

'No sightings then?'

'Some unlikely ones, but we're following up everything we're offered, however far-fetched.'

'Surely someone local must have seen her, in broad daylight, on an open road.'

'If so, they haven't yet come forward.' And anyway, Yeadings thought, who notices a youngster with an adult in a passing car? One assumes they belong together. He preferred not to mention that casts of tyre tracks in soft leaf mould by the river path were under microscopic examination.

He followed Winterton into the comfortable sitting-room and accepted the offered Scotch, since he wasn't strictly on duty but waffling around on the off-chance. 'For what it's worth, I traced that old note addressed to your daughter,' he began, taking up a place on a sofa with the other man facing him.

'Really? After so much time?'

'It was Mrs Clifford Hook who wrote it.'

'Olive? Good Lord, I'd quite forgotten her. Yes, of course. After Caroline left she was forever pestering me about Julie. Imagined I'd let her adopt the child.'

'She'd not long lost a baby of her own, I believe.'

'That's why I put up with it for so long, but finally I warned Hook she was getting out of hand. The poor woman needed professional help. He wouldn't have had far to turn for the right treatment. The means to deal with her were on his own doorstep by then.'

'But he wasn't a medical man himself, just trying to manage a revolutionary medical situation. Perhaps he felt that calling on the doctors under his management would have left him personally vulnerable.'

'She was a sick woman. That was why she ended as she did. He neglected her needs.'

'So she killed herself. How exactly?'

'An overdose of something. I don't know the details.'

Winterton clearly found the subject distasteful, so Yeadings took another angle. 'Did he share her love of children?'

'Perhaps. He always made a great fuss of Julie as a baby. Rather clumsily. But more rationally than his wife.'

'Tell me about him.'

'You surely don't see him as—'

'An abductor? I don't yet see anyone as that. We have to consider everything and everyone before we can narrow the frame. I met him this afternoon for the first time and I felt he was under considerable strain.'

'That could well be. He's a small man who took on an immense responsibility. It was when the SHSA was set up. They picked on him because he had enthusiasm and what they saw then as vision.'

'SHSA?'

'Special Hospitals Services Authority, when the old prison-asylum system was condemned and a new set-up replaced the medical governors with managers, to bring them in line with regular NHS hospitals.'

Yeadings remembered well enough. The incoming managers would have seen it as a crusade. The psychiatric staff and the nurses (still regarded as 'screws' by the inmates, being members of the Prison Officers' Union) had resisted the new order. But the reforms had been established and the whole concept of high security for psychiatric care was changed, with the emphasis on treatment rather than restraint.

'It all went too far, of course,' Winterton grunted. 'See what the results are—such laxity that Ashworth Hospital, for example, became a moral sewer and was threatened with the same "change or close" order which the previous government served on the old rigorous system.'

And at Craythorpe Park Hospital it lay with people like Hook, Yeadings reflected, to balance the needs of medicos, patients, nurses, public opinion and the government. Small wonder his own equilibrium seemed at risk.

'He's met with tragedy enough in his personal life,' he reminded Winterton.

'Caroline used to call him a born loser. You'd never have taken them for brother and sister. She was four years older, a much stronger character. Where she stood up to rigid parents he allowed them to damp him down. It set the pattern for his whole life. Some people are capable of change, but the obstacles he met didn't bring out the hero in him. He crumpled.

'It's no exaggeration to say he worshipped his sister, but it wasn't in his nature to follow her lead and break out of his rut. He was socially inept. Even his wife…'

'His wife,' Yeadings reminded Winterton as he hesitated in mid-sentence.

'Olive was Caroline's choice for him. Not so much a friend of hers as an encumbrance. Caroline tossed her to him and he picked her up like an obedient spaniel goes after a stick and brings it back, wagging its tail.'

'What were Olive's feelings in this?'

'She was a romantic in thrall to Caroline. Perhaps she saw marrying Clifford as a substitute for being close to her goddess. You might say his was a courtship of inertia. That sort of thing is not so very uncommon.'

'And now he's widowed, alone.'

'I'm afraid we've lost touch. After his wife's death Clifford gave up the large house that came with the post and took a smaller, newer one on the hospital grounds. I asked him out to dinner twice but his unease was almost infectious. Both times he arrived late, left early on some unlikely excuse, and it was hard work getting a conversation going. After that I'm afraid I gave up trying.'

'Could he and Julie have met recently?'

'No. She never goes out without me or the mother of one of her schoolfriends.'

'But if they met by chance, would Julie go off with him?'

'No. She would barely remember him. It was so long since he'd been here.'

Yeadings stiffened as a dull thud came from upstairs. In the following silence they both stared upwards, Winterton tensely defensive.

Then visibly he relaxed. 'Made me jump,' he apologised. 'The wind must be rising. I left the bathroom window open. That'll be something blown off the window-sill.'

Yeadings rose and thanked the man for his patience in filling in some gaps. 'Not that what I've learned appears to lead anywhere, but you can't really tell at this point.'

At the door he turned back. 'One other thing. About Olive Hook's death as suicide. Did you find that verdict acceptable?'

Winterton looked uncertain. 'Why not? From what I heard, she was quite unstable.'

Yeadings nodded as if satisfied and gave a final glance round the room. 'I see you have the equipment set up for monitoring incoming calls.'

'Yes, it's been tested.'

'So we shall hear instantly if any demand for ransom comes through. You know the importance of keeping the speaker talking long enough for the source to be traced?'

'Yes. I'm glad to do anything at any time if it will help get Julie home safe.'

But suppose she is already home? Yeadings suggested to

himself as he switched on the ignition. Winterton's explanation for the noise upstairs hadn't convinced him for a moment. You had to keep in mind that the man was a fiction writer with a ready imagination.

Could Julie still be in the house but moved elsewhere during the police search? Yet why? Unless Winterton needed time for signs of physical abuse to fade and the child to be coached to give a distorted version of events.

Alternatively, had Julie somehow learned the details of her mother's running away and blamed her father for it? So was her own disappearance deliberate, intended as revenge on him? Angus Mott had already pointed out that Julie's preparations for a picnic echoed her mother's plans on the day she'd disappeared.

As he swung the car to re-enter the lane, Yeadings glanced back at the house. All the upstairs windows on this side were closed, but at one he caught the flutter of a white curtain as a watcher moved quickly away.

Outlined in the front doorway Winterton raised a hand in acknowledgement to him, turned slowly and went indoors.

NINE

THE RANSOM CALL CAME at two thirty.

Winterton had been asleep. In a bewildering nightmare he was soaping himself down in a cast-iron bath while a line of naked men queued beside it. Although he sensed more than saw them, his eyes being fixed on the scummy water, he knew they were strangers. And their bodies were insubstantial, like tattered muslin translucent hangings swaying in a draught.

He was still afraid of them as he groped for the receiver and put it, ice cold, against his ear.

'Winterton,' he gasped.

There was silence, not even breathing. Supposing it to be a wrong number, he was about to drop the thing and sit up in bed.

Then came the laughter, low and scornful.

'How are you feeling now?' the caller demanded.

It was almost certainly a man, but the words weren't fully voiced. Something not much more than a whisper, and it terrified him, sounding strangled and demented.

'Who is this? What do you want?'

'I am the voice of your absent conscience, Daniel. And what I want is satisfaction.'

Again the weird laughter, then a metallic click as the phone was hung up at the far end.

'No!' Winterton shouted. 'Listen!' But the line had been cut, leaving only a slow, steady whine.

He sat there, sweating and shivering. The man was playing with him. This was the first little prick of the épée. There would be other calls, because he hadn't properly started yet. He hadn't made demands. He hadn't even referred to what he'd done.

The man knew him, could count on him being here, within reach, at any time of the day or night that the bastard cared to repeat the torment, while he himself was totally in the dark. How long would he draw it out before he stated his intentions, made his specific demands? And what would be happening to Julie while the maniac took his time playing cat and mouse?

The police would have used their intercept line. But the message had been too short. They'd no chance of tracing the caller. He hadn't sounded the sort of fool who might overlook the 1471 facility. His number would be a withheld one. No; more likely he would have used a public phone box and was already driving away into the night, totally anonymous and undetectable.

Sleep after this was impossible. Winterton made his way downstairs, fearfully turning on lights all the way to the kitchen. Every window was closely curtained, but he had the gruesome sense of a watcher outside following his every move, gloating over his patent horror.

He filled the kettle, forcing his hands not to tremble. Before the water had quite boiled the phone rang again. He lifted the receiver off the kitchen wall. 'Yes,' he said into it. He had never before been afraid to give his name.

It was DI Mott, sounding as though he hadn't been to bed. Perhaps they took it in turns to go nocturnal. Did they work shifts, like uniformed police? Winterton was conscious of despair that it wasn't Superintendent Yeadings. Not that he could have made any difference. The taped conversation would be processed in just the same way, enhanced, analysed and run against recordings of known child abductors.

'Yes, yes,' he said impatiently across Mott's attempts to reassure. 'How often will he do this before he comes out in the open?'

Mott hesitated. 'I doubt he'll trouble you again tonight.'

No, he wouldn't need to. Not repeating the call would be the finest torture. Winterton knew he should try for some way of switching his mind off, get some rest, but it was impossible—because it was Julie, his little girl, that the man was holding. Pray God the bastard wouldn't hurt her.

Next time, he promised himself, I'll insist on her speaking to me. I have to know she's—

But then wouldn't that prompt the man to make her cry out? How could he ever risk that?

'Mr Winterton, would you like someone to come out and be with you?'

'I don't want that. In case the house is being watched. He mustn't know the police are listening in.'

'Is there a friend you could contact who would keep you company?'

'Nobody I could stand right now. I'll be all right. I'll get a grip on myself.'

When Mott had hung up Winterton found the trembling had stopped of itself.

A friend who would come in and comfort him? Ironic, that. There was nobody. Julie's mother was the only person who could possibly have understood how he felt now.

Caroline. That was who it was all about, of course. What he'd done to her. He didn't need anyone to explain what the caller meant when he called himself Winterton's absent conscience. He could as well have called himself Nemesis.

Yet how could he possibly know? It had to be guess-work. There was no proof. No clue left behind.

If he had really known, he'd have no need to kidnap Julie. The man could have turned to blackmail instead and not risked raising a hornet's nest. It would have stayed just between the two of them.

Perhaps it hadn't been so smart to have the police listening in.

Ignoring the heated kettle he reached for his garden shoes and shrugged on his Barbour from the scullery peg. He knew Mott was right about the caller not ringing again tonight. He would deliberately be left to worry himself into a blue funk. That's the way he would have written it himself in one of his thrillers.

He told himself there was a point in leaving the house. It gave him the illusion of being, even minimally, in control. If, by some perverted chance, the bastard did ring, it would wrong-foot him to find his victim wasn't available for taunting.

Patting a pocket to ensure his torch was there, he extinguished the downstairs light and cautiously let himself out into the moonless night.

'WHAT DO YOU THINK?' Yeadings asked his elite team as they met at eight a.m. 'Was it genuine or a hoax call?'

'Mischievous at the very least,' Mott said decisively. 'If it's the real thing then the caller has some special knowledge about Winterton that's not evident to us.'

'Yes. That bit about being "your absent conscience." Mind, we shouldn't make too much of Winterton's reaction. If an unknown roused anyone at two thirty a.m. and made the same insinuation, most of us could recall some peccadillo, or worse, to fit the bill.'

'But what's Winterton done that's so shameful? The man seems such a dodo—doesn't go anywhere, do anything—

just bangs away at his books and accumulates royalties,'
Beaumont grumbled.

'More sinned against than sinning?' Yeadings suggested.

'Unlucky, anyway,' Z gave as her opinion. 'Maybe he's
one of those types that things just happen to.'

'Even things going bump in the night—or the evening,
actually.' Yeadings was remembering the thump on the
lounge ceiling which wasn't—as Winterton had claimed—
caused by something blown off the bathroom window-sill.
He mentioned it to the others now, and included a description of the watcher upstairs who'd darted behind a curtain
as he'd driven away.

'So Winterton could be a closet Romeo, hiding a woman
in his bedroom. Not that that's criminal or unreasonable.
In fact it's what we'd expect, his wife having left him eight
years back, with no permanent replacement,' Mott considered.

'But why the secrecy?' Z asked.

'Because he's a prig,' Beaumont declared, 'and he
doesn't want it known that he's using a tom.'

'It would help to know who it was upstairs,' Yeadings
sighed. 'I'd have given a lot then for a right to search.
Suppose the woman, or whoever, is part of the thing Winterton's supposed to have a bad conscience over? She could
even have a connection with the caller who rang up a few
hours later.'

'I'm not sure,' Z doubted, 'that when he's desperate over
his daughter's safety he'd be bothered with keeping up a
sexual liaison.'

Beaumont snorted. '"Keeping up a sexual liaison." Call
a spade a spade, Z, can't you? But then, being a woman,
how would you know what he'd do when he's tormented
by demons?'

Yeadings chose to overlook the signs of a coming spat.

His two sergeants were given to jostling each other these days. It hadn't happened when Z was still a DC in the team because her general usefulness had overcome Beaumont's chauvinist prejudice. But now, with both of equal rank, any time she hit a target he'd let off a burst of rapid fire for fear of being over-looked. Never having displayed notice-able ambition until she threatened to overtake him, Beau-mont was misdirecting the energy that should go into the job into sniping.

'Whoever it was in the house,' Yeadings regretted, 'she—or even possibly he—hadn't left a car parked out front. Though it could have been on the rear apron, or even concealed in the double garage beside Winterton's. He's only got the one Merc now, hasn't he?'

'But maybe his visitor walked from the main road bus stop, or Winterton drove out to collect her.'

'This was before dusk,' Yeadings reminded them. 'Some-one just might have seen her or him. That's something to follow up.'

He found it interesting that none of the three had con-sidered the possibility that first sprang to his mind: that the person upstairs in Winterton's house was Julie herself. That could imply that his suspicion was way off the mark; or maybe they would come round to consider it when other possibilities were exhausted. He'd leave it for the moment.

'I assume there are no takers for the phone call being a put-up job to throw us off whatever track we're supposed to be on?' Mott suggested.

'Logically it would be a track to Winterton then,' Z said. 'And if he was in cahoots with whoever rang him they'd not have dragged in that bit about his conscience, with us listening in.'

'Unless it's double bluff, to make us think it wasn't a set-up,' Beaumont objected.

'He may be devious,' Yeadings said, 'but that's taking it a bit far. Anyway, to more certain matters. I've identified the writer of the letter Z found in Julie's cache and it led me to the uncle, Caroline's brother, Clifford Hook. It was his wife, dead some time back, who wrote to Julie, wanting her to come and stay. And you might care to know that Hook is convinced his sister is dead, murdered by Winterton. So either he won't accept that she ran off with Morgan or he has reason to believe that her death has occurred since then.'

'In which case why not Hook for the two thirty a.m. caller?' Mott said eagerly. 'What's he like?'

'I'd like to hear your opinion on that. So find some reason to rattle his cage, Angus. And take Z along. As Beaumont told us, he's in charge of Craythorpe Park High Security Psychiatric Hospital. Tackle him at work and ask if he minds your taping the conversation. You may decide he's kinky enough to have made the phone call to Winterton, but it doesn't mean he has to be Julie's abductor.'

'If he isn't, and yet he made the call, he must have a vicious streak, knowing how devastated his brother-in-law would be,' Z said grimly.

Yeadings nodded. Mott gathered up a sheaf of reports. 'Beaumont, when Z brings back the tape of Hook's voice, I want you to arrange an oscilloscope comparison with the recorded phone call. That voice will have been disguised in some way, but despite any assumed accent, some basic speech patterns will still be there underneath. And while you're waiting for results on that, send our uniformed detail looking for a sighting of Winterton's visitor, on the road or on any bus that stopped near the driveway of Long Gable at any time yesterday.'

Yeadings watched them disperse, then sat plunged in thought awhile, going over their discussion. What Beaumont had said about Winterton hung on in his mind: the dumbo who had no interest outside his writing.

No; what Beaumont had actually called Winterton was 'dodo'. 'Dumbo' had slipped into his mind because earlier either Katy or Winterton had said his sister called Hook that. Both starting with D.

And, Lordy, yes; hadn't that initial bugged him all those years ago? 'D' was how the missing note to Caroline had been signed, the note her assistant had opened because Caroline was late to work.

Simple enough when you knew the answer, or the probable answer. Not that it could matter now, so long after. The note merely said he hadn't come up with some information she wanted. And he'd ended, gauchely, *Lurv you,* with the initial D. D for Dumbo. Hook, in fact.

So, back to Beaumont's dodo, Winterton, whose chosen life was writing fiction. How far did he project himself into his characters, unconsciously dropping clues to his own personality in what he made them do?

The question made all the more interesting his own conversation with Nan the previous evening just before bed. She had been relaxing over a nightcap.

'Remember you asked if I'd ever read anything by Daniel Winterton, Mike?' Nan had run a forefinger thoughtfully down the misted tumbler's side and delicately sucked the moisture off before going on.

'The way you spoke of him he sounded rather scary. The dust jackets had put me off, but in the end, perversely, it made me want to read one of his novels. I found a recent one in paperback and bought it.'

'Good. I assume you've dipped into it. What did you find?'

'A bit of everything. It was disturbing, certainly. Not the classic good guy versus evil one scenario, but compassion and cynicism at odds with each other under a deceptively calm surface. He's sensitive, and subtle. His main character was alone a lot and reflected on events. As he must do himself, I suppose.'

She drained her glass and reached for a book on the side table, removing a used envelope inserted to keep a place.

'Listen to this bit, "He saw himself stumbling on, enclosed, and caught up by shreds of doubt like cobwebs in his brain. Cobwebs of his own spinning." And further on, "His eyes followed the tracery of golden light on the oak tree's weathered bark. Sunshine, he thought gratefully. Then, unsure: the sun—so vital, but dangerous too. All the important things in life bring their own danger."

'Fear of a deeper reality behind everyday things. It's as though the man's fear spreads until he becomes afraid to move. But he overcomes it, ploughs on just the same. He knows his mind is disintegrating, but he simply goes on going on. Desperately brave.'

Yeadings had her read it through a second time, then commented, 'He's saying that someone really brave is well aware what fear is and deals with it. That's a truism which he's constructed that character around. It doesn't mean he lives up to it himself. A writer can't be every one of the characters he uses.'

'But that is simply all that the book is about: surviving treachery, honestly facing his own nature and accepting what comes. There was enough of him in it to make the ending convincing. It was sad, tragic even, but it left me feeling that life wasn't totally awful.'

Yeadings considered her. The book had gripped her enough to keep her reading all day until she reached the end. That was quite something for the dutiful Nan, normally cramming in twenty-five hours' domestic and child-chasing duties daily.

'You said this was a recent paperback? What's it called?'

'It's this year's, published in hardback twelve months before.' She showed him the title page: *The Long Way Home*.

So it was relative to the man as he was, seven years after Caroline's desertion, but before this threat to Julie. It sounded a quietly triumphant book, seeming to imply that the writer too accepted how things were. But now, with Julie gone, he would hardly be writing in the same vein.

Last night that had all seemed loosely peripheral to the present case, but now in the light of day he was aware of the total structure. Winterton might have changed with circumstances, but he was the same man throughout, one who externalised his emotions in a particularly public way, even if they emerged encoded in fiction. The books in sequence had to chart his progress. They carried some kind of truth about him; either what he essentially was or what he would have liked to be.

Again Yeadings found himself thinking back to the earlier disappearance. He was curious to know how life with Caroline suddenly gone had first affected Winterton, and what had come through in his writing. The man was not an unfeeling block of wood. Shocked by his wife's disappearance, almost immediately he must have feared he'd have to identify her body as victim of a car crash; finally he had learned that she had deserted him for a younger man she was infatuated with, and had cleared out their joint account.

That was a lot to take. Storyline enough to inspire a novel. So what had he done with the scouring experience—suppressed it, or worked it out in the way he knew best?

The compulsion to follow this up gave Yeadings the excuse to bypass his paperwork and drive to the local public library. None of Winterton's books were left on the shelves, but the computer there gave a list of his works. He appeared to have produced a novel regularly each year since 1987 and all were still available for borrowing somewhere among the county branches. The librarian punched in a request for information and they found that of the two Yeadings particularly wanted, one was still on the shelves in Great Missenden and the other at Burnham.

And this, he thought sardonically as he accelerated on their trail, is the nearest to pulsating action that I get these days!

He had been careful in his choice, going for the dates the books were being written, and that meant allowing almost a year for the work to be finished and as much again for each to be printed and marketed. The earlier one had been completed immediately before Caroline's disappearance, and the other published two years later.

Returning, on impulse he made a detour and found himself by a field gate, gazing down over sloping pasture towards the converted cottages glowing golden in the sunlight. Behind, through sparse willows, he caught the glint of water. There was no sign of Winterton about the grounds.

It occurred to Yeadings that he might find the man changed in some way since the anonymous phone call. If so, that could help to answer some of the questions he had about him.

He reversed the Rover fifty yards along the country lane and turned in at the drive to Long Gable.

The front door stood open to the comfortable brick-floored sitting-room with its bright cushions and watercolour landscapes. Simple and unpretentious, a room to relax in. But how could Winterton be comfortable now?

Yeadings reached for the knocker and made his presence known. Its brass was cloudy, as if whoever cleaned the place had given up. He remembered Z telling him that Winterton had cancelled the twice-weekly help, unable at present to stand the village woman's sympathy.

Somewhere farther in he heard a chair scrape on wooden boards and Winterton appeared, in his slippers. 'Superintendent, come in.' He moved back and Yeadings was waved into the study where a blank computer screen glowed. He saw where Winterton had pushed away his chair from the work station. There were no papers on the console; just a used mug, its inside brown-ringed with the stains of strong coffee.

'You heard about the phone call?' Winterton assumed.

'Yes. How did it leave you?'

The man hadn't expected that question. He thought a moment, then said, 'Unnerved.'

'There was nothing specific. No actual threat; no demand. Did you feel it was genuine?'

'Oh yes. Felt it certainly. Couldn't prove it, though. The speaker didn't identify himself in any way.'

'He gave us nothing to work on. But if it wasn't a hoax, he'll call you again.'

Winterton made a gesture with his hands. Impatient? Hopeless? Yeadings couldn't tell. If he'd been in the man's shoes he'd be mixed up too, anxious for progress and at the same time afraid for what it might involve.

'Is there anyone who could be with you for a day or two?'

'I'm better alone.'

Yeadings doubted it, but wouldn't argue. He made general conversation, sounding out his way before he broached what he'd come for.

'You once wrote,' he said, 'that all the important things in life bring their own danger. What were you thinking of then?'

His question didn't faze the man. He looked up at a corner of the ceiling and waited, choosing his phrases deliberately. He was, after all, a writer, a wordsmith.

'Every move we make, every decision, has its risks. The more significant the choice made, the greater the potential danger.'

'Is that why you never remarried?' For a moment Yeadings thought he had overstepped the permissible, but Winterton answered easily. 'I was fortunate with Caroline, but I'd never take that risk again. I'd never even consider it.'

'Even for Julie's sake?'

Mention of the child's name reopened the wound. For a moment Winterton looked shattered. 'Do you think I don't know how deprived she is? Do you think I haven't felt guilt over it?' His eyes became hooded. He looked away, struck the arm of the chair with one hand, the fingers curved into talons. 'Look, Superintendent—'

'I've taken up too much of your time,' Yeadings said, rising. He gestured towards the blank screen of the word processor. 'I hope I haven't stemmed the flow.'

'There is no flow.'

No; the father in Yeadings could see that. Until the child was found and restored unharmed there'd be no kind of life for this man. Certainly nothing creative.

But wouldn't there be the same block if he was full of guilt—if he was responsible for his own child's death?

The man was driven by demons. But what demons?

As Yeadings drove home Winterton's voice echoed in his head. Referring to his marriage, he'd been 'fortunate with Caroline'—and then came an admission of guilt. But guilt for precisely what? Was that only the usual guilt that came with any sort of grieving, or something more? And by what twisted reasoning did the man feel fortunate in having married a promiscuous woman who would eventually desert him and their small daughter? It almost smacked of masochism.

TEN

BACK AT THE OFFICE, YEADINGS threw out stale coffee, made fresh, cleared his desktop and settled in to read, hoping to be left relatively undisturbed. The only interruption came almost two hours into his studies, when the telephone rang from its new position on the floor. Yeadings groped for it and came up breathing hard.

The voice was vaguely familiar. Surely he'd heard it just recently; that accent…

The man identified himself as the detective sergeant from one of the Newtowns in Wales. The Gwent one. He hadn't found Morgan, but came up chattily with a suggestion of his own.

'Of course I'm not implying your informant meant to deceive you, Superintendent, but we do find people outside the Principality make this mistake. Newtown and Newport, see. Both in Gwent. Get a lot of muddling, one way and another. So I gave a friend of mine a bell down there, Newport that is, seeing as we'd drawn a blank on a Barry Morgan here, like.'

'And?'

'Well, he couldn't trace a local *precisely* by that name, but he had a family that'd come up from the Cardiff area years back.'

What in the name of local geography? Yeadings was asking himself.

'*Barry,* see? People who move on sometimes call their

kids after the place they were born in. And Barry docks are right there...'

Give me strength, Yeadings silently demanded heavenwards; and save me from the wordy Welsh.

'So he asked around, this mate of mine, and he ran the family down. Spot on. Real name's Lewis Morgan, not Barry. Just that his family called him that, see? His father had the same baptismal name, which could have caused a right royal mix-up. Only the old man's dead now. The old mum's still there, with a couple of daughters, but young Barry, he's been away for donkeys' ages. Turned up a few years back looking for a job and then disappeared again. Nobody knows where he is at present. England they suppose. That any use to you, Superintendent?'

Yeadings drew a deep breath and thanked the Newtown sergeant civilly. He'd have to accept that Barry Morgan, whether the one quoted or not, wasn't at present in the land—or the town—of his fathers. Which got the case precisely no distance forward.

As a wild shot he enquired what sort of job Morgan had been looking for.

'That was something I wasn't told, sir. How about I contact Newport again and find out for you?'

How about it indeed. Not that it was likely to lead anywhere. Yeadings repeated his thanks and broke the connection.

He was left disconsolately flicking an elastic band, which had appeared from nowhere on his desk, and recalling the only time he had ever driven through Newtown, Gwent, returning from the Pembroke peninsula. He and Nan had gone on holiday there with Sally before Luke was born, and unknown to either of them, the poor little mite had been developing mumps on the journey back. The whole day-long journey home was through a steady downpour.

All he remembered of Newtown was a crowded car park, inadequate women's toilets and an overall greyness. It was perhaps understandable that a police sergeant landlocked there should welcome a request from Thames Valley as something to light up his dreary existence.

Yeadings refilled his mug and returned to Winterton's book. There was a lot of talking in it, but he wasn't entirely sure the words fitted the actions. It was as though he glimpsed a shadowy hidden agenda all through.

When eventually Mott returned, having sent Z off to duplicate the tape of Hook's recent questioning, Yeadings had just finished skimming the first book. Briefly he explained how it struck him.

'And Winterton couldn't have meant the reader to grasp anything ulterior, because at the end he didn't pull it all out and expose its significance. Maybe he wasn't aware of it himself.'

'That sounds like a stab at amateur psychology.'

'Which I'm no way qualified to spout on. And I'm not a great reader of fiction. All the same, I'm used to listening to people's voices. I'm getting more than one here from the written words.'

'Are you saying you think he's schizoid?'

Yeadings considered that. 'No, I'm not, but he's very imaginative. He may be capable of deceiving himself.'

Mott seated himself opposite, and Yeadings slid the book over, open at a page towards the end.

The DI read aloud: 'The woman was cowering now against the locked door, hands to her face, fingernails split where she had clawed at it before turning defensively back to him. Her face was distorted by fear. She was out of her wits; the ice-cool princess gone crazy.

'"I like you crazed," he said, advancing on her with the camcorder, and smiling thinly. "I have always wanted you.

I need to keep you. Forever. And you must love me, only
me. For that I have to make you share my pain."''

Yeadings closed the book as Mott made a grimace of
distaste.

'That must have ended the conversation.'

'In a way it does. Because then he rapes and kills her.
But the two voices go on, in pillow talk. This book's open-
ended. You're left to decide if the character's gone schizoid
or there's a ghostly companionship.'

'Weird. Still, I guess it suits some tastes.' Mott was reading the cover advertisement: 'A tense, twisting tale of baffled antagonists slowly, exquisitely, killing each other, day
by day. Chilling and compulsive.'

Yeadings nodded. 'It's all of that. *Circe's Circle,* the one
that made his name, possibly his fortune. Anyway it went
into two reprints in the first three years. And he completed
it just six weeks before Caroline disappeared. It leaves me
wondering...'

'If that's how he wanted to treat her? Lucky she left him
when she did.'

'His ice-cold princess. Yes. And yet...'

Mott waited while Yeadings hunted for words to express
his doubt. 'As a child or a teenager, didn't you ever invent
somebody, have imaginary conversations with a person
you'd built a whole story around?'

'Not me,' Mott claimed, sounding totally feet-on-the-
ground. 'Writers maybe.'

'Even future middle-aged detective superintendents who
boast a Wise Woman granny?'

'If so, maybe you should be doing a Daniel Winterton
and making your fortune at it. Whether he was thinking of
his wife or a fictional woman, all that that garbage tells me
is what a vicious mind the man has.'

'But fiction may be as far as it goes with him. Writing

it out may have been enough in itself. I haven't a doubt
that it was Caroline he was thinking of. He even describes
her in the early chapters. She's exactly like the photograph
he gave us when we were searching for her.'

'Has he ever written since about tiresome little girls who
need stern correction?'

Now who was being imaginative? Yeadings regarded his
DI evenly. 'Not to my knowledge, but it's something you
might look up. There's a writers' directory somewhere
which lists books. If you hunt out the relevant reviews
they'll give you some idea of the storylines.'

'Shall I get Z to…?'

'I'd like you on this. With your prejudices at full throt-
tle.'

Mott understood. The Boss liked Winterton and didn't
quite trust himself to see the worst in him. The hard-man
role was delegated to himself.

'But we know what happened to his wife. She wasn't
raped and killed. She went off with the toy boy neighbour.'

'And then what? Nobody seems to know what happened
to them afterwards. Suppose Winterton encountered her
again, in the full knowledge of all she'd done to him? Remember, Hook is convinced Winterton murdered his wife.
Now where did he get that idea?'

Mott stood up. 'I'll get on to it.' He scowled at the closed
book on the desk. 'It looks like someone's going to be
spending a lot of time reading in the next few days. I
thought we were hard pressed to find a lost child.'

A few minutes after Mott's departure Z arrived with
Yeadings' copy of the Hook tape. She set the cassette
player going and, at his invitation, helped herself to a mug
of black coffee.

'Ill at ease,' the Boss commented as Hook's voice came
through.

'He seemed a nervy sort of person, sweating freely, and he blinked a lot. I don't think it was just because we were there. Actually, Angus gave him a reasonably easy time.'

'Because he didn't see him as a wicked uncle. Did you?'

Z wasn't committing herself. 'I'd like to see him under different conditions, but he struck me as—an inoffensive bumbler, out of his depth, pretty stressed out by the job, not far from breaking point.'

They listened to the interview being interrupted by a knock at Hook's office door. Someone entered, apologised for choosing a bad moment and reluctantly left when not invited to stay.

'A doctor?' Yeadings asked.

'One of the management staff, younger than Winterton. Fancies himself, rather. A lizardy sort of face with a black goatee beard. He seemed on familiar terms with Hook. Calls him Clifford. He was curious,' Z said, 'and clearly wanted to be told what our meeting was about.'

'Mm,' Yeadings said as the recording finished. This time Hook hadn't confided any run-up to his wife's suicide; simply the bald statement.

'Nothing new here. Much the same ground as I covered myself. Exasperating repetition for the man, twice in two days, but maybe he's accustomed to explaining himself over and over to the mentally challenged—or whatever it's correct to call them these days.'

He gestured towards the library book. 'Let me bring you up to date on this.'

Z listened intently while he described it. 'And the other?'

'*Worm's Way*. The cover blurb says it's exciting, full of intrigue. A lively plot in which subtly delineated characters interlock in conflict and the underdog finally triumphs.'

Z considered it. 'That doesn't sound as disturbing as the first.'

'More objective perhaps. He must have started it some months after Caroline left him, but there's little sense of trauma. By then, I suppose, he felt the pressure was off.'

Z looked uncertain. 'Do you mean he was relieved she was gone?'

'Why not? Maybe he found he preferred his own company. Except for Julie, of course.' Yeadings rose and went to stare out of the window before continuing.

'And in her case, I'd say that the loss has shaken Daniel Winterton to the core.'

AT CRAYTHORPE PARK High Security Psychiatric Hospital there had been an outbreak of fighting among patients at visiting time. Hook was informed as soon as Mott and Z had left. He dispatched Len Grover to get a full report.

As so often, the trouble had started among the sexual offenders, provoked this time by a beautiful young male visitor. Oppressive heat building since midday under a felty sky had set ragged tempers on edge. Some kind of electric storm was finally inevitable.

'Apparently,' Len reported back, 'this lad was allowed to wander off alone in the garden and a couple of inmates joined him for a spot of opportunist petting. It got competitive and one of them had a kitchen knife in his pocket, so he stuck it in the other's groin, but not before he'd been clocked with a lump of granite himself from the rockery. They're both in surgery getting stitched up. Also three others who relished the idea of a free-for-all. The visitor is complaining he's mortally offended and threatening to go to the papers with his story. Sir, I think you'd better see him and stop it developing.'

Hook closed his eyes and gripped the near edge of his desk. 'Later, perhaps. I—'

His own visitors had been gone no more than ten minutes

and, interrupting them, Len had hovered long enough to confirm his suspicions. They were plain-clothes police, male and female of the species. He dropped his official correctness and laid a gentle hand on the other man's shoulder. 'Clifford, you're looking crook. Let me get you something. It's this heat. You need a fan on in here.'

'I'll be fine. As you say, it's just the heat.' He lifted his head, baffled by the need to cope with a new crisis. 'But how did a knife get out of the kitchen? Had anyone reported it missing?'

'It wasn't a sharp one and nobody missed it. Look, I'll go and sort it for you. Then you can interview whoever when we know what's what. And I'll have a word with the visitor involved. I'll see he's given VIP treatment in the doctors' rest room. It's ten to one he's got a police record for soliciting and won't want publicity himself. He could be just mouthing off to cover his backside.'

Grover's choice of imagery was unfortunate. It had slipped out unintentionally and he managed to control his grin before Hook saw it. He replaced it with an expression of gentle concern until he was out of the office.

At the door Hook called him back. 'Thanks, Len. What would I do without you?'

'Manage just as well as you did before.'

Hook doubted it, although certainly Len's competence owed much to the improved staff training he had introduced himself. It had been tough at first breaking down inbuilt prejudices against the patients, referred to then as 'lags' and 'nonces' but Len had been fertile ground, quick to pick up the essential differences between the old regime and the new enlightened outlook. Perhaps being brought up in Australia made him more open-minded. Hook had faced some opposition in moving him sideways from nursing to management, but Len Grover had proved his worth and, now promoted to his personal assistant, he was totally trustworthy. He was a strong upholder of Hook's authority against challenges from medical staff or union reps. And beyond that, he had become almost a friend. There was no one else Hook dared speak so freely to or whose opinion he so relied on.

Tomorrow would be soon enough to look into the afternoon's incident, when Len had it already sorted on paper. Meanwhile, since he did indeed feel 'crook', as Len so oddly described it, he would perhaps call it a day and go home.

Passing through the outer office, he informed his secretary where he would be and that no calls were to be put through to the house except in an emergency. 'If you're in any doubt,' he said sharply, catching her about to question this, 'consult Mr Grover. He will advise you.'

He walked back to the house and found the BMW parked in the driveway, where Len must have dropped it off earlier. He reached under the far-side wheel arch to retrieve the ring of keys from on top of the tyre. The car could stay out overnight. He was too weary to garage it.

Back at the house he knew that his fermenting thoughts wouldn't let him rest. He had kept an old store of Olive's pills in his bedside cabinet. She had refused to take all prescriptions for months before she killed herself, accusing the doctors of wanting to kill her. Then, ironically, had used the things to do it herself.

He supposed he should have thrown them all away, but he was a natural hoarder. Now, if they could guarantee him instant oblivion, he would have felt safe enough taking something, but he dreaded the brink of consciousness as a zone of fearful confusion. This was no moment to risk it. The second police visit had already released dark memories like rampaging demons.

He seldom knew a full night's sleep. Even as a boy he had suffered from what Caroline called 'the two o'clock blues'—a time of night that should never be experienced, a mental trough when you awoke questioning every decision you'd ever made and grieving for every lost opportunity.

And now there would be so much more to fret him: guilt and anguish over having failed Caroline; much the same over Olive; even more concerning little Julie. But any shame he felt must be nothing to what Winterton should have to suffer.

The house, closed up all day, pulsed with accumulated heat, but as he opened a window the sultry outside air puffed in with an almost sulphurous hint of coming storm. He eased off his jacket and hung it over a chair back. The cotton shirt was sticking clammily to his back. He removed it, dropped it in the linen basket and filled the bathroom basin with cold water, bending to splash it over face and shoulders. It struck with an almost painful shock and then he was shivering with fever.

His head, in a steel-like clamp, felt bloated with dull throbbing. There were hours of intolerable daylight left to be endured, and then interminable night. He lay on the stripped bed and moaned with frustration, his body burning again, and the mattress incapable of soaking the heat away. He must take something, anything, to give him respite. He swung his legs down and padded back into the kitchen, dragged a chair towards the cupboards, climbed unsteadily up and reached for the sealed bottle.

DS Zyczynski stood at the open door to Yeadings' office and left it to him to acknowledge her or not.

'What is it, Z?' he demanded, not looking up from his reading.

'DI Mott has had to go over to Windsor on that fraud case, sir, but he'll be back right away. And I've just had a phone call regarding the morning Julie disappeared. An angler saw a large, light blue saloon parked where the tyre tracks were found, out by the river.'

Yeadings looked up, his brows thunderous. 'Why the delay before he reported it?'

'Guilty conscience. His fishing licence had run out three months back so he shouldn't have been there. But he mentioned seeing the car to his wife, and she insisted he should ring us. She's just back from staying with her mother.

'I've asked for him to be brought in to identify the make of car. He had cycled right past it, but he has no interest in anything on four wheels and claims he can't tell a Porsche from a go-kart.'

'Winterton's Merc is a large pale saloon.'

'Silver, I'd call it.'

'So would I, but do we know if this cyclist would? Z, grab yourself another coffee and take a seat.'

She sat. 'I'll forgo the coffee, thanks, sir. I'm limiting my caffeine after midday.'

He looked at her assessingly. 'Trouble with sleeping? I hope you'll not suggest I change to decaf.'

'I wouldn't dream of it, sir.'

'Exactly so. A man needs his fix.' He raised the black caterpillar brows in an expression of mock innocence. 'I understand that Max Harris is in the neighbourhood.'

To cover her hesitation he rushed in with, 'Because if he is, and you don't have anything more entertaining planned for tonight, Nan and I would be delighted for you both to drop by. For a meal, that is. Nothing special. Say seven thirty or eight, then we'll just be getting child-free.'

'Thank you, sir. That would be great.'

'Good girl. Give Nan a ring, will you, and say there'll
be two extra.'

At which he slyly returned to his reading, leaving Z,
fuming, to drop the probably unwelcome news on his wife.

In fact, Nan had been thinking of making apfelstrudel,
mainly to keep Sally amused. The humid heat had made
little Luke cross all afternoon, and under the circumstances
perhaps baking wasn't the brightest idea, but Z's call now
made it essential.

She scrabbled in the freezer for pâté and pulled out a
family pack of pork loin steaks. She had shopped for fresh
vegetables that morning, had Conference pears, strawber-
ries, cherries and fromage frais, so saw no problem there.

It was months since she'd set eyes on Max, although she
had chanced on Z near the market last week and pulled her
into a teashop. It would be good to have their company,
even if Mike had some ulterior motive in inviting them.
Like picking the columnist's brains about Winterton's literary connections?

DANIEL WINTERTON TOOK IN the carton of groceries and
checked his pockets for change to give the delivery boy.
He discovered he was down to his last couple of tenners
and a handful of silver, and remembered he'd intended
drawing cash on his way out to lunch with Julie on Monday. Already that seemed months ago.

The delivery boy, wobbling sweatily up the long gravel
lane on his bicycle, later described the driving as 'like a
bat out of hell'. The silver Merc had shot past him on to
the village road in a flying spray of gravel. Questioned later
on whether he could identify the driver, he was sure it was
Mr Winterton because he'd recognised the car, but pressed
to be more precise he was less certain. It was someone who
could have been him, seen from the back and hidden by

the headrest. Finally, reminded that he'd said the car was driven at speed, he admitted he really couldn't say who was in the driving seat, man or woman. Or indeed if anyone else had been in the car.

When Superintendent Yeadings called Winterton's number at a few minutes after three thirty p.m., the ringing continued without the answerphone cutting in. It surprised him, but the man could be in some distant part of the house or garden, having forgotten to switch through. Surprisingly casual, if Winterton was expecting a second call from the abductor.

Yeadings decided to leave it and try again, which he did twice before suspecting something was amiss. He then rang through to Control for a patrol car to check on the house.

Twenty minutes later the report came in that Long Gable was empty. Since the front door was imperfectly latched, the constable had walked through the house, shouting to announce himself. There was no response. He was satisfied that the owner was absent. On checking the garage he had found that also empty.

Winterton, it seemed, had done a runner.

ELEVEN

YEADINGS SWORE UNDER his breath. There had been every reason to expect Winterton would stay at home close to the phone. Any instructions from the kidnapper would have been automatically intercepted and himself alerted, but there had been none. That Winterton had taken matters into his own hands threw a new light on the man.

But perhaps the kidnapper had made contact by some other means to set up a rendezvous; or turned up in person, forcing Winterton to leave with him. But in that case his Merc would have remained at the house—unless, of course, Winterton had been instructed to follow the other's car, needing his own for returning with Julie.

In that case the kidnapper must have revealed his face. So did it mean that Winterton had known his identity all along but for some reason failed to admit this? Because of some hold the man had over him—the quoted bad conscience?

It wasn't beyond possibility that he would agree to keep the police out of negotiations, under threat of harm to his daughter. But unless he kept a large secret hoard of banknotes in the house, how could he hope to buy the kidnapper off? Would some action be demanded of him, rather than money?

Whatever he'd contracted to do, his complaisance couldn't guarantee he'd get what he was hoping for. In which case Yeadings had a grim suspicion that a search for the man could now end with finding his body.

Or suppose it was the two thirty a.m. phone call itself that had eventually panicked him into flight? The man who'd mentioned his 'absent conscience' could have proof that Winterton had engineered his own daughter's disappearance.

Disappearance or death? There was still a chance of the child's body, not his, being eventually found.

THE ALL-POINTS ALERT WENT OUT to seek, observe and report on the silver Mercedes, but on no account to approach or challenge. The Chilterns helicopter was put on alert, to await instructions. A message went out to Mott's team to contact Yeadings only by land line. Then he went through to Control to wait for something to happen.

He found action enough already, with a report coming in of a multiple RTA at a contraflow on the M4, drawing in Traffic Division and emergency services over a wide area. With the normal build-up of home-going traffic all westbound lanes between Exits 10 and 12 were now choked solid, with inevitably a handful of nutty egotists trying to escape by reversing down the hard shoulder and so blocking access for ambulances, fire appliances and police. It took all of DI Bellamy's cool to issue fresh instructions on alternative routings, while Yeadings silently fumed that his own requirements were second-ranked.

When at last a line became free, more trouble was reported. A bank raid at closing time in Beaconsfield, raiders still on the premises, gunshots heard and hostages held. Senior officers and Area CID were attending, with an Armed Support Vehicle ordered to the scene.

Fifty-seven minutes after the report that Winterton had gone missing, his car was observed speeding on a 30 mph

stretch of the North Orbital, half a mile short of the Maple
Cross access to the M25.

Outrunning the modest patrol car, the Mercedes hurtled
into the clockwise flow and streaked for the fast lane, headlights flashing, hitting over a ton where it reached a clear
patch, weaving when caught behind a dawdler doing ninety.

As the report came in Yeadings swore quietly under his
breath. Winterton was panicking. This was no planned journey to a rendezvous. The man had surely gone barking
mad.

Hertfordshire force was alerted as the vehicle left the
Thames Valley. Under lowering storm clouds the chopper
zoomed into action, loaded with thermal imagining equipment, and continuously radioing positions to the patrol cars
in pursuit.

Inevitably it would end in one of two ways: capture or
a bloody crash. Yeadings was praying there'd be no damage caused by police driving. Statistics for civilian casualties from car chases were growing horrendous.

Three motorway police cars were distantly on the Merc's
tail when they received instructions to move up and identify
themselves. With sirens and flashing lights they cut a
swathe through other traffic as they gained on the speeding
car, preparing for a coordinated interception ahead.

'He's making for the M1 junction. Two others will cut
him off at Exit 21,' DI Bellamy predicted calmly, then
dropped momentary interest in Winterton and returned to
controlling the M4 pile-up where two fire appliances, working on a tanker's fuel spillage, were preventing ambulances' approach to casualties on the eastern edge.

'Three known dead so far,' Bellamy said tersely. 'A &
E departments from Reading to Slough are notified of imminent arrivals. ETA for medics and surgeon four minutes
to the scene.'

This threefold burst of activity had abruptly swamped Control after a period of comparative calm. While one communication line dealt with the multiple RTA on the M4, another must remain open for developments in the bank raid at Beaconsfield. Armed robbers were still on the premises there and hostages had been taken. Against these situations Winterton's fate was small beer and currently out of area.

It was no place for himself, Yeadings regretted. He'd leave all this adrenalin boost to Bellamy's team, and clear off to his office. The outcome of Winterton's flight would be relayed to him in time.

Time, though. He sensed something a tad mystifying there. What had Winterton been up to since leaving home? Fifty-seven minutes had elapsed between discovering that he'd flown the coop and his car being spotted out on the North Orbital. And what the devil was he doing so far south before making this lightning dash for the northbound M1? It made little sense; there were a dozen more direct routes.

One thing was clear. Driving so insanely, he couldn't have Julie with him in the car. Or if he had, she must be past all feeling. It looked bad.

Yeadings put out a call to Mott's mobile. He had reason enough now for a detailed search of Winterton's house without a warrant. A Scenes of Crime team was to meet the DI out at Long Gable.

Passing the CID office Yeadings had observed Z perched on the corner of a desk while a shabbily dressed, middle-aged man with a bald cranium peaking through sparse, straw-coloured hair peered at a VDU screen. Yeadings went back a few steps to get a view of the screen himself and saw diagrams of car types slowly scrolling. The man, he assumed, was the angler, and he raised his eyebrows in Z's direction.

Behind the visitor's back she turned her palms upwards, shrugging. So, a typical Joe Public; it seemed that the angler circulated with his eyes half shut and his mind geared in neutral.

'When you're free, Z,' Yeadings murmured and continued on his way.

She appeared some twenty minutes later, to find Yeadings still unenlightened on Winterton's fate. 'Any joy there?' he asked her.

'His name is Bingham. He works at a DIY store in Chesham. He showed slight interest in three separate makes of car. The one he saw on the afternoon Julie went missing could be any of them, so he said. And they're as different as a Ford Granada, a Mitsubishi Challenger and a Jaguar S. But he is certain about the colour. I showed him a decorator's paint swatch and he picked out Azure.'

'So it wasn't Winterton's car. His Mercedes is definitely silver. And at present the Lord only knows where it is.'

Z gave him a questioning glance and he shrugged. 'I'd better bring you up to date. Whether due to endemic madness, the lunar phase or zodiac influences, Thames Valley has suddenly gone barking mad. We have three simultaneous major incidents, and the least important is Winterton doing an O.J. Simpson towards the M1. I'm expecting to hear at any minute that he's been pulled in or ended as an RTA statistic.'

'Why run? Has he gone to meet the kidnapper?'

'If he has, then he's kept it dark from us, and by now the cars on his tail will have blown it for him. But I think not. He'd never risk drawing police attention by speeding if he was on his way to a deal. We shan't know exactly what he's running from until we catch up with him.'

Z looked uneasy. 'But if the kidnapper hadn't allowed enough time for Winterton to get wherever he had to be—'

'I told you, we don't know that the kidnapper did get in touch. There wasn't a second phone call. For that matter, we've no real proof that there's a kidnapper at all. Winterton could have set up that night call himself.'

'Maybe he *wants* to attract attention. If someone's hidden in the car, holding a gun on him…'

'He'd be forced to drive more modestly. I think we have to accept that the man's on the run.'

'In which case—'

'In which case I'm afraid we're back to considering seriously whether Winterton has made away with Julie himself. That's why I'm having his house turned inside out.'

WHEN DANIEL WINTERTON first started making money at an interesting level he had decided to transfer his banking affairs to the Beaconsfield branch. He wasn't personally known there, so this ensured a greater sense of privacy; and besides, it was an attractive town with a number of decent eating places. As a result he had become accustomed to solitary visits for 'browsing and grazing', as he called it.

Today was different, and he cursed the need to drive so far. With a kidnapper's demands imminent it was essential to get there before closing time and start transferring a considerable amount from shares to cash. It was something he should have done that first day, after Julie had failed to turn up by nightfall.

He had a small-town mistrust of city brokers. To his mind, too many antennae were fine tuned to checking on them and speculating on the information extracted. Until now he had regarded the more cumbersome bank service as a guarantee of anonymity, the only publicity that interested him being purely of the literary kind and financed by his publisher.

Now he felt trapped by his earlier unnecessary caution

and was desperate to get the chore done and return home
for any further message from the kidnapper; because this
time surely he would be getting specific instructions. The
man must be as anxious for payment and to hand Julie over
as he was himself to have her safely back.

There were cruel moments when he saw her quite
clearly. They flashed upon him like vivid photo stills. She
was lying in half-darkness, trussed and gagged on a filthy
mattress in a dank cellar. Her face was smudged with the
grimy tracks of earlier tears, her lovely blond hair in a
greasy tangle. The first sharp terrors were over; now she
was curled tight with misery and trying hard not to cry
aloud.

He'd done the scene himself in one of his early books,
piling on the crude detail, running to steel manacles chafing
a young woman's wrists to cuffs of dried blood. And the
villain had indulged a fine taste for mental torture.

Now he dared not recall it; yet the images kept recurring
in varying frames of horror. His own creation. Now his self-
inflicted hell.

Reaching the bank barely in time, he braked the car at
the street corner, mounting the pavement with his nearside
wheels. He'd overshot the street end and, in reversing a
couple of feet, he felt his rear bumper make contact. As he
scrambled out there was a cry of protest from a girl in the
vehicle behind, but he waved impatiently and hurried on.
Let her come and have it out with him later.

He reached the bank's door as a teller was approaching,
eyes on his wrist, counting the seconds. And from behind
Winterton someone else was thrusting past, a woman dragging a small child who was sulkily resisting, knuckling its
eyes and grizzling.

'Excuse me,' Winterton said firmly, moving in front
again towards the counter.

And then he saw the ugly snout of the shotgun raised almost under his nose as the door slammed behind; twin steely nostrils gesturing him aside while the supposed teller closed in behind, poking something small and hard against his ribcage.

'Over by the wall. All of you. On your faces! Spread yourselves.'

Then he saw there were others being herded towards him. Simultaneously there was a sharp clang and sheet-metal shields had dropped to isolate the counters—except for one opening, where the barrel of a gun was already clamped under the window and aimed at the terrified clerk only twenty inches away.

Everything now was happening in slow motion; only his heart raced in overdrive. He stared at the man confronting him and in place of a head saw a grotesque outsized onion where a nylon stocking flattened and distorted the man's features. More hideous to him than that, however, was his own gibbering fear. It took an effort of will to make his legs obey him, sidling crabwise in the direction indicated, hands held high, to drop heavily to his knees and then prostrate himself.

This couldn't be meant to happen. He didn't belong here. Enmeshed in a drama of his own, he had been spun off into an alien one, more immediate and dangerous, where he had no control, could make no move at all. He was as helpless as Julie must be, gagged and bound as a prisoner. He was a victim now too, impotent to protect himself or her.

Dear God! he thought, his cheek pressed harshly into the bitter-smelling vinyl of the flooring, must it end this way? Suppose these madmen kill me and Julie never gets found?

He had for so long acted the puppet master, creating and

manipulating his characters, regarding his actual surroundings as much the same malleable material.

But this was real. Here he had no power to make things come right in the end. No choice. He couldn't foresee or avert whatever was to follow.

A sudden burst of firing beat about the walls, becoming deafening as its echoes were hurled back, indistinguishable from the shots themselves. Despite the threats he rolled on one shoulder to stare up disbelievingly. The third raider, panicking as he struggled to free his gun from the gap beneath the teller's window, had knocked off the safety catch and released the automatic action. At close range, rapid fire was spraying the staff area. It went chattering on until the magazine was exhausted.

The girl seated in the teller's place opposite had had half her face and one shoulder blown away. As Winterton watched, appalled, the rest of the body slithered bloodily away to disappear below the counter. He caught a glimpse of red-brown hair in a ponytail and thought he recalled her, a pretty girl not long out of school. A daughter. Someone's Julie.

The gunman, aghast, screamed crazily, 'No! No! *No!*' He was still struggling with the gun as though it were a live thing thrashing in his hands.

The taller raider back by the door stood petrified, his handgun hanging forgotten by his side. The one who had threatened Winterton as he came in was the only person moving. He stayed fiercely in charge, backing against the wall and swinging the sawn-off shotgun in an arc to petrify the room. 'Stay down!' he roared and Winterton dropped again on to his face.

The man's crepe rubber soles squeaked alongside as he approached the tellers' counter. He spoke in a contemptuously controlled voice to the hysterical man and there came the sharp sounds of two open-handed slaps and a caught breath before the shouting became a low blubbering. There were terrified animal squealings from bank staff beyond the barrier.

'You lot,' the man ordered with ice-cold menace, 'keep your hands high and get back against the wall. Who has the key to this door? Bring it over. I'm coming through.'

The bastard was going to carry on, Winterton realised. It made no difference that the girl had been killed. Demoralised, he felt his own guts go into spasm and knew he must vomit but swallowed hard to force the bile back.

Against hysterical sobbing there came the cool click of a lock being turned, a scuff of soft soles and, closer, the continuous anguished grief of the unintentional killer. That one could be discounted as a threat; he was wasted. So, surely, was the automatic.

Winterton forced himself to be rational. Two gunmen remained operative, one with a revolver, the other a twelve-bore. There were probably seven or eight bank staff out of sight and four customers beside himself prostrate to the near side of the counter. One was the child, making odd clicking sounds as he fought for breath. An asthmatic. That was all the poor mother needed. Not a hero among them all.

'Oh my God, my God,' moaned the killer. This time he was left to wallow in shock. The leader was beyond the barrier with the safe opened and was holding his gun on three of the staff as they shakily fumbled its contents into a canvas sack. It still left the taller gunman keeping guard over the customers and a way free to the street door.

Coward, Winterton accused himself in shame. For all that the scenario was familiar he couldn't risk making a move. This wasn't a product of his word processor. Here, outside imagination, he had no control.

And he'd only one life to lose. Until now he'd had a spare one for each book, and the sure knowledge that he could outlive every cliffhanger.

He mustn't be destroyed here. It wasn't his world. He had to submit, because he must survive into his own reality, for Julie's sake.

Leaving his hands spread to either side of his head, he stiffened his neck and lifted it slowly to check on the farthest prisoners. Two pensioners. From three metres away he could see the tremors that shook the old man. His walking stick lay out of reach where he'd fallen and one leg looked cruelly twisted. The woman lay like a beached whale, still as death.

An old man and woman, a young mother, a child, and himself a coward. There was no hope there. They must all continue to lie passive until the raiders had collected sufficient loot and left. Pray God they'd be satisfied then and there'd be no more bloodshed.

The killer's sobbing cut suddenly, and there was a brief silence, overtaken by sudden, animal anger. 'You bastard!' he screamed at full force. 'You said they were blanks. Steve, you shit, you swore they—'

'Shut it!'

The leader's voice came from nearer, with chilling menace, but the impassioned killer was past reason. Winterton raised his head again in time to see the two men grapple and sway above him, one clawing at the other as the shotgun's stock swung and landed a smashing blow on the killer's skull. He swayed a moment, staggered, his gloved fingers raking the other's face and ripping the fabric of the mask. Then he dropped heavily and lay unmoving.

The stocking had torn in the middle, exposing a jutting nose and Neanderthal brow. The man paused only to kick away the fallen body and swing again towards his prisoners

on the floor. With his free hand he pulled the nylon away
from his mouth and spat. His eyes met Winterton's and
swept on towards the crouching woman who was staring,
appalled, and clutching the child to her chest.

In the man's cold gaze Winterton read his own sure death
and hers. They could never be left to identify him.

He laid his head flat again and waited for it to end, empty
of fear for that moment and strangely sad that the last thing
he should ever see was a swirling pattern out of focus on
the vinyl floor, distorted into a leering face. All his life
reduced to this.

Shockingly the bank's alarm bell set up a clangour out
in the street. Rattled, the two gunmen turned on the staff
who stood frozen. It wasn't clear who had leaned on the
button, but they were all to share the guilt.

The robber called Steve waved the other through the door
to the open-plan office. 'Take the bags. You there, show
him the back way out.'

Winterton gently raised himself on one elbow, grimaced
at the woman, pointed towards the counter and watched as
she silently crawled towards its cover, the toddler hugged
against her side. Then he followed, lying against the child
to conceal him. He could do nothing for the old couple but,
not having glimpsed the gunman's face, they might pro-
voke him less.

Protected by the counter, Winterton could only guess
what happened next, hearing the muffled sounds of footsteps and grunting. It seemed none of the staff was being
a hero as the gangsters immobilised them and made their
escape into the rear passage. Now, he imagined, it could
be only minutes before help came and the nightmare was
over.

The taller man came back and dragged the unconscious
robber out, the heels of his trainers squeaking against the

vinyl floor. Then, after a short silence inside the bank, made
more pronounced by the dinning alarm on the street, there
were running footsteps and the two gunmen were back in
a frenzy, balked by the automatic locking device that had
sealed off the rear steel door. 'Switch it off, you shit!' the
leader shouted wildly at someone unseen. 'You must be
able. What if there was a fire? Do it. Do it now!'

It was a man trying to answer. It sounded as though the
other had him by the throat. 'I c-can't. S-someone has to
use a key from outside.'

Now was the time, Winterton knew, that things could get
really bad. He heard the shotgun explode and covered his
ears with his hands.

THELMA HOBBS HAD ALREADY made two sweeps of the
kerbside parking along this street and now was writing fu-
riously on her pad and slapping parking tickets under the
windscreen wipers of three cars that had overstayed their
time.

She liked her outdoor job for its regular hours, didn't
mind the occasional rain and had no compunction about
grinding the road hogs.

The silver Mercedes at the far end had arrived since she
last came round, and apart from the bloody thing having
two wheels on the pavement and sitting square over the
double yellow lines, it overlapped the street corner. She felt
special satisfaction in writing out the ticket for that rich
smarty.

The Shogun parked behind it, with a young woman in a
baseball cap at the wheel, was also over time, but she was
now hemmed in and couldn't choose but to sit tight till the
oaf in front came back. Thelma decided that might be punishment enough for the present. She'd pick up on that one
next time she offended.

Thelma tugged her meter-maid's hat more firmly over one eye, turned the corner and strolled on, checking the next line of parking. That was when the bank alarm went off right behind her, so that she nearly jumped out of her skin.

Not that it hadn't done so before when some thickhead had fumbled the wrong button; and it didn't signify anything that the bank was now closed. Everyone knew that work went on inside long after the public were herded out. Nobody around her seemed in any way disturbed by the cry of wolf, and Thelma's obsessive enemy was the motor car and its many offences. What she heard next, however, brought a rush of adrenalin: a full-throated roar that she recognised as a Le Mans start. Tyres shrieking with massive acceleration, a hand leaned hard on the horn as the silver Mercedes took off and flashed into the traffic flow.

That style of departure usually marked her arrival, didn't follow her ticketing the culprit.

Deprived of confronting her prey, she would take it out on the Shogun she'd passed up on. If the girl in the baseball cap hadn't driven off by the time Thelma got back there she should have the next ticket. It would round off figures nicely for the end of the day. The job was twice as satisfying if you met your customers face to face—the personal touch, after all.

Thelma flipped open the pad of tickets and ambled back. The Shogun was still there, but her full gratification wasn't, because the girl, obviously tired of being hemmed in, must have abandoned the car and trotted off on foot.

With the ticket duly made out and attached to the Shogun's windscreen, Thelma Hobbs turned the corner again and made her way down the next row of cars while the bank alarm, unabated, became gradually dimmed by distance.

It did occur to her at one point to wonder dreamily what she might have done if the alarm had been a genuine one. It suggested a quite heroic role which, however unlikely, would have lit up an otherwise rather ordinary day.

TWELVE

TWO MARKED POLICE CARS were the first to arrive at the bank, closely followed by Beaumont in his Vauxhall, having heard their sirens from afar and followed in their wake. Next came Superintendent Jenks of Uniform with a sergeant equipped with a loudhailer.

This was excitement enough to get a small crowd gathered, keeping the constables busy herding them back, closing the street to traffic and securing the area with strings of blue and white plastic tape on iron bollards. The alarm bell continued its din throughout.

'Cut that bloody row,' Jenks ordered. 'We can't hear a damn thing else.'

An Armed Support van screeched to a stop and disgorged a number of navy blue uniforms topped by baseball caps. Each man, clearly labelled POLICE in white, hugged a Heckler & Koch semi-automatic or wore a heavier, long-barrelled Sniper rifle from a shoulder sling.

The van was swiftly reversed towards the parked Shogun and run over the pavement under the offending alarm bell. One officer vaulted on to the vehicle's roof to sever the wiring. The following silence was shattering.

As the armed officers fanned out towards allocated firing positions, two slats of a vertical blind at one of the bank's windows were briefly pressed apart and a masked face peered through.

'Good,' Jenks declared, observing from a distance. 'So

they know the size of their problem. All we do now is simply follow the knitting pattern.'

'STEVE,' THE TALL MAN with the pistol groaned, 'we've had it. The getaway's there but Pat's scarpered. There's bloody filth all over the place.'

'Shut it! No names.' The other man finished covering his lower face with a dark handkerchief and shouldered him aside. He stared between the slats and swore fiercely between gritted teeth.

'Hostages,' he decided, and looked round at the bodies on the floor. 'We'll demand a police car. Take the woman to the door and keep well behind her. You—' and he pointed the shotgun at Winterton, '—get up. Now, when I tell you, open the door slowly and stay clear. No clever tricks or I take you both out. Get it?'

He wouldn't, Winterton tried telling himself. He can't kill us in full view of anyone outside. They'd never let him get away. And they don't know out there that someone's already dead.

But, even making sense, that didn't stem the fear. His hands were shaking as he faced the bank door and reached for the lock. Behind him he heard the woman jostled into position and then the child started choking over its screams.

The woman became useless then, out of her mind, squealing hysterically and tearing at the man until he pulled free to pistolwhip her and she collapsed to the ground, out cold.

'Bloody hell.' Steve, disgusted, moved in on Winterton with the sawn-off. 'It'll have to be you, then. And you're a larger target.'

'It won't work,' Winterton tried to explain, his voice wobbling as he struggled with the door. 'This lock'll be on automatic too.'

The gang leader marched back into the staff area, levelled his shotgun at a middle-aged man and demanded, 'Where's the bloody override system?'

Shakily the man pointed to a small junction box at knee height below the counter.

'Fix it or I fix you. This is your last chance. I shan't fire into the floor this time.'

The man limped across to the box, opened it with a key from his inner pocket and switched off the circuit. At the door Winterton felt the latch give under his fingers, took a deep breath and stared hard at the man called Steve. If he wasn't the one to pull the trigger, would it be the police?

FIFTEEN MILES NORTH-EASTWARD on the M25, things hadn't gone to plan. While the pursuing police cars were gradually closing up ready for the ambush at Exit 21 for the M1, at the last instant the Mercedes streaked across the intervening lanes and rocketed out on the previous exit, 20.

The pursuit cars overran, swerved, screeched to a halt on handbrake turns and shot, head on, into the following traffic. Two collided with the contraflow and one wove through to pull up on the hard shoulder.

An articulated lorry had struck the first police car sideways on; the smaller vehicle overturned twice and landed on its roof with fuel spilling from the tank. Its driver struggled to free his jammed door while the remaining driver bellowed into his handset for emergency backup and to relocate the useless ambush ahead.

BACK AT CONTROL, DI Bellamy was white-knuckled. While the multiple pile-up on the M4 still demanded maximum attention from Traffic, the bank raid at Beaconsfield was turning into an elaborate production of *Aida*. And now they had two cars out of action on the M25, officers injured and a thorough balls-up of netting Winterton's runaway car. He fired off instructions with little of his customary cool and snarled, 'Better tell the super that his chap's still free.'

'Right,' Yeadings acknowledged when the message came in. He wasn't alarmed, although Winterton, as a car-chase fan in fiction, seemed to have a remarkable taste for the real thing. He'd just pulled a fast one and out-thought the pursuit, but it was only a matter of time before they caught up with him.

Time, though. That reminded him that Nan would be expecting him back. Not only him, but also Z and Max Harris for dinner. And he'd sent Z off to drive the angler home after his fruitless effort to identify the pale blue car.

Beaumont had just phoned in from standby on the Beaconsfield bank raid, and with Mott searching Long Gable, it left only him on the ground. It might be an idea to look in again on Control and keep an eye on how the Winterton debacle was shaping up.

He arrived to an electric atmosphere, in time to catch the chopper pilot's report that the Mercedes had performed a full circle and re-entered the ring motorway in an anti-clockwise direction. Bellamy now had to throw in more cars to surround him on that route. But from which feeder roads?

Winterton wasn't proving the mild, domesticated type he'd seemed, but suddenly Action Man in spades. His tactics to date were those of a skilled getaway driver. Certainly they were too sustained to be the outcome of panic. He was thinking with his wheels.

Yeadings wasn't so sure that the impression he'd built of the man now fitted the reality.

IN BEACONSFIELD, Superintendent Jenks was bringing Control up to date on the siege situation outside the bank. There had been no further sign of movement inside, and no one had picked up on a police call put through to them by telephone.

Bystanders were being questioned and two witnesses had mentioned an earlier burst of rapid gunfire. Opinions varied between hearing eight and twenty shots.

So at least one of the villains had an automatic, probably taking a clip of ten.

So far no request for medical aid had been received. In fact the robbers had ignored all messages by loudhailer. A section of the armed backup had now reached the bank's roof by way of neighbouring buildings and was in position to cut off any attempted escape at that level.

Jenks's voice broke off. 'Hang on. Here we go. The door's opening. Someone's coming out. Two men. The front one has a white flag. No, it's a torn-off shirtsleeve!

'Now he's halted. They're using him as a shield. He's one of the hostages. There's a pistol to his head.'

At Control DI Bellamy grunted. A pistol. Previous to this Jenks had spoken of the single discharge of a shotgun, after bystanders had reported earlier automatic fire. The array of firearms might be motley but they had to be taken seriously. These guns were not just for show.

As the link with Jenks cut off, attention rapidly switched back to the M25 pursuit. Police cars from Exit 21 were streaking south to join the remaining one, which had re-entered by Access 20 anticlockwise. But before the Mercedes was sighted there came a suppressed exclamation. 'Traffic building up ahead. There's a pile-up. Yes. It's the Merc. He's off the road. Two lanes are closed. Emergency Services...'

Yeadings grunted as his own mobile became insistent and he lost the next terse orders. He stepped back through the doorway and took his call in the passage outside. Beaumont's excited voice came over. 'It's Winterton. He's *here,* sir, at Beaconsfield. He's the hostage they've got at the bank!'

'Right. Stay there,' Yeadings snapped. And then, to himself, 'So who the hell is that in his Merc?'

There was no mystery. It had to be the gang's getaway driver who'd seen the police reaction and made off. Whatever fate he'd abandoned the others to, getting away was clearly his personal priority. Any surprise came later, from 'him' being a woman.

Which shouldn't amaze me, Yeadings told himself. Roadwise, hadn't women the edge on men these days? Although strictly speaking their record was for safe driving.

Safe she hadn't been. And from the first medical reports it seemed she might not pull through, after all her fine display of unconcern for other road users' lives. However, like anyone else, she was entitled to the best surgical and inpatient attention available. She was just one of four critical cases the ambulances took to Casualty at Watford General.

'Off our patch, but there's still enough happening on it,' Bellamy muttered. 'And your man Winterton gets to be a priority after all.'

Poor devil, Yeadings thought, switching rapidly back to viewing him as victim, not suspect. Concerned with getting into the bank before Friday closure, he'd probably left the Merc's keys in the ignition. Maybe the original getaway car had some defect; whatever, the gang's driver had panicked at the alarm bell when the others didn't join her, and she'd seized her chance. She would have heard the gunfire and thought at least one of them was down. So she saved what she could of the situation—which was the proverbial number one. It might help matters on the ground if Superintendent Jenks warned the other gang members, as persuasion to cut their losses and give in, that the woman was already held.

He learned they were still holding out and had answered the most recent phone call by demanding a marked police car with uniformed driver for their escape, plus a guarantee of no harassment.

Not the brightest villains apparently. The longer the siege went on the more the weekend traffic would build, until they had nil chance of making their way through unimpeded, though a flashing blue light and a siren might help. The next demand they'd make would be an instant flight from an airport. He wondered what preparations they'd made in advance: passports and bookings? Maybe they had the necessary papers with them. Or maybe they were caught with a foot in the air.

Dodgy, either way. He hoped they weren't desperate enough to shoot their way through to hijacking a tourist-packed plane. There could be carnage in a crowded airport concourse.

It was turning into an extended job for uniformed branch, Traffic, and Armed Response personnel; also action stations for Heathrow and Luton Security. Meanwhile, Superintendent Jenks must deliver complex delaying tactics with Dutch-uncle calm. Then everyone must sit tight until the professional negotiator came on scene.

Meanwhile, Yeadings decided, until the shrink arrived it might hearten Winterton if he displayed himself discreetly and gave an enigmatic nod from across the way. While it wasn't possible to see into the bank, those in there would surely be keeping an eye on what went on out in the road.

Heading for his car he met his woman DS in the corridor. 'Z, there are developments with Winterton. I'll explain as we go, and you can ring my wife from the car. Tell her dinner's off for tonight. Things are getting complicated.'

Z found that Nan took it calmly, certainly with less irritation than she felt herself. Evidently last-minute cancellations delivered second hand weren't new to her, whereas the woman DS had now twice been dropped into doing the Boss's dirty work. Yeadings himself had continued to drive with a blandly innocent expression after offloading the call.

'Sir, I was coming to tell you...'

'Fire away then.'

'I took Bingham home and he—'

'Bingham?' Yeadings' eyebrows shot high.

'The angler who couldn't identify the light blue car.'

'So?'

'When we were almost there he remembered something more. After he'd cycled past the car he'd stopped and looked back because he heard a noise in the bushes, and he noticed the radiator grill. He said it had two squarish chrome frames set in like nostrils. It had slipped his mind until then. Two nostrils, sir. That should make it a BMW.'

This in itself was not ground-breaking—but Z had sounded as if there was more to come. 'What kind of noise in the bushes?' he demanded.

'A rustling of leaves and a grunt, he said. He assumed it was someone from the car who'd got taken short, so he looked away and walked on.'

'A grunt, Z.'

'Yes, I wondered. He couldn't time it exactly. Never wears a watch when fishing. But he thought it was between twelve thirty and one. The grunt could have been Julie with someone's hand over her mouth. Or simply some dog on the loose, rabbit-hunting.'

'A pity he's so proper. In this case we could have done with a peeping Tom.'

THE CLEARED AREA ROUND the bank stretched halfway along each of two streets at right angles. Yeadings walked under the police tape which a saluting constable lifted for him and went across to Jenks.

Z accosted a uniformed man wearing Traffic Day-Glo who stood beside a row of civilian cars at the kerb.

'Did you radio in their licence numbers? We need to know who's inside.'

The man produced a list. 'The Shogun in the front was reported stolen three days ago in Lincoln. Could be the one the gang's been using. But the driver seems to have scarpered.'

'That fits,' Z agreed. 'We've an unknown woman injured in an RTA on the M25. The Merc she drove belongs to the hostage shown with a gun to his head.'

'I heard he's the father of the kid that's gone missing.'

'Bad news travels fast. I suppose that means you've seen DS Beaumont around.'

Z glanced across at the knot of senior officers and recognised her oppo's slouched figure on the fringe. He raised a hand and she went over. His Pinocchio features were as wooden as ever.

'Carlton TV and BBC News are on their way,' he warned. 'Mr Jenks wants hostages' relatives identified and informed before they see anything on the box. Can you cover?'

'I've got a probable hostage list here,' she offered. 'One car's registered to an Arnold Frome living in Watlington Road, the other to a Ms Angela Drayne of Widmer End. We'd have to use your wheels, because I came with the Boss. And we may find there's no one at either address. I'll check first that I'm not needed here.'

Yeadings looked up as she approached and grunted at the request. 'From the list of car owners it seems there's a woman held inside. Also there will be women bank staff.

So I want you to stay, Z. It could all blow up at any moment, and we don't yet have a WPC on standby. Tell Beaumont to inform family at both addresses and return ASAP.'

'Is there any movement yet?' she asked when she got back.

'Theirs or ours?' Yeadings hedged. 'There's a strong case for status quo until we know if anyone's injured. Technical backup is trying for audio intercept round the side of the building. Meanwhile we're directing all attention in this direction.'

'Do we know who the gang are?'

'They haven't introduced themselves,' Yeadings said mildly. 'Their driver wisely had no ID on her, so we'll get nothing from that end either, until she comes round. Which could be way off, if ever. The man sheltered by Winterton was masked and remains anonymous. He had a pistol, so he's no member of a legitimate gun club. Thanks to recent brilliant legislation, only the baddies now have access to handguns.' Yeadings had a low opinion of all politicians.

'There must be at least one other villain inside keeping things quiet. He'd most likely be the one who spoke on the phone to Superintendent Jenks. Voice not familiar, and a Midlands accent. He denies anyone's wounded and now wants the Armed Support Vehicle's tyres deflated as with all other vehicles, before a fully tanked police Land Rover is provided, plus an unarmed uniformed driver who's to be sent into the bank for frisking. Mr Jenks is holding out for all hostages to be released first.'

Yeadings sighed, easing his collar in the humid heat. 'If he gets anywhere with that, it qualifies him to sort out the Balkans.'

UNAWARE OF ANY DISASTER beyond his own emotional crisis, Clifford Hook lay staring up at the shadowed ceiling of his bedroom. He longed for the coolness of night to bring relief, yet dreaded the onset of its long, wakeful hours.

All afternoon distant thunder had rumbled inconclusively over the Chilterns with sporadic sheet lightning. The storm itself seemed torpid, incapable of breaking.

Whisky hadn't helped. His head throbbed and pumped more heavily. Instead of being drowsy he was overcharged, his nerves jangling. Light penetrated his eyelids, throwing up a screen for imagined horrors. He saw Julie's face drawn with pain, and couldn't bear the accusation in her eyes.

Words echoed from a childhood faith he thought he'd long outgrown: the garbled confession as, his face pressed on the backs of his hands and his bare knees pricked by the carpety church hassock, he had tried to concentrate on forgotten sins. He could smell again the pew's dusty wood-work and feel the fine India paper of the prayer book under his fingers.

'Forgive us our sins. The remembrance of them is grievous unto us, the burden of them is intolerable.'

And it was, literally, intolerable: a burden he could never be free of. How could he face the knowledge that through him the child had been destroyed—as Caroline had, years before? He should have spoken out before it came to this.

Because there had been no physical proof, only this hear-say account brought to him years later through a third party, he had done nothing when he might have saved her. Her monstrous father with his evil lies had been left unpunished.

Even now, when the police had come to his office at the hospital, he had stopped short of outright accusation. He had simply insisted that Caroline was dead, but the police still believed she had run away with a lover.

He should have spoken out, even if he could prove nothing; even if they thought he was improvising in a vindictive outburst against his brother-in-law. It was true he hated him, but it was no fabrication. He knew Winterton had murdered Caroline as surely as if he had seen it happen. And now the evil man had killed for a second time, destroying his own defenceless and innocent child.

Hook acknowledged he was a coward. He must face himself as that, and now it was too late to reverse what had happened. The child was gone. Whatever she did or said that moved Winterton to this final, unspeakable act, it could not happen again. Her suffering was over. The man had no one near him left to destroy.

Hook knew of serial killers here at the hospital. Their terrible histories had gone through his hands. They were offered treatment because they were sick, and over a long period could possibly be cured. Daniel Winterton wasn't like them; he was an unforgiving man who judged and coldly acted out the sentences he imposed.

Certainly Caro had deceived her husband, but wasn't that a lesser sin than murder? And surely he had long known how she was, while the anger built up inside and he planned his revenge.

Caro had never deserved a violent death. Her beauty had been her curse. It made her too desirable, and she had given way to the men who admired her.

It was like an ancient parable. She was the woman taken in adultery. Her husband had come upon her in the act, and her lover had abandoned her, taking payment to go away and say nothing about the vicious treatment Winterton had meted out. But he hadn't stayed silent forever.

There were still times when Hook could not believe it himself. It must be some gothic horror he'd seen on TV. Or he had experienced it in a nightmare. We make our own dreams—don't we?—for mysterious reasons the mind cannot comprehend. And a day or two later, confused and hung up on it, we wonder, was it really true or did I only dream it?

Sometimes he was ready to accept that he had invented the whole Morgan story to punish himself for having failed that wonderful sister, not being close enough for her to have confided her fears and needs to him. He had loved her too much, and demanded too little. Worse, he had failed to warn her off when she had begun that fatal affair with the treacherous young man next door.

If he had come upon her like that himself, in Winterton's place, wouldn't he have felt the same? Outraged. Murderous. He thought he could actually see himself confronting the lovers, attacking her, striking her down and then pleading with the man to—

No. That could never have been. He mustn't let his imagination run wild like that. It wasn't himself; it was Winterton. Daniel Winterton had been Caroline's killer.

And then Julie, that flawless image of her mother… Much, much later she had somehow guessed the shocking truth, and her father had to silence her.

A flash of lightning lit the room and pierced Hook through to his nerve ends. A single crash of thunder followed straight after, while the curtains blew in on his bed like some predator leaping on carrion. He heard the sudden hiss of rain on tarmac, gusting like gravel against the window panes. He staggered from the bed and leaned out, elbows on the sill to feel the harsh cold striking through his hair, chill runnels tickling and snaking down his cheeks and behind his ears.

At last the heat had broken. Things must be better now. He could weep unseen in the rain and hopefully come clean.

THIRTEEN

OUTSIDE THE BANK the storm broke as savagely, huge raindrops blackening dusty surfaces in seconds and sheeting across the empty space cleared between the crime-scene tapes. Police ranks broke as the senior men dived for cover in opposite doorways or parked cars. Sensors brought street lights on and the early August evening was instantly night.

This was going to make things harder, Yeadings decided. For themselves and for the gang attempting to escape. Regrettably also for any of the innocent road users later getting in their way.

He turned up his jacket collar and made for the communications van. Inside they were working to enhance the intercept from the bank.

THE ROBBER WHO HAD BLASTED the cashier was moaning as he started to come round. On his knees, he started to crawl back from where he had been dragged. Steve went over and toed him in the ribs. 'Get up! Here.' On him he dropped a length of flex cut from a computer printer. 'Start tying their hands behind. That one first.' He nodded towards Winterton. 'Then the bank lot.'

He continued past, confident there'd be no more resistance, and pulled aside two slats of blind to peer through. Rain bucketing over the window obscured the road outside, and he stepped back in alarm as the black sky burst with jagged lightning like a giant incandescent root, exposing him like a stage spotlight. The following crash seemed to shake the room, then rumbled off in the distance.

'Shit,' he said. 'We'll not drive through that lot. We sit tight and wait.'

'That'll give *them* more time. They'll set up an ambush.' The taller, more silent one was panicking now. 'Let's take a chance. Make a dash while they're rattled.'

'There's no fucking car, shithead!' He knew they'd placed marksmen, but he wouldn't admit as much with the hostages listening. It might give someone ideas about being a hero. He didn't want any more action inside. He was trying like mad to blank out what had already happened. That way maybe the others would too.

He stared at the ceiling. 'What's upstairs?' He swung his shotgun in an arc on the bank staff huddled against the far wall.

'It's a flat. Nobody lives there at present. It has an entrance from the yard at the back. There's a steel door.'

Not that we'd get out into the yard to try it, Steve thought bitterly. The override to the automatic security had released the front door lock but the rear door was still immovable.

There was another chance. Although they couldn't get to the roof by way of the flat's steel door, it didn't mean they couldn't get *out* through it from the flat. And even if doors and windows were reinforced in the bank, the ceiling looked like ordinary gypsum plasterboard. Above it there should be crossbeams supporting the upstairs floor. He knew well enough from repairs to buildings of this kind that beyond those beams would be nothing more than wooden boards covered by carpet or vinyl flooring.

He looked over to where the staff and customers were now all safely secured, except the frail oldies. 'Pile up desks in that corner,' he ordered his men. He gestured upwards with the barrel of his sawn-off. 'That's the way we get out. All we need now is an axe and a saw.'

IN THE COMMUNICATIONS VAN they now had an audio fix on the bank's interior. The man's voice came over clearly, followed by low-key mutterings and the scraping of furniture on flooring. Yeadings handed back the headset and nodded to the technical sergeant. 'That should keep them busy for a while. I'll find out what chance they have of any tools being on the premises.'

'Pretty unlikely,' Superintendent Jenks commented. 'They'll not get far with a couple of nail files and a bushel of paper clips. Meanwhile I think that's the negotiator arriving.'

Peering through the wash of rain over the van's rear window, he opened the door and ventured his balding dome a few inches into the deluge.

A tubby man covered in shiny black plastic emerged from the newly arrived car and splashed across to where Jenks waited, heaved himself in and apologised with the single word, 'Monsoon,' as he swept off his sou'wester.

'Morton.' He introduced himself in much the same tone and offered a pudgy hand.

Yeadings yielded up his place at the radio desk and prepared to go about his business. There were bodies enough in this cramped kennel, and he was aware of a doghouse waiting for him at home.

Experience of shrinks warned him that there could now be a long-drawn dialogue interspersed with far from pregnant pauses. When the action came it would be instant and vicious: alien territory for his comfortable, desk-adapted body.

Among uniformed reinforcements arriving were two WPCs, so before leaving Yeadings dismissed Z. 'Tomor-

row,' he told her, 'I want you to check that Winterton's
house is left exactly as it was. I don't want the man any
more upset than he'll be already, once we get him out
safely. Angus will stay on there to the end tonight, but he
doesn't know the house as well as you do.'

'Has the search turned up anything, sir?'

'I haven't debriefed Angus yet, but he's disappointed so
far. He needs a couple more hours. When Winterton's eventually rescued I'll have him sent for a medical check-up.
Anyway, get off home now. I'm sorry we had to cancel the
meal.'

'Right, sir.' Although she'd taken refuge in a doorway
across from the bank, she had been caught in the first downpour. Her cotton shirt felt plastered to her shoulders and
her sandals squelched with every step. The thought of a
shower and a fleecy towel was foremost in her mind. And
next came Max, who had to be told that she couldn't keep
him on at Beattie's any longer.

Beaumont had drawn a blank at both addresses relating
to the parked cars and had just returned to the siege scene.
He offered to drive her to pick up her own car.

'I spoke to the neighbours,' he told her. 'The Fromes are
an elderly couple who go everywhere together. The old
chap's got Parkinson's and the wife has heart disease. The
other woman's a single mother. She'd have her little boy
with her. He's a two-year-old and gets asthma badly. With
Winterton that makes five, plus the bank staff of probably
eight. Unlucky thirteen. I guess things aren't too good in
there right now.'

The rain had turned steady and the thunder was increas-
ingly distant. With the soaking came old scents off pavement, painted woodwork, cement and car bodies, all indi-
vidual, slightly astringent. Not a totally unwelcome kind of
urban freshness; but it made Z suddenly long for the coun-

try, to smell a beanfield, honeysuckle, cut hay, even dried
cowpats.

It was symptomatic of the changeover from cop to civilian. When she was tired she was all nostalgia. Caught
up in the nitty-gritty of law enforcement and the seamy side
of investigation, you could have a little too much of the
here and now.

She picked up her car and near home stopped off at the
corner shop which stayed open late. Despite the hour there
were seven or eight Gujeratis gathered there for a lively
discussion, which broke off as she entered. After a second's
marked silence they resumed more quietly in their own language and she felt their dark eyes following her round the
shelves.

She chose half a dozen basics and at the pay desk offered
her basket to a beaming child of nine or ten proudly in
charge of the till. He had all the assurance of a bossy male
adult, the object of admiring giggles from three little girls
sitting on the floor behind him.

'No, no!' A woman in purple tunic and green shalwar
clapped her hands to shoo the boy away, as though she'd
only then noticed him. She left the group and came round
the counter to serve, smiling to reveal symmetrical gold-
filled canines.

Defensive because she knows I'm the Bill, Z registered.
As if I've got time to beef about under-age employment.

She smiled at the woman. 'Your children?' she asked.

'These four, yes. I have two more. One girl older, also
a baby boy.' Her singsong hadn't yet acquired the drab
local accent. She was an incomer.

'You must be proud of them.'

She obviously was, but lowered her dark eyes.

God, I sound patronising, Z thought. Now I can't even
talk straight about kids.

In the car, buckling her seat belt, she noticed the rear-view mirror had been knocked crooked when she'd got out. Now it reflected the upper half of her own face, with the day's make-up worn off. Two small red dots beside the bridge of her nose angrily marked where the dermatologist had removed the rodent cancers. They stared back at her like the eyes of some tiny malevolent beast.

Cancer, she thought; barely visible, and he'd said it wasn't a real baddy. All the same, he'd decided to remove the things right away under local anaesthetic. And until then I was only bothered whether that woman's vicious nails were going to leave permanent scars. You could never know what lurked round the corner.

She grimaced at her reflection and firmly straightened the mirror. To hell with the past. Tomorrow she had to check that Winterton's house had been left in good order. She doubted Angus would have turned up anything incriminating there, but the search had to be made. A missing child was what really mattered, and she wouldn't spare herself in the search for Julie.

She carried her groceries through to the kitchen. Beattie was sitting there in her dressing gown, her tired feet in pink fluffy slippers propped on a stool. She was hugging a mug of hot chocolate. On her black and white portable television Newsroom South East was just coming to a close.

'There's a terrible thing,' she said with relish. 'I guess that's where you've been, ducks. Couldn't see you in the crowd, though.'

'The bank raid? Yes. What's the latest?'

'Some special bloke's been talking to the robbers on the phone. Seems it's going to take some time.'

Z turned from restocking her half of the fridge. 'Is Max still out people-watching in the local pub?'

'No. He's gone back to London. Said he had some business to attend to. Not that it fooled me.'

'Really?' Z turned back to her landlady, who had switched on her shrewd face.

'Well, it's not exackerly comf'table here, is it? I'm surprised he put up with it at all.'

Z waited for more. 'I've been thinking,' Beattie declared, 'and I've made me mind up. I don't have to stay on in this crummy neighbourhood with all that lovely lolly sitting there in the bank. One thing my sister knew was how to enjoy her last years, and I know she'd approve. I'm gonna sell up here and get somethink better. I've already been to the agents.'

'But you love this house.'

'Used to. It's not the same, though. This kitchen, fr'instance. It felt so cosy once. Only now I keep remembering she died here. Flew all that way from South Africa to pass out at my kitchen table. And she didn't mince her words over how I lived. Thought it was a right pigsty. She'd want me to use her money to get somethink really nice. So I'm gonna stretch me wings.'

Beattie going upmarket: which leaves me where? Z wondered.

The old lady put her feet down, stood and reached up to the mantelpiece for an envelope. 'Here. It's from your young man. And there's a bouquet in a bucket of water out in the scullery. I thought it'd be better there in the cool.'

Max signing off? Z asked herself. Was she to lose him as well as Beattie? Both in one evening?

'Cheer up, ducks. It's not the end of the world. He's very fond of you. Only he wasn't comfortable hanging around all day and half the night with nothing to do. Then that on-off dinner with your boss. He said he shouldn't have come bothering you when the job was getting sticky.'

Z scanned the few words in Max's sloping script. 'He wants me to come to London as soon as I'm free.' It was almost as though Max guessed how she felt about having him here.

'You'll do that, won't you? He's a lovely man, and you're so right together. You'd go a long way before you found another one like him.'

'He'll do,' Z conceded, smiling. 'He's funny and he's clever and he's kind. He's just himself, not bothered with an image. That's a relief, and pretty rare.

'Since joining the force I've become such a cynic. I can't risk trusting strangers. When someone attractive comes along I find myself wondering just what con he's putting over. I watch some historic pageantry and I'm expecting it's a false front for some disreputable deal. Once the job gets hold of you everything and everyone is a potential phoney.'

'Maybe you'd like to settle down and get married.'

'I don't think that's in the cards. But if you're giving up this house, Beattie, I might look for a flat big enough to let Max keep a room on, for when he comes this way.'

'You wouldn't move to London?'

'No. For me London's a place to go to, not live in.'

'Good,' Beattie said with satisfaction, 'because I've seen just the place I want to buy. It's enormous, so I could divide it into four good flats upstairs and keep half the ground floor for meself.'

She faced Z with a smug little smile. 'And ackshally, you're gonna love the upstairs one that looks out towards the river.'

Z was dumbfounded. 'How long have you been planning all this?'

'Months,' Beattie informed her gleefully. 'And I've worn me legs to stumps going round all sorts of properties. But the right one's only just come on the market. O'course, you'd have to approve or there's no deal.

'Here.' She scrabbled under a cushion and drew out a sheaf of agent's notices. 'Them's the perticklers. You take them and read them later. Tell me tomorrer what you think.

'You're looking tired, ducks. Why don't you run a bath while I fix you a nice chicken omelette you can eat in bed?'

Why don't I? Z silently agreed. She felt ready to be counted out.

Upstairs her two rooms retained all the heat of the day, Beattie having closed the windows at the first distant rumble of thunder. The BBC had said there'd be heavy rain, and for her anything from that source came close to a royal decree.

Z knew she would miss the old dear if they broke up. Since promotion she could have afforded a decent studio flat, but had come to count on her landlady's occasional company. Just seeing a light under Beattie's kitchen door when she came in at night gave her the same sense of belonging as a dog's welcoming bark.

These days Beattie was full of surprises, from the brilliant red-dyed hair (which clashed with her taste for shocking pink in the Cartland tradition) to this latest dissatisfaction with the home she'd prided herself on. Once a dresser for the old Windmill Theatre, and later a trained beautician, she had squirrelled away her modest wealth to buy this terraced Victorian house on retirement. It had been all she wanted in the world until her sister, twice married to big money and twice widowed, had returned from South Africa to look down on her acquisitions. Now it seemed that Beattie was to take a leaf out of the sister's book and head for the *dolce vita*.

Tired enough to switch off instantly once she'd parked

the empty tray outside on the landing, Z fell almost instantly asleep, helped by Beattie's half-bottle of good Merlot.

OVERNIGHT NEGOTIATIONS continued between the bank raiders and police, culminating in an attempted breakout at four a.m. As day broke the police Land Rover arrived as requested, and its uniformed driver was allowed through the bank's front door and frisked for hidden weapons.

Some twenty minutes later he was the first to come out, with the taller robber's pistol to his head. Then came Winterton as Steve's shield and finally the elderly couple hobbling together ahead of the third gunman who had retrieved the useless automatic.

Police demands for the bank staff, the two women customers and the child to be sent out in advance had been denied. Released, they could have disclosed that the teller was dead and then the opposition would have hardened.

Exhausted by fruitless attempts to break into the upstairs apartment, the gunmen were by then desperate. Emerging on to the pavement, the little cortège moved into the Land Rover's cover. The first two stepped up, Steve moving Winterton aside until the others were in. But as the elderly woman reached up, she appeared to slip, disappearing between the wheels.

Beside her the enraged husband staggered back, brandishing his stick and knocking the automatic out of the man's hand behind him. In the general confusion Winterton backheeled Steve, catching him a cracking blow on the kneecap. At that point a loudspeaker demanded surrender and floodlights sprang out to reveal a circle of marksmen moving in. Dazzled, hostages and gunmen raised their hands and waited to be sorted.

The early morning news bulletins were brief enough, promising later details of the successful police action and the gunmen's arrests. The press had been kept at a distance, but a blanketed stretcher was shown being loaded into an ambulance. A separate view of a mangled Mercedes was described as the robber's getaway car which had fled the scene.

By then Z was on her way to Long Gable.

WINTERTON HAD REFUSED hospital treatment. After a full examination by paramedics he had insisted on being driven home, Mott's searchers having by then left the house. Z arrived at eight o'clock to find Winterton in pyjamas and dressing gown, still not having gone to bed. The sleeping tablets he'd been given were on the kitchen counter, untouched.

'I can't rest,' he protested, rubbing a hand across his inflamed eyes, then rasping it over his chin. 'I know with all this publicity there won't be a call from the kidnapper, so I've unplugged the phone, but sleep's impossible yet.'

She understood well enough. He was still high on adrenalin.

'It's shock,' she said comfortingly. 'The sedative would help. But at least take things quietly or you'll suddenly go out like a light.'

'Shock, yes. Everything's so sudden. It's been like this for days. So unreal, ever since I found Julie wasn't here.

'Before—with Caroline—I had all the time in the world. I had only to act and it all fell into place. The worst was over.'

Again he rubbed a hand over his face, knowing he'd lost her. He went on haltingly, as if to himself, but he meant her to understand. 'The suffering, the decisions. Having to face what we were to each other. There'd been two dimensions, you see—love and...'

She couldn't follow him. He seemed to be rambling. Two dimensions? Love and what? Its opposite?

'Hate?' The word was forced from her, barely more than a whisper.

He looked up, startled. 'Never quite that. *Shame*. She shamed me. It was—as if everything she did, every slight, made me bleed deep inside. So I did what I had to do.'

'And then "the worst was over"?' Her running away with Morgan? That didn't fit what he'd said. Did he mean that *killing* her had brought relief, not guilt?

'I'd waited so long, thought so hard about it, until I knew it was the only way. I knew exactly how to go about it. I was in total control, had to stand firm. So that Caroline could never leave me.'

A physical chill ran over Z's flesh. She felt the hairs on her neck stiffening, standing erect. She remembered a whitewashed interview room and another's confession, half gloating, half supplicating. Stafford Manders, the serial child-killer, explaining himself, his needs, to Yeadings, and all the time dreamily smiling: 'I couldn't let them get away, you see. I loved them. They were mine.'

'You don't see, do you?'

Winterton—also a child killer?—stared at her, into her. For an instant she had lost all sensation and was defenceless against him. His pale eyes had grown huge in the flat, bloodless face. 'Love,' he said. 'Love is the strongest force ever. When all else is pared away, it remains, pure and unspoilt. Terribly innocent.'

No, she didn't understand and never wanted to. That way lay madness. Her mind refused to follow. Desperately she wanted…she needed Yeadings here. He should be in her place. At least some part of him might understand. He had never been a victim, as she had. That made a difference. He was inviolate.

'Let me show you.' The man held out a hand towards her. She was powerless to move. Either to follow or to run.

'It's all right. I'm going to show you.'

He smiled, and his face was illumined with a saintlike fervour. 'You must come through and meet my Caroline.'

Z forced herself to her feet. Hesitantly she went after him, her mobile phone clutched behind her back.

FOURTEEN

THE CALL INTERRUPTED Yeadings in mid-sentence. He grunted, lifted the receiver, caught the urgency in Z's voice, and shouted for Mott to follow as he plunged out for the car. 'Long Gable,' he instructed the DI, buckling himself into the passenger seat. This was one occasion when a younger man's reactions might be faster, and to hell with the speed restrictions.

Town streets and country lanes went by in a blur not entirely the outcome of his mental state.

At Winterton's house, pulling up with a spray of gravel, they made for the open front door. Mott leaned on the bell, but Yeadings walked straight on in, through the empty lounge.

Across the sunny kitchen Winterton was a dark shape on the window seat, bent over a woman at his feet, her head between his knees. His outstretched hands...

Not strangling. Caressing.

And it wasn't Z's cap of dark curls but long, whitish blond hair pinned up on top of the woman's head.

Winterton looked up. 'Superintendent, I'm glad you've come. I want you to meet my wife.

'Caroline, this is the man who will find Julie for us.'

From the corner of his eyes Yeadings caught a slight movement and saw Z leaning against a wall, sickly pale.

'Sir?'

He moved swiftly across and guided her to a chair at the table.

The other figures stayed motionless. He went closer and saw the woman's eyes wide open.

She wasn't dead. But she wasn't properly alive. He reached for his mobile and quietly gave the address, ordered an ambulance.

Caroline—if it was Caroline Winterton—clung to the man's knees. 'No! No,' she pleaded. 'Don't let them! He can't send me away.'

Daniel bent closer over her, whispering, still gently stroking.

'Sir,' Z said shakenly, 'she's been here all the time. There is a cellar. It's blocked up from inside the house, but you get in from the inspection pit in the garage.'

'And that's where...? Dear God Almighty. *Eight years* he's kept her down there?'

He stared at them both, absorbed in each other. If Winterton was mad, what would his wife be after all this time?

Now Winterton became aware of him again and was trying to explain. 'At first it was all right because she fought me at every step, and that was what I needed. Every attempt at defiance justified me. She went out of her mind with anger, couldn't believe that this despised, uncomplaining husband who had fit in with her agenda could suddenly make demands of his own.

'No, that's wrong. I made no demands, I simply isolated her from the world that had made her what she'd become. And I withheld any close contact between us, any opportunity for retaliation.

'She had all she needed to be reasonably fed and sheltered. The choices were simple, she could eat or go hungry—and yes, for a while she did even try starving herself, but boredom beat her before it affected her health, and then meals became the highlight of her day. She could sleep or stay awake, submit or rage, break everything around her or make herself comfortable there, speak when I appeared at the hatch or ignore me. Those were her options. I never explained, never asked for anything. I supplied the means for her to live a perfectly hermetic life and discover herself. It was her forty days in the wilderness, but for her it took over three years.'

'Three—before she broke?'

'She began to change.'

'You broke her in, like a wild horse.'

'She started to turn back into what she was when I first knew and loved her, before the monster phase. And she became content. It was what she wanted. I was all she wanted.'

Yeadings, watching him, recognised the smile. He was at peace with what he had achieved.

'And this at risk of becoming a monster yourself.'

Winterton rested his gentle gaze on him. 'Do you think I was unaware of it? There was a later phase, when we both realised what was happening to us—that we had parallel roles. Holding her there made me as much a prisoner. I didn't dare go away, or be ill, or fail our routine in any way because her life depended on me. Symbiosis. It was something we suffered together. We began shyly, hesitantly, to talk, to hunt for the truth. It was a revelation.'

He seemed to stop there, as if the story was complete. Then he saw Yeadings was expecting more. He considered him. 'I know you once negotiated a hostage situation, Superintendent.'

'Some years back.'

'Yes. Well, in this case the time factor is unusual, longer even than the captivities in Beirut. It wasn't like that stupid business yesterday at the bank. That was a kind of clumsy accident. It had no place in our lives, except as a threat to force the wrong ending.'

In the silence Yeadings asked, 'You saw a parallel with the hostage-taking in Beirut?'

'Because our situation had meaning. It was a long instruction for us both. My prisoner began as alien to me, and I saw I had a principle to follow, no matter how long it might take. But I practised no humiliation or torture—beyond the denial of liberty. And I discovered that with the outer world excluded, there develops a unique intimacy between captor and captive. An affinity develops, an overwhelming need, a love. We reached a stage when we were no longer antagonists, but could respect both the symbiosis and each other's separateness.'

Yeadings seemed to relax a little, although he made no movement. 'And it was then you remembered that at some time you had once cared for each other enough to marry.'

'To choose to spend the rest of our lives together, yes. Perhaps I might claim that we rediscovered that love, but it wouldn't be quite true. We were involved in—obsessed by—something deeper and much more powerful, something spiritual, like a conversion, so that it had to continue for the salvation of us both. At last she—Caroline—had discovered motherhood. That is the only way I can describe it. Because by then *she* had broken *me*. I knew the obscenity of what I had done. I was the one she had to protect and comfort.'

Yeadings had closed his eyes at the pain in the man's face. Now when he opened them he saw the woman had turned and was kneeling. She held Winterton's two hands between her own.

'And that was the moment of nemesis,' the man said. 'You can't do a horrific thing like that without punishment.

So whatever justice, or God, there is, I have brought this penalty on us both.

'*Julie* has been taken away. *Our daughter* is a prisoner somewhere, and I can't trust whoever…'

He freed his hands to cover his face, rocking slowly backward and forward in grief. 'It is *my* fault. Perhaps I hadn't loved her enough, being so involved in this other secret life. Someone is doing to her what I…'

Or even worse, Yeadings thought.

Mott stirred impatiently beside him and Yeadings could sense waves of disgust coming off him. But there had to be as many witnesses as possible to what had been said. A male witness, because Z, as a modern woman, must have condemned the caveman action outright.

THEY HAD ALL MOVED INTO the sitting-room and Caroline now lay quietly on a sofa, her head in her husband's lap. There had been little conversation while they waited, Winterton seeming to accept that in this new phase he had no right of choice.

Or no need of choice? Yeadings wondered. The man had already achieved what he had set out to do. He appeared less apprehensive of their future than the woman, comforted by being with her, yet still with half his mind a prey to fears for little Julie.

Even in that he had seemingly surrendered responsibility to Yeadings ('This is the man who will find Julie for us.') What would become of these two if he failed them?

Almost silently the ambulance arrived, its blue light strobing through the room. Yeadings heard the paramedics' shoes crunching on gravel, then they were with them, looking for the injured.

Strictly, Yeadings knew, the two should be taken separately for taped interviews, but there were difficulties there.

Neither was on a quite normal plane mentally. It could be dangerous to part them, especially in the woman's case. She wasn't ready for exposure to strangers. All the while Winterton had been speaking she hadn't looked at anyone but her husband. It was as though Z, Mott and he didn't exist for her. When she recovered—if eventually she did—which Caroline would emerge, the new over-sensitised one or the other?

He nodded the paramedics outside and explained the needs were psychiatric. He would have to consult a professional on whether the woman was competent to be questioned or not.

'Meanwhile,' he warned, 'they must be kept together, at least until both have been assessed.'

While the paramedics radioed back for directions, Yeadings returned inside. No one had moved. He explained the arrangements he was making for them, still addressing only Winterton. Then he corrected himself and turned to Caroline. 'Do you understand?'

She seemed to shrink a little in facing him, but nodded. 'So long,' she said, 'as Daniel's with me.'

His two detectives left the house, Yeadings instructing Z to follow the ambulance and ring him when the Wintertons were settled in. He checked on windows and doors, locked up and pocketed the key.

Mott had strode past without a word, making for the double garage where both doors were already lifted. Winterton's Merc was missing and the inspection pit was exposed.

He hunkered to peer down at its timbered sides. It was stoutly lined with what looked like old railway sleepers and only lightly stained with oil droppings from the car.

Gingerly Mott eased himself in, crouched and explored the surfaces. A shadow fell over him and he looked up to see Z. She was stooping to pass him a plastic card. 'Winterton said there's a horizontal slot at the far end of the left side, between two timbers.'

Mott found it and thrust the card in. Silently the wall of the pit slid open for a distance of three feet or so. Beyond was a short flight of aluminium steps down to a lit passage.

He removed the plastic, and the steel shutter, lightly clad with timber, returned to its former position. Mott climbed out and used his mobile to ring Control, ordering a guard on the house, the site to be secured and SOCOs to examine the underground quarters.

When Mott reached the car, looking thunderous, Yeadings was already belted in the driving seat watching the ambulance pull away.

At last the DI found words to relieve his anger. 'The bastard! He'll plead diminished responsibility, spend a few months in his brother-in-law's holiday home for nutters and be free on the streets again. And still we don't know what he's done with the little girl.'

Yeadings looked across at him. 'You heard what he said about Julie. He has no more idea than we have where she is or who's got her.'

'The man's a psycho. He could have disposed of her and deny to himself that he's done it. Keeping anyone imprisoned down there for *eight years* isn't the action of anyone sane.'

'Certainly it takes some believing,' Yeadings said hollowly. He shifted in his seat uncomfortably. 'I once read of a husband in America who kept his wife locked up for almost thirty years. Maybe it happened in wild country and was as simple as chaining a dog to a kennel. But this is altogether different. Winterton planned it minutely over a period, rebuilt the house little by little to accommodate the crime, must have sound-proofed her quarters, saw to every intricate practical detail himself. Given the inhumane intention, such premeditation is nothing short of evil. And yet the man seems…'

'So what can we get him on?'

Yeadings sighed. 'Abduction, false imprisonment, waste of police time.' He put the car in gear. 'And what good will it do either of them if he's sent away for a long stretch?'

'What's sauce for the goose… Dammit, we thought he'd killed her. He might just as well. She's a complete mess.'

'And unhappy?'

'What d'you mean?'

'You saw her. Suppose when she's questioned she refuses to admit she was imprisoned, if she says she chose to stay down there?'

'She's not that crazy. You can't believe Winterton's word on that.'

'No doubt we'll see. But she's been this way for some years now, reconciled to whatever restricted life she'd made for herself, and dependent on mothering Winterton—or so he claims. And we did find her loose in the house. I think that lately she's been allowed the run of the place when no one was about. He's been gradually training her to face freedom. It was Caroline upstairs that evening when I called and something fell on the bedroom floor.'

'She could have been tied up and was trying to get in touch with you.'

'No. Everything went quiet after that, and she was able to get to the window to watch me leaving. I believe him. By then she was a willing hermit.'

'I'll never accept that.'

'I find it hard enough myself. But then nothing like this has ever happened to me.'

They drove on to the designated hospital where the Wintertons were to be held, and arranged for a WPC to remain on guard in the corridor. On her arrival, Mott returned with Z to base and Yeadings left for an emergency meeting with the ACC (Crime).

The latest news left the senior officer dismayed but clinging to the message he'd prepared for the interview: that lack of progress in the hunt for Julie didn't justify the costs already incurred over chasing wild geese. There was little kudos to be gained from claiming an old case was now solved, when it had been officially closed so long ago.

'There will be new charges, sir, and I believe the two cases are connected,' Yeadings insisted. 'If they're handled in the right way we could bust the Julie case within hours.'

'It can't be too soon. I want that house pulled to pieces if there's any chance the child's still hidden in it.'

That hadn't been what Yeadings had in mind, but one allows an Assistant Chief Constable the last word.

BY MORNING Z HAD JUST about come round to accepting what she'd witnessed. As the team gathered in Yeadings' office she leaned across to the old file open on his desk and lifted from it a glossy print of Caroline.

'She's paler, heavier and fleshier now, but her face has barely aged since Winterton gave you this photograph all that time ago. It seems impossible. You'd think there'd be more visible signs of what she's been through.'

Yeadings swung in his office chair and thumped with his fist on the desk so that the coffee mugs juddered. What sympathy he'd shown for the man on the previous evening had been overtaken by anger. 'He's broken her spirit, she's totally dominated. How much do you suppose she suffered before she got like that? She must have fought like a wildcat before she gave in.'

'She's a wildcat still when anyone tries to part them.

They tried that at the hospital. She's terrified of everyone but him, terrified of being helped. It's unbelievable.'

'Oh, believe it, Z. We've all heard how it happens. This is the Stockholm Syndrome, but taken to its limits. Jailer and prisoner inseparable. What a job for the shrinks. They'll be queueing from here to Adelaide to study the case and get out the first book on it.'

'Maybe,' Beaumont suggested, 'she's best left the way she is, as the tamed shrew. Let time sort her out. But what the hell will she do when we get Winterton put away for a long stretch for abduction and holding her by force? From what the SOCOs says she had every home comfort down there.'

Mott looked sour. 'Books and CDs, a selection of videos which Winterton considered proper for her, but no television in case it corrupted the new-version Caroline. There was even an exercise bike. And it seems she'd taken to making her own clothes as a hobby—no doubt his idea of occupational therapy. Do you call that home comforts for a one-time businesswoman?'

Yeadings grunted, ignoring the question. 'I received a message from him late last night. He wanted to talk, so I went out to the hospital and taped the conversation, with the WPC as witness. His wife was asleep in the same room, heavily sedated.'

Mott looked grim. 'What did he say?'

'He made a full confession of how he pulled off the snatch. He's a devious beggar. Barry Morgan was in it with him, well paid to sell out the woman he'd been stringing along. They arranged for Winterton to catch them together at Pollards Mount, the house which Morgan was supposedly showing to her as a Mrs McQueen, and where the two used to meet. Winterton acted the betrayed husband, waved an empty revolver and made Morgan tie Caroline up. Then the two men dumped her in the back of Winterton's hired car, which Morgan drove back to Long Gable, dropping Winterton off beforehand to pick up Morgan's car from the station in order to dispose of it before resuming his afternoon alibi. Are you with me this far?'

Beaumont was rubbing one side of his nose. 'But Caroline's car, sir. According to the case notes it was later stolen from a Heathrow car park. Winterton's story leaves it abandoned at Pollards Mount.'

'Temporarily, Sergeant. If you read the whole account, you'll recall that Morgan had ridden his bike to work that morning, claiming that his car had developed some fault. In fact it hadn't. The bike was one of the folding kind that stow away easily. Later, when he dropped Winterton off at the station to swop cars, he transferred it from his own Fiat to the hired car which he then returned and cycled back to Pollards Mount to drive off Caroline's BMW. Then, with her passport, luggage, the flight tickets, holiday bookings and the joint account passbook, he picked up the blonde stand-in, following Winterton's instructions.'

'How come nobody spotted the hole in Winterton's alibi?'

'Because he slipped back to his desk at the Colindale without anyone there checking how long he'd been at lunch. Why should they? All of them had their heads down reading.'

'And Morgan's car? Where did Winterton dump it?'

'An unremarkable one. He'd only to leave it in a London street with its keys in the ignition to be sure it would dispose of itself.'

Z nodded. 'So Barry Morgan was bought off? This explains how he could suddenly afford a luxury holiday in the Canaries. The man's totally heartless. As far as he knew, Caroline would be killed by her husband when he got back from London, and buried in the garden.'

'Ruthless and dangerous. He left Caroline trussed up and gagged in the locked garage as ordered, safe from observation from the nanny and the child who'd been sent off for the day.

'Our immediate task is to find him, because he could well be imitating the crime Winterton coached him so well in. I believe he's the one who's holding Julie, as backup to blackmail. He knows Winterton is a good source for cash. A damn sight more so after all this time, when he'd be feeling safe from investigation. Because, don't forget, Morgan will still think Caroline was murdered. It's important he should go on believing that, so I've ordered a clampdown on any information regarding last night's development. If he discovers she's still alive it makes a nonsense of his hold over Winterton. He may panic and do Julie some harm.'

'So where the hell is the man?' Beaumont demanded. 'Eight years. You can't have a colder trail than that. How could he stay unseen that long? He'll have changed his appearance. Maybe he's been living abroad.'

'He'd have to come back to pull off the Julie kidnap. Angus, I want a check on incomers at airports, ferry ports. See if he needed to renew his passport, and if so where and when. We know the earlier one was made out to Barry Morgan, but his correct forename is Lewis. He may have gone back to that. And there's his family in Gwent.

'Beaumont, get off to that address in Wales and start digging around. I don't need to tell you what to look for.'

Z glanced at her watch. 'Sir, I'd like to get back to the hospital. It could be that Caroline Winterton remembers something of Morgan's background. They were lovers before her husband bribed him to sell her out.'

'I doubt she'll talk to you, Z.'

'She will if Winterton persuades her. He's got everything to gain if Morgan really is our man.'

'Try it, but you may find the doctors will prevent you. And keep in touch. I may want you elsewhere in a hurry.'

Z ARRIVED AT THE PRIVATE suite to find it empty but for the uniformed woman constable who was sitting on the window-sill drinking coffee from a polystyrene beaker. The two single beds and the matching armchairs were empty.

'It's all right,' the policewoman said hurriedly. 'They're having a joint session with the shrink. He'll give me a buzz when it's over and I'll be escorting them back up here.'

'Right.' The psychiatrist had certainly moved in on the case pretty smartly. Z hoped Caroline wouldn't be put under such pressure that she'd clam up before Z could question her herself.

'Funny old mess-up,' the WPC commented. 'I suppose Daniel Winterton will go down for false imprisonment.'

'If the Prosecution Service accepts we have a valid case. There's little chance Caroline will give evidence against him as she is at present.'

'I thought we got his full confession. That must count.'

'Except that the way he tells it he used no force at all once Barry Morgan had bundled her into the house. He tells it like the Horse Whisperer—all done by kindness and trust. I imagine they've both got a convenient memory about the unhappy early stages.'

At least we can throw the book at Morgan once we've found him, Z thought with satisfaction. No court is going to feel much compassion over his part in it: accepting a massive bribe to trot his alternative blonde off to the Canaries on Caroline's passport, having emptied the joint account with Winterton's blessing and possibly coming back later to threaten the man he thought had pulled off his wife's murder. And then, according to the Boss, Morgan could also be responsible for Julie's disappearance.

FIFTEEN

Z LEFT THE SUITE TO GET COFFEE and a Danish, which she took back to the car. It could be a longish wait before Caroline was fit to face a second interview.

She sat listening to Thames Valley Radio's music and chat, only glancing up when two men returned to the car parked next to her own. From a back view the stockier of the two looked familiar. As he was clipping himself into the driving seat she caught his face in profile: square, pallid, fleshy. Clifford Hook, Caroline's brother.

The man with him was younger, lean and dark-skinned, an ethnic Asian, talking with rapid hand movements, palms uppermost, long thumbs jabbing outwards. He seemed to be protesting volubly.

Under present strictures Hook would have been denied access to his sister, so there was no call for him to be here. He wasn't a doctor, just the manager of a high security psychiatric unit. So did that mean that the man he'd brought with him was the shrink called in by—?

By whom? Who would have the authority to order examination of the Wintertons at this early stage? She was pretty certain Yeadings hadn't been a party to it. So was it the consultant here?

Or had the two men bluffed their way in, one with credible medical credentials and the other determined to see his sister whether it was officially sanctioned or not? In any case, how had they known where the Wintertons were being held, since the Boss had ordered a clampdown on information? Telephone tittle-tattle between staff at the two hospitals? That seemed possible, because the case must have aroused medical curiosity. Any leak could have started from here.

She flung open her door, but the other car was already drawing out of the gates. There was no point in following it. She could guess where they'd be returning. Better to get to the Wintertons and see what damage, if any, had been done. She gave a last glance back at the disappearing car, automatically memorising its number plate. A BMW, pale blue, several years old but well kept, and registered in Oxford.

Then a mental image flashed up: the angler Bingham cycling by a large pale blue car, empty and parked half hidden among the trees. From his description of the radiator grid she had identified it as a BMW. Bingham had claimed he saw the car at lunchtime on the day Julie disappeared.

Since Hook had been driving this one, it was more likely his than the other man's. She remembered there had been an earlier pale blue BMW too, owned by Caroline, stolen from an airport car park and written off in the joyriders' fatal crash. Maybe his sister's old model had so impressed Hook that he'd bought a similar one.

It was instantly clear to her who had snatched Julie. The Boss was on the wrong track imagining Morgan had come back. Hook was the one determined on avenging the sister he'd adored and whom he insisted Winterton had killed. And the disguised voice of the telephone threat fitted that belief better than a missing person like Morgan.

So what would Hook do, now his sister had reappeared alive? If he released the little girl, wouldn't she give him away? Uncle or not, the charge would still be abduction. He daren't let her loose, unless he'd kept his identity secret while he'd held her. And what had he done now to Winterton?

Z hared back into the hospital, evaded the clerk at reception and stabbed at the lift button. The indicator showed the lift stationary at the Winterton's floor. She stabbed again, ineffectually, then darted for the stairs. The receptionist was starting to phone, but called angrily after her: a replacement since Z had come in before.

Out of breath she reached the right landing just as the second wheelchair was being backed from the lift. Winterton looked bewildered, his wife almost insensible. The two porters swung round aggressively as Z appeared, but the WPC intervened. 'It's OK,' she shouted. 'She's one of us.'

A middle-aged woman in a white coat stepped out last from the lift. Her plastic name tag described her as J.G. Marshall, MD Psych.

'Are you responsible—?' she started in on Z.

'No, you are. Why did you let those two men in?'

'I should like your name, Officer.'

Z whipped out her warrant card, quoting it aloud while the woman groped for spectacles that hung from a gilt neck chain. Her voice was acid as she denied the men had had access to her patients. 'I left orders for sedation and complete bed rest without intervention. This the visitors tried to override, but I was informed in time and no direct contact was made,' she claimed stiffly.

'I'd like a word in private,' Z told her.

'Perhaps that would be as well.' She turned to the WPC. 'I repeat, *no one* except myself, Nurse Hennigan or her replacement is allowed inside their suite, whoever they claim to be. And no order will be given to transfer the patients elsewhere. Is that understood?' Then she gestured towards the lift, stood back and made room for Z.

The door of her ground-floor office stood open and papers scattered on the floor showed how instantly she had run out at the emergency call. Z recognised there was no room for criticism here. A closed-circuit video screen high on the wall opposite the desk showed a monochrome image of the Wintertons being helped back into bed.

'I'm sorry,' Z said. 'The fault wasn't yours, and I guess the receptionist allowed them in as medical personnel.'

'She won't again. Sergeant, were you involved in sending these patients here?'

'Yes. I was at their home when Mr Winterton produced his wife.'

'In which case I need a full account from you of what was done and said at that time.'

'So does my boss. You shall have a copy when I file my report. We wish to cooperate with you as much as I hope you will with us. But I have to ring in immediately, because I believe I have a lead to the kidnapped child. Unless I'm ordered elsewhere I'll be back immediately.'

From the car Z contacted Yeadings and described Hook's attempt to bring in his own specialist. Then as she put her point about the car she heard Mott's voice in the background quietly swearing.

'Leave it with us, Z,' the Boss told her. 'You're off duty now. Go and keep your lady shrink happy.'

Back in Dr Marshall's office the atmosphere had warmed. 'What do I call you?' she asked Z, smiling now. Z told her. 'No forename? And you let everyone abbreviate you to an initial?'

'It doesn't depersonalise me. We're a close team. My name's long and we take short cuts when we can.'

'Short, ah! So now will you have a short, or something longer?' She had unlocked cupboard doors to reveal a fitted drinks cabinet. Z surveyed the bottles and asked for a vermouth with lemonade and ice. 'Off duty,' Yeadings had said. He must have foresight.

'I'm Janice,' the doctor said, pouring herself a large single malt. 'I've finished for the day, thank heaven, and since you're accustomed to writing reports, you may help yourself to my keyboard, if you can stand me watching over your shoulder. Tell it how it happened, and I'll ask my questions at the end.'

THE HOUSE WAS IN DARKNESS apart from twin globe lights at the porch. Automatically Hook had headed for it, then realised he did not want to be trapped there trying to placate Aziz. Nor could he drop the man off now and expect him to walk back. He sat a moment staring at the house, feeling no fancy for returning to its cold shadows. He drove on past and took two right turns back to the staff car park at the main building. Aziz was still seething at having been drawn into a crass professional indiscretion.

'Leave it for now,' Hook pleaded. 'There's no great harm done, and I've more important worries.'

'Mr Hook, I am not happy at leaving it for now. There will be a formal complaint. Dr Marshall is a very senior lady and I have my professional reputation to consider. I had no idea that you had not been invited to take me along for a consultation. You deliberately misled me.'

Hook suppressed a groan. The man had fallen over himself to have a part in the case. True, it was a little irregular to rush in on his sister, but as her closest relative he should have been instantly informed of her arrival. It was one of the hospital porters who had phoned the news through, an ex-employee of Craythorpe Park keen for recognition.

It had shaken him. Caroline—alive, after all this time. He had thought at first it was some grotesque mistake. It must be her body that had been recovered.

But the man had been adamant. Mrs Caroline Winterton was listed as a patient. He had helped to carry her in.

It was incredible, wonderful, but appalling too. Of course he was anxious to see her and know what state that monster Winterton had left her in.

He finally summoned enough authority to rid himself of Aziz, went through to his office, turned on his desk lamp and pulled down the blinds at the Victorian bow window. A red light was flashing on the answerphone. He pressed to get the messages, and there were three: two from the tabloid press wanting his version of the patients' knife fight on the grounds, and the last from Griffiths at the Department of Health. He slumped in his chair and put his head in his hands. Trouble on every side.

He had sat unmoving for some time—he had no idea how long—when he heard a tap at his door. His arms were stiff as he tried to sit up. His assistant slid in.

'I saw the light from outside. Why aren't you at home? I turned up at eight and there was no one there.'

He'd forgotten. Tonight he'd planned a special meal for the two of them: duck pâté from Sainsbury's with rocket salad and hollandaise fillets of Scottish salmon with creamed potato, peas and baby carrots. Afterwards, a frozen tiramisu.

He'd never much bothered with food for himself; was prepared to use the canteen or have meals delivered from the hospital kitchens. But with a gourmet to entertain, it made it worthwhile. Grover's friendship had turned his whole life round.

'I guessed you must have forgotten. But where were you? I sat on the steps waiting for over half an hour, then went for a walk.' He sounded waspish, when what Hook needed then was to be comforted.

'Sit down, I've got...' Hook stared at him vaguely, unable to finish.

'Something's happened. Tell me.' Now the voice had changed, more wary. 'Maybe I can do something.'

'It's my sister. It's Caroline. She's turned up. After all this time, she's alive.'

There was a startled silence. 'Your sister's dead. We know that. You can't believe anything Winterton says. He killed her and disposed of the body, but the police couldn't prove it. The man's a vicious liar. He should be put away.'

'No, they...' He shook his head wearily, then looked up resentfully. 'Where were you when I needed you? I had this phone call to say she's in hospital, and Daniel too. The police are holding them both there. They're to be examined by a psychiatrist. So I took Aziz across to see her. I don't understand, but it seems...'

Grover was on his feet, the neat lizard face transformed with an unhealthy flush. His eyes seemed to bulge. 'Clifford, get a grip on yourself. This woman who says she's Caroline—what did she say?'

'We only glimpsed them, didn't get to talk to them. A doctor stopped us. It was embarrassing. No one was supposed to know she was there. The police wanted it suppressed. Listen, you have to find out what really happened. You told me Morgan said he'd—'

'Clifford, you're not well. Not well at all, old man. Let me run you back home. You'll be better in bed.'

'I'd not sleep. My mind's all churned up.'

'Then I'll get you some tablets to help, strong ones.'

Hook ignored him and ploughed doggedly on. 'Now Aziz says he'll be reprimanded for professional misconduct, and he blames me. Oh God, I've been stupid. But I had to see Caroline. I thought if he got through to see her

I could slip in with him. I never meant to make trouble for him.'

'Poor old Aziz. Tell you what. Scribble him a note. Just say how very sorry you are, it was all a mistake and you'd been misinformed. Do it now and you'll feel better. I'll slip it under his door and we'll sort it all tomorrow. You don't want him panicking and doing anything silly to drop you in it. Come on, old man, let's get you home. No great harm done, and once you've slept on it you'll find it will sort itself. Here, write on this and then I'll drive you back.'

YEADINGS TRIED TO CONTACT Chief Superintendent Harper for uniformed backup. Since the overtime expended on the bank raid Harper had decreed he must authorise anything further himself.

He was attending a cricket club dinner in Farnham Common and, accompanied by background stamping and ribald cheering, seemed to have difficulty in grasping what the CID man was saying over the phone. Eventually Yeadings was referred back to the night duty inspector. 'See to it yourself, Yeadings, there's a good fellow. You really don't need me coming in.'

Harper was right: he was not needed. Even useless. But Yeadings had thought he'd want a hand in the kidnapper's capture, even a word in a microphone if the press swarmed early.

'Was he…?' Mott began.

'"Tired and emotional," as it's said.' Yeadings threw the euphemism at him as they made their way out. Mott had grabbed what was to hand. With the engine running, a uniformed sergeant and constable waited in a marked car drawn up behind Yeadings' Rover. Three more were on standby.

Enough time had been lost already, Yeadings thought.

Thank God they hadn't the delay of getting a warrant, since the search was for a missing child.

Yeadings waved the patrol car ahead and, with blue light flashing and siren braying, they cut a swathe through the late evening traffic. In a bare twenty minutes they saw the mental hospital's roofs against the skyline.

Behind its high outer walls Craythorpe Park lay silent under a sliver of moon. At the gate lodge the night guard stared at the police car, barely noticed the warrant cards and looked grim at the mention of Hook's name. Then he opened up and started to ring through to announce them. Mott waved him off and accelerated away. 'Go left and then right at the far end,' the guard shouted after them.

Deep shadows from overhanging eaves patterned the grim stone of the older buildings. The newer, single-storey ones used for therapy and recreation were of yellow brick and grouped socially with trim lawns and garden beds between. Knee-high, white-painted signboards indicated the purpose of each.

Two hundred yards along the perimeter road they met the outer wall again, turned right and pulled up before a seventies double-fronted house with a sloping terrace and stone steps leading up to double doors. Twin globe lamps threw light over their maroon-gloss panels, but inside the house was in darkness.

Nobody answered their knocking. 'Guard the front,' Mott told the uniformed men. He ran to the rear and shaded his eyes to peer into the nearest window. With his ear against the glass he could make out a telephone faintly ringing indoors: the gate guard still trying to raise Hook.

'Deaf, lying low, or absent?' he grunted. Then with a silent prayer that he wasn't rousing the hornet's nest of a police complaints inquiry, he lifted an ornamental pot from its plinth, shook out its root-bound geraniums and shattered the nearest large pane. He climbed through and opened the front door to the others.

The ground floor appeared empty. No one answered their calls. In the kitchen prepared vegetables lay in a bowl of water on the work surface. Everything was neat and clean. It looked as if whoever kept house for Hook had left him to get his own supper. And he wasn't home to eat it.

Yeadings went through to the study and drew the heavy curtains before turning on the desk lamp. No need to advertise to Hook as he returned home that there were visitors waiting.

From upstairs Mott called urgently, 'Boss!'

Yeadings made for the staircase. Already he could hear his DI jabbing at his mobile. As he reached the dimly moonlit bedroom, Mott was barking out instructions, ordering an ambulance and SOCOs.

Dear God, not little Julie?

The hump in the bed was more substantial.

Hook's face was grey; no visible breathing. On the bedside cabinet stood an empty glass and two bottles. The larger bore a picture of a white horse and had a trace of whisky left in it. The small one, lifted by Mott in his handkerchief, was empty and bore the hospital's pharmacy label.

'How is he?' Yeadings demanded. His hand shot out to feel the neck for a pulse. 'He's alive. Let's get him breathing, then walk him.'

It wasn't until the paramedics arrived that the note was found. It had fallen to the floor and been kicked under the bed. Yeadings handed it to Mott. 'Handwritten and signed, but with no date. Just that he's sorry. He'd meant it for the best.'

'Sorry for trying to top himself? Or does it also cover taking Winterton's daughter to force him to confess what he'd done to Caroline?' Mott demanded. 'So where is Julie?'

But Yeadings, piling the discarded duvet back on the mattress, was unfolding some fabric that didn't match its checked pattern. A scrap of floral-printed voile. A child's summer dress.

'This was in the bed with him,' he said grimly. 'She has to be here in the house somewhere.'

DAWN WAS BREAKING BEFORE they called off the search. There was no other sign of the child. The cellar held nothing more than junk furniture, empty packing cases and several cartons of wine supplied by Oddbins. Few of the upstairs rooms were furnished and clearly the man lived here on his own. All walls sounded solid. The single outbuilding held only normal gardening equipment, a rope hammock and an old croquet set.

'We may have to wait until Hook's able to talk,' Yeadings told Mott. 'But meanwhile I want all inmates and staff kept indoors under observation and the grounds toothcombed.'

The ambulance could have taken the unconscious man to Wycombe General, but the intensive care unit there was over-loaded and, since there were doctors at Craythorpe Park accustomed to dealing with drug overdoses, the decision was made to keep him there, in isolation. Yeadings left him in his single ward, washed out, wired and tubed, already under chemical detox, with the outcome uncertain. A constable sat outside his door, ready to take a statement when, or if, he came round.

'It was a serious dose, but you got to him early,' the doctor in charge told him. 'We've washed him out but can't tell yet what tissue damage has been caused. The alcohol won't have helped, but it seems he didn't drink all that much. It can't have started as a full bottle.'

'And the chances?'

'Fifty-fifty. So we keep at it.'

WITH SO MUCH POLICE ACTIVITY now on the site it wasn't possible to prevent speculation. It was clear to everyone that a rigorous search was being undertaken and that the original centre for it had been the administrative manager's house.

The flashing blue lights and unaccustomed sounds had disturbed staff and patients. Yeadings, accepting a return lift to base by patrol car, looked back and saw clustered faces staring curiously down from the dormitory windows. He would have to put out some anodyne statement to prevent the spread of panic. Police uniforms could stir up bad memories for some of the offender inmates, many of whom would be shambling uncertainly along the borderline of sanity. Couldn't risk anyone throwing a wobbly. If he had to choose a venue for a delicate inquiry it would certainly not be a high-risk psychiatric hospital.

The sun had risen over the height of the outer wall, signalling the start of another humid day unrelieved by the storm that had gone before. Yeadings changed his mind about leaving, quitted the car at the gate lodge and started walking back to the main building, pressing out his home number on his mobile.

Sally answered and he felt a tightness in his throat at the sound of her slow, childish voice. He hadn't expected her to be up so early.

'It's Daddy, love. Sorry I wasn't home before you went to bed. Did you miss me?'

'Mummy said you were busy. I kissed her twice instead.'

'Good idea. Give her another from me. Is she there?'

'In the bathroom. Luke's been sick. It woke me up. I'll get her.'

He heard the metallic clank of the receiver put down on the hall table and Sally's slippers scuffing across the hall tiles. After half a minute Nan came on. 'I hope you found time for some breakfast. How about the little girl?'

Her priorities were not, perhaps, the same as his own: food could wait. 'We're still looking. Expect me when you see me, eh?'

'Right. Take care.'

Some wives, he reflected, clicking off, would demand chapter and verse, but Nan had been trained to emergencies. Luke's upset couldn't be serious: Nan was taking it in her stride. She knew how to keep her cool—and other people's. Now he hoped the nursing staff here would have learnt the same wardside manner.

His approach had been observed, and a grey-suited man was waiting for him at the open door of the main building. Of medium height, slim, dark, good-looking, with a rather diamond-shaped face, he would be some seven or eight years younger than Yeadings himself. His pale complexion contrasted dramatically with the black, collar-length hair and trimmed goatee beard. 'Superintendent Yeadings?' he queried. 'My name's Grover, Len Grover. I'm Mr Hook's assistant, covering in his absence. I understand he's receiving emergency treatment. Can you tell me how he is?'

'I'm not a medical man, Mr Grover, so I can't venture an opinion. Perhaps you would show me to his office?'

The man's manner was smooth. That and his penetrating dark eyes gave the policeman the impression of a Svengali. If he had said he was a doctor Yeadings would have guessed he went in for a spot of hypnotic sedation.

The office was close at hand. Once inside, Hook's assistant waved Yeadings towards the bay window and planted himself behind the paper-strewn desk.

'Have you begun working here this morning?'

Grover considered the question, looked at the open files before him and said, 'I was just about to start, but I can put myself at your disposal, Superintendent, if you need me.'

'I need the room, actually. If you require any of these files, will you leave me a list of which ones you've taken before you go?'

Grover rose hesitantly. 'I imagined you would want to question me about Mr Hook's state of mind. I must have been one of the last people to see him last night.'

So the man already guessed it was a suicide attempt. 'Were you both on duty together?'

'We need to hand over, you know.'

'At what time would this be?'

'Quite late. I had closed the office soon after six, as usual. After that one of us is on call for emergency decisions.'

Yeadings considered his manner a tad uppity, considering he had claimed to expect being questioned. 'How often is there any emergency which would merit your being disturbed?'

The man's mouth tightened. He was getting rattled because the right questions weren't coming. He wanted to gossip about his boss, not office routines.

'You understand, Mr Grover, that I need to get an insider's view of the place and how it runs.'

'Yes, of course, Superintendent. Perhaps I could explain what happened after I left. Mr Hook was on call last night, but I discovered he had left the hospital grounds. Wasn't available, I mean.'

'How did you discover this?'

'I'd been invited to dinner at his house, on site. I arrived to find the place in darkness, waited outside for over half an hour and assumed he had forgotten our arrangement. I checked the garage and saw one of his cars was gone.'

Grover was getting into his stride. This was the story he'd had ready to spill.

'You say ''one of his cars.'' He had another, then?'

'He has two. A three-year-old Nissan and an older BMW which he'd bought second-hand. He sometimes lends the older one to members of staff, so I wasn't really worried to see it gone. But I've noticed how absent-minded he's been of late, so I rang the gate lodge and was told he'd driven out some hour before, with one of our medical staff as a passenger.'

'Dr Aziz.'

'Yes, Superintendent. Naturally I found this disquieting, so I changed the rota board and put myself on call in his place.'

'A wise precaution.'

'When I stay over I use a bedroom in the building across the quadrangle, since normally I live outside the hospital. Perhaps because of the unusual circumstances I found it hard to sleep. I don't know what time it was when I got up for a drink of water. After midnight, I think. The moon was shining in through a gap in the curtains. When I went to shut it out I looked across here and saw a light on in this office. So I flung some clothes on and came across. Mr Hook was here in a distressed state.'

'What clothes did you put on? The suit you are now wearing?'

The quiet inquiry halted him. He looked startled, perhaps needled at the irrelevant interruption. 'No. I put on what I'd worn the day before. Shall I continue?'

'Please do. You say Mr Hook was distressed.'

'Extremely so. He told me that he had received information that his sister, whom he had believed dead, had suddenly reappeared and, together with her estranged husband, was in an Oxford private hospital under psychiatric care.'

'Wasn't Mr Hook relieved to hear she was still alive?'

'Utterly confused, incredulous, but he had decided to see for himself, taking Dr Aziz in the hope that he would be able to get to Mrs Winterton's bedside.'

'Did he succeed?'

Grover challenged Yeadings with a hard stare.

The superintendent nodded. 'Yes, this part of the story is familiar to me, but you're telling it well. Do please go on.'

'I only know what Mr Hook told me. It had made trouble for Dr Aziz, who was upset at unknowingly having overstepped professional etiquette.'

'He'd thought the request came from Mrs Winterton herself? Yes, I see. Mr Hook was being very open with you. He obviously has confidence in your discretion.'

There was a flicker in the dark eyes. 'I had the impression that he was talking partly to himself, but also to keep me at bay. It was as though—maybe I'm being fanciful, but it seemed that it wasn't just the Aziz thing or his own absence from duty that had really upset him. He was still willing to justify his actions there. But he was utterly frantic, desperate, as though he had done something much more serious and wished he could turn time back. He kept saying, ''My God! What have I done? I'm finished!'''

'You assumed that his distress was more for himself than for his sister?'

Grover hesitated. 'Both, I'd say. It was related in some way. He was furious with his brother-in-law. He said that imprisoning his wife all that time was evil and vicious.'

'Worse than the murder he'd previously accused him of?'

Grover frowned in concentration. 'He recalled something from way back, when Caroline had once been kept from playing tennis with a—a male friend. She'd complained, "This bloody, boring rain! Day after day, keeping us penned in. God, how I hate doing nothing!"'

'And Winterton had been there. He'd turned back from filling her glass and said, "Yes, it's your idea of hell, Caroline, isn't it? I must remember that."'

'Clifford said that even then it had sounded like a threat. It had stayed in his mind ever since.'

Yeadings considered this, drifting about the office, occasionally lifting some object, examining it and replacing it, while Grover sat silently watching. 'Do you believe Mr Hook disliked his brother-in-law enough to do violence to him?'

'Mr Hook isn't a violent person, Superintendent. But sometimes he gets desperate and acts wildly without thinking. Then someone has to cope with any unfortunate outcome.'

'Which you see as your role.'

'I do what I can. I have learnt to deal with patients who are stressed, and Mr Hook has been under colossal pressure for some time. Last night I tried to calm him, but he said he wanted to be left alone. I didn't like leaving him, but he insisted.'

Grover covered his eyes with one hand before he went on. 'From my window I watched the lights stay on here for another twenty minutes. But he didn't leave the building at once. I waited until at last he came out by the front door and went stumbling off on foot towards his car. I assumed he would return to his own house.

'Then, this morning, I found there were keys missing from inside the safe here.'

'We found two sets in his pockets.'

'They would be his own private keys and the top-security set. I believe he'd used the second set to open the pharmacy drugs cupboard, because this morning the dispenser found its steel door left unlocked and a bottle of sleeping tablets missing.'

SIXTEEN

YEADINGS MET UP WITH HIS DI in a small side office which Grover had offered for police business. There he relayed to him the conversation with Hook's assistant.

It was essential to get the unconscious man to talk as soon as he came round, but meanwhile the search of the entire hospital complex had to be completed.

'If Julie's still alive,' Mott said, 'though with Hook's suicide attempt it seems unlikely she is, he'd have kept her somewhere close, to have access for feeding her.'

A police van had arrived with a complement of uniformed officers for the general search, followed closely by a dog van with handlers and two German shepherds on leashes. There were so many buildings, some of the older ones unused, closed off and waiting for demolition, that anywhere that the patients and staff did not regularly penetrate must be considered possible places in which Julie might be imprisoned.

Mott's first move had been to check each of the keys from the two sets found in Hook's clothing and match them to known locks. When that was done all keys were accounted for. It was chilling. Either Hook had another key hidden or Julie could be put away more permanently.

Two spades, among the tools in his garden shed, were bagged for Forensics. Both were suspiciously clean and gleaming, but the shafts bore a dozen or more smudged and overlapping marks from hands.

Yeadings, having returned to the management office, consulted the duty register and discovered that according to initialled entries, Hook had been on duty at the hospital over the period when Julie was thought to have disappeared.

Not that this was a hard-standing alibi, in view of the man's dereliction of the evening before. He could have made a habit of expecting Grover to take over during his irregular absences. Yeadings looked up the gate guard for the midday shift on the day in question, searched the database for the man's particulars, found he was currently off-duty and set off to interview him at his home in the village.

The man's name was Protheroe, a wizened monkey of a man whom he found in rolled shirtsleeves and braces turning over a potato plot in his back garden. He moved towards a teak bench, produced a tin of tobacco, pipe and matches and set about the slow, calm lighting-up ritual which Yeadings had so often in his smoking days used to get a suspect gibbering on the edge of his seat.

The entrancing scent of latakia and moist shredded leaf floated out in a blue haze, mixing with the hint of a familiar perfume from a line of fresh washing blowing above their heads. Without a pipe of his own to fondle, Yeadings' big hands hung down uselessly between his knees as he sat perspiring gently in the hot sunshine. Disciplining himself to slow down to the man's calm pace, he suggested amiably, 'I guess you get to know everyone going in and out of the hospital grounds.'

'Know who they are, right enough. Can't say as I exackerly *know* them.'

'Recognise them, and their cars?'

'Those that belong there, yus. Get to reckernise quite a lot of visitors too, the regulars. Newcomers, strangers— well, I give them a good looking-over.'

'Suppose someone unexpected is driving a car that's familiar?'

'Happens now'n again.'

'Do you just let them through?'

'There's two things, see. The car, you reckernise that first. Then, close up, you look to see who's driving it. I talk to everyone, coming or going, make sure they answer me back. Gives them a chance to warn me if anything's wrong. Wink at me, like, or cross their eyes. Then I'd poke about in the back, see if anyone's hiding under a rug or something.'

'Has that happened?'

'Twice,' Protheroe said calmly. 'One stowaway had a knife. The other had some copper piping with dry bloodstains on it. If I let any of the patients get by me without the proper pass I could lose my job. And it's a good one.' He waved his pipe to include his garden and the little brick semi. 'This all belongs to the hospital. I know when I'm lucky. And who wants dangerous nutters let loose outside?'

Yeadings rumbled appreciatively. This man was thorough. He would make a good witness. 'Do you keep a log on who goes in and out?'

'We have to. But I remember as well. You can check me against the book any time over the last week or ten days.'

'That's quite an accomplishment. I want you to take your mind back...'

And the result was negative. According to Protheroe, not only had Hook not left the grounds at all on the day Julie went missing, but the BMW had also not gone through.

'You're quite sure?' Yeadings insisted.

'I told you. You can check with the book. I can't speak for others on other shifts, but that car hasn't gone out or come in for over a fortnight while I was on gate duty.'

Yeadings thanked the man, admired the sturdy feathered tops of his rows of carrots and took his leave. Driving back he speculated on Hook's leaving the car elsewhere and going out on foot at the required time. Even then he'd probably be noticed by Protheroe, unless he'd left very early. But surely during the daytime there had to be someone senior left in charge of the management office? If not Hook, then Grover.

He drove back and ran Hook's assistant to earth in the staff canteen. His memory wasn't as immediate as the guard's.

'Not to worry,' Yeadings said bluffly. There was more than one way of skinning a rabbit. He could use the keys he'd lifted at Hook's house to let himself back into the office and consult the daybook.

On arriving there, however, he found two female assistants at work. And the daybook exonerated Hook entirely. Not only had he made several entries over the morning in question, but he had remained on duty over lunchtime to escort a patient's widow to the mortuary for identification. Yeadings was satisfied; you don't go arguing with a silent witness. A corpse has authority of its own.

'So,' Mott said gloomily when he was told, 'we're on a hiding to nothing with Hook as the kidnapper. I really thought we were going to clear up on this. It looks like a simple stress-related attempt to kill himself, and thank God he didn't mention police harassment in his final note, or I'd be facing an official complaint from his family.'

'He hasn't any family that we know of. But if the car the angler saw wasn't Hook's BMW, there has to be another pale blue saloon car locally that we haven't traced. Not that it was necessarily connected with the kidnap. And with Hook eliminated we're right back to square one.'

'Bang goes our only suspect left,' said Mott sourly. 'But

I don't see how he got his hands on that dress of Julie's. I still don't want to call off the search here.'

'No,' Yeadings said sharply.

'No?'

'No.' He didn't know why he was so sure about that. If Hook was out of the frame then what reason remained to suppose Julie could be hidden somewhere in the hospital grounds?

'Of course,' he considered, 'it could be the same BMW, and someone had borrowed it.'

Not every guard on gate duty would be as scrupulous as Protheroe. But Mott had been wrong about something, which made Yeadings hesitate, thinking of babies being let out with the bathwater.

Mott was waiting.

'He wasn't our only suspect,' Yeadings reminded him slowly.

'Not still thinking of Barry Morgan?'

'Why not? Who else do we know of who's personally linked in any way to the Wintertons? Suppose the sighted car actually was a BMW almost identical to Caroline's. Morgan would remember the original. Julie might, too. I saw enough photographs of her with it in those old albums Winterton showed me. Suppose Morgan got hold of a car like that and Julie somehow got to see it, still dreaming her mummy would turn up one day.'

'And Morgan the voice on the phone threatening Winterton before demanding the big pay-off? But Boss, there's been no trace of him. He could be in Adelaide or Timbuktu. We don't even know he's still alive.'

'Back to my office,' Yeadings ordered. 'I've some long-distance calls to make.'

Before contacting the Newport, Gwent, police station again, Yeadings put through a call to Z's mobile and

learned that there were no developments with the Wintertons, and that, for the present, police questioning had been
completely banned by the shrink in charge.

When Yeadings did get the Welsh number he learned
that Beaumont had made good time down the M4 and was
brought to the phone. 'What have you got?' Yeadings demanded of him.

'What you asked for—his job inquiries. It seems he'd
blown most of his money bumming round Morocco and
needed to get a job of some kind. There was nothing for
him locally, but according to a mate here he'd applied to
for a reference, he'd gone across to Northern Ireland,
wanted to train as a nursing auxiliary in Belfast. Which it
seems he did—until he broke his collarbone in a crash in
a friend's car. Which brought him home briefly to Mummy.
He was patched up, went off again and there's been dead
silence ever since.'

'That's the first time we've had any mention of a friend.
Till now he's seemed a loner—unless the friend was female.'

'This buddy was Senior Charge Nurse at the same hospital. Local plods there broke the news directly by phone
to the Morgan family. I'll fax you all details when I've
traced the *Belfast Telegraph* write-up.'

'Good. Let's hope he's still employed in the same sort
of job. With all the data available we should be able to
trace him at some hospital in the UK. Aim to get back here
tomorrow, but meanwhile sniff out anything else that's going and fax it.'

Yeadings turned to Mott. 'I'm off home now and I suggest you do the same while everything's quiet. Get some
rest. I've a feeling it's all going to blow up soon, maybe
when the Wintertons have had time to pull themselves together. Till then it's the waiting game, and I need to think.'

He arrived home to find Nan baking in a kitchen over-heated despite open doors and a whirring fan. He could hear the children distantly shouting in the garden.

'Why pick such a steamy day for all this?' he asked his wife, kissing a floury cheek as he squeezed past from the fridge with an iced juice.

She stopped rolling pastry and stared back at him. 'Your fault. Sally felt let down when we had to cancel Z and Max Harris yesterday. I'd promised she could stay up and have half an hour with them. So, as penance, I told her to invite some friends.

'We've got a children's tea party at four thirty. Fun and games, sandwiches, tartlets, cakes, jellies and competitions. If you don't want to chicken out I'd be glad of some help with the garden treasure hunt. You'll find prizes and clues in that basket over there, together with a map of where to plant things.'

'Great,' Yeadings told her, 'provided I can snatch an hour's kip first. I'm dying on my feet. And Sally can have her Z. I'll order a replacement to cover the Wintertons. She's still in Oxford at their hospital.'

'Wintertons—plural? Hospital? So you did get young Julie back?'

It startled him that so much had happened since he'd last been in touch with Nan. 'No,' he said curtly. 'Julie's not found, but the long-lost wife is. I'll explain when I've sorted a few things.' He was aware of leaving Nan staring, open-mouthed.

He rang base and found that Mott was still in the office, able to switch the duties to free Z.

'Your fax is through from Beaumont,' Mott told him, 'but I don't see that it gives us any lead. Just what he said on the phone. Except that Morgan's friend was the driver in the traffic accident and got killed outright. I'll leave a copy on your desk.'

'Fine. Now get home when you've sent Z here. We need her this afternoon for a children's party.'

He checked on Sally and Luke, then went into the downstairs shower room to rid himself of his professional life.

With a stream of cooling water over his upturned face it should have been easy, but images continued to flash on the screen of his closed eyelids: Hook's ashen face, the homely guard working at his potato patch, the pale blue BMW, the double set of keys, the drugs cupboard left open, the pale blue BMW. And yet again the pale blue BMW. The damn thing's image wouldn't wash off him. So why?

Because—but for Hook being in the clear—it would have fitted in so beautifully. His pale blue BMW parked where it would be just visible from some point in Winterton's garden. Where it could be pointed out to Julie by someone coming to the open front door— 'Look, your mummy's car. She wants to talk to you.'

He could almost see the little girl in the passenger seat, excited at the promise that she would see her mother at journey's end. And the driver beside her ought to have been Hook. She might have accepted a lift with him, her mother's brother.

Nobody else fitted the bill, but Hook couldn't have been there, couldn't be in two places at once. So either they had the time wrong or the car. Perhaps both.

Their only other suspect was the elusive Barry Morgan. Three-year-old Julie had known him, one of the pair who rented the end cottage, so, despite the passage of time, not strictly a stranger. There were even photographs including him and Peg Harbury in the albums Julie had access to. Aged eleven she could have accepted him as a special friend of her mother's, if she'd ever seen the two of them together.

Barry was another element, like the pale blue BMW, which would have fitted so well. Except that no one had seen him in the locality since the day Winterton had paid him to run off to Lanzarote while Caroline was holed up in the newly completed cellar.

But it had to be Barry. He alone knew that Winterton's account of Caroline's desertion was an invention. And since she had never reappeared until now, he would have supposed Winterton had murdered her and hidden the body, so making him an ideal subject for blackmail.

But Hook too, had been convinced that Caroline was murdered. Was it possible Morgan had got in contact with him and given him that idea, admitting that the blond woman he'd eloped with was someone else?

The idea was so startling it had Yeadings stumbling out of the shower and groping for a towel. With it precariously tucked under his armpits, and still streaming water, he ran back and grabbed the kitchen phone.

He still wasn't sure how far his reasoning had taken him as he again stabbed out the number of Mott's mobile, but he knew the need was immediate.

Barry a nurse, and Hook running a hospital; Hook's older car—the BMW—sometimes on loan to members of staff!

Barry Morgan had to be *there,* in touch with Hook. Even working with him? Or using a middle-man—the so-helpful assistant who'd been moved sideways from nursing to management? He would have been off duty when Hook was on, could have borrowed the car, fitted Hook up, not realising the office daybook would give Hook an alibi—or, over-confident, not believing the police would ever consult it. He should have removed the page: it would have been assumed that Hook had done so, covering himself.

And something about Hook's suicide attempt had been niggling at Yeadings. It was over-elaborate. Hook had had no need to take drugs from the hospital pharmacy, with all those of his dead wife's still in his medicine chest at home. Grover had drawn attention to the drugs cupboard left open, and he could have unlocked it as easily himself.

Mott came on the line. There were traffic noises in the background. He was taking the call while driving home.

'Angus, why the hell didn't we check out all the Craythorpe Park personnel files for Barry Morgan?'

'We did. He wasn't there, Boss. I covered all the male nurses myself.'

'And management?'

'There weren't any files on them.'

'You mean you weren't offered any. They have to exist. That assistant of Hook's—Len Grover...'

'*Who?*' Mott swore. There was a sound of tyres shrieking on a metalled surface and a blast of hooting.

Yeadings waited, hearing his own heartbeat suddenly loud, feeling his bath towel slipping.

Sally was there beside her mother, rolling out a remnant of pastry, her eyes on him huge with amazement. Yeadings seized two ends of the fluffy cotton and made a half-knot on one hip.

'Boss.' It was Mott, sounding calmer but breathing hard. 'That was the name came through on the fax. Len Grover was Morgan's friend in Northern Ireland, killed in the car crash. I saw Hook's assistant at Craythorpe Park but never heard his name.

'Look, I'm turning. Can you have a patrol car meet me at Craythorpe? The search team have gone home. We need to protect Hook. He's been set up. Someone put that child's dress in his bed and doped the man. If he pegs out Grover will feel safe enough, but if there's any chance of Hook recovering…'

'Sh—' hissed Yeadings and swiftly changed it to, 'Sugar!' Nan and Sally leapt back as he swept by, one arm extended for whatever clothes might come to hand.

As he braked his Rover by the doors to Craythorpe Park Hospital, Mott's Saab screeched up behind. They both raced inside. The management office was empty but for a female clerk fussing with a potted hibiscus.

'Grover?' Mott demanded. She was struck speechless.

'Where's Hook been taken? Show me. Is he still here?'

She came alive then, brushing past them and waving for them to follow. The hall lift failed to respond. The indicator showed it lodged at the second floor.

'Unloading,' the girl supposed. The two men hared for the stairs with her close on their heels. 'Second floor,' she panted.

Hook had a small room to himself, hooked up to an IV drip of some clear fluid. A catheter line ran from the bed down to floor level and entered a plastic bag of strangely vivid urine. On the wall behind was a whiteboard with scrawled readings of his quarter-hourly test results. This was a place well accustomed to emergency detox.

The man tapping the drip feed had his back turned but at their hurried approach his head swung round, the dark, goatee beard brushing the white coat.

Mott threw himself at him in a rugby tackle as Yeadings flew at the unconscious man's wrist and tore the IV needle from its straps. There was a glassy tinkle as a syringe fell to the floor and rolled under the bed.

Grover—Morgan—whoever—had gone down hard, his head catching the IV stand and taking it with him. Mott knelt ungently on him, forcing his arms back. 'Lewis Morgan,' he said between gritted teeth, 'I am arresting you for

the attempted murder of Clifford Hook. You have a right
to remain silent, but...'

He didn't. And his language wasn't refined.

A MALE NURSE DRESSED THE CUT on the arrested man's
cheek and forehead. Yeadings had dispatched Mott downstairs, as much to cool his temper as to await the police
escort. He appeared calm enough himself but his voice was
steely as he offered the injured man the options.

'We know you have the girl. I don't have to labour the
point that if she is found alive and well things will be less
hard for you in the long run. Every minute that passes from
now on you may regard as adding a year to your final
sentence. Now, where is she?'

'I don't know what you're talking about. What girl?'
Grover spat out.

'It's adding up all the time,' Yeadings assured him. 'And
we have the whole book to throw at you. Apart from the
syringe with which you attempted to finish Hook off,
there's your telephone call to Winterton on tape. And I'm
sure we can turn up your forged application for a vacancy
here in the name of your friend killed in the car crash.

'How is your collarbone, by the way? Must be well
mended for you to hump a lively little eleven-year-old
around. It's only a matter of time before we find her. But,
as I mentioned, time's something that's as little on your
side as hers, so...'

Morgan groaned. 'I never used force. She came willingly. She recognised my voice.'

'Save your explanations for the tapes. Then you'll be in
the capable hands of Inspector Mott. For myself I have a
prior engagement.'

'I didn't hurt her. You wanted to know where she is.'

'Right.' Yeadings drew a breath of relief. 'Come and show us, then.'

Two patrol cars were now behind Mott's, and one of the four constables inside was a woman. The DI nodded her back into the second car, pressing the handcuffed prisoner into the rear of the front one. He slid in beside him.

Following Morgan's directions, they circled the central lawn, turning off towards a cluster of old buildings on the hospital's perimeter. They had been among the first examined and the search had drawn a blank.

'Turn off here,' Morgan said as they drove past, then muttered something under his breath.

'What's that?' Mott demanded.

'It's not my fault she wouldn't eat, bloody kid.' Morgan almost shouted it.

Gutsy, the way her mother had started off, the DI thought. How long would it have taken to break her down?

The road ran alongside a wilderness of knee-high grass with four or five straggling fruit trees long grown wild, the remains of an orchard which reminded Yeadings of the ancient apple tree of Julie's secret cache.

There were tracks through the long grass, and flattened patches where patients free to roam had set up little camps, as children do.

'The Wilderness,' Morgan said. 'We have to get out and walk through.'

He led them by one of the tracks to a small prefabricated hut that had a single square window with cracked panes and a padlocked wooden door. It had already been searched.

'Key's round my neck,' he muttered, and Mott groped to pull it out on a cord.

'A bit risky, wasn't it? Anyone could break in.'

'Not after the row Hook made about the window getting

cracked. Put the fear of God into the patients. He wanted the place cleared for a cricket pitch and to use the hut as a pavilion. More waste of money, so the board got the plans shelved.'

Morgan wasn't playing dumb anymore. A reaction had set in and the words were tumbling out almost euphorically. If his wrists hadn't been cuffed he would have waved them in.

The place was empty but for an old motorised mowing machine, two used oil barrels and corner cobwebs. Morgan nodded at the mower. 'Underneath.'

They pushed it across towards the window. The exposed floor showed the cracks of a square trapdoor. There was no bolt or hinge, so one of the constables prised the lid off with a screwdriver lying nearby. It lifted away leaving a dim cavity barely eighteen inches high between floor and flattened soil. There was an acrid smell of musty hay, sweat, urine and human faeces.

'Filthy little cow,' Morgan spat at her.

The hole wasn't entirely dark, they saw now, because of cracks in the boarding of the hut's walls, and where light showed there was some movement of air. Yeadings leaned over and made out the pale shape of something close-wrapped in canvas like a karate suit. Only it was worse. He hadn't seen one of these since a prisoner had gone berserk a few years back and the medics had had to restrain him.

'Get her out,' he ordered.

It was difficult because of the cramped space. The child seemed barely awake, and when the ties of the straitjacket were undone her arms stayed set stiffly in the same restricted position. Packing tape covered her mouth and continued right round over her long blond hair. However carefully done, getting it off was going to hurt.

'Bastard! Bastard,' Mott ground out, turning on the man, fists balled. 'A child. What did she ever do to you?'

Morgan was cowering against the hut wall. 'She bit me, the little cow! *She drew blood!*'

'I'M GLAD I WASN'T THERE,' Z said sombrely as the details were allowed out after the children's party. Mott had just joined them on the patio for drinks, after booking Grover in and reporting upstairs.

'Explain to me,' Nan begged. 'Surely Hook recognised Morgan when he came back as Grover? It was only eight years later, after all.'

'He must have changed a lot,' Mott said. 'Morgan had been blue-eyed and clean-shaven with fair hair, according to his original description. So he disguised himself by growing a beard, dyeing it and his hair black, and wearing dark-coloured lenses. The real Grover had been an Australian and Morgan occasionally produced a convincing hint of "strine." The rest was due to ageing. Quite a good disguise job, I'd say. Anyway, it's not clear whether Hook ever saw Morgan up close when he used to visit his sister.'

'But Julie recognised him?'

'He said it was his voice. She's a very musical child. Also he'd removed his lenses, so his eyes were the same. He asked her how she liked his new beard. And after eight years she wouldn't have been very clear about his hair.'

'Anyway, we got him,' Mott said with satisfaction.

'It's not,' Yeadings reflected sadly, 'a case of all's well that ends well. The three Wintertons are reunited, but for how long and in what condition?'

'Our part of the job was fine,' Mott insisted. 'We've got Morgan for what he did to little Julie, and that's all we're responsible for. Now we've got to present it as a watertight case. The rest is up to Crown Prosecution. And the shrinks.'

'Not to mention the judge,' Z offered. 'Whoever deals with Morgan can't be too tough on him for my liking, but Daniel Winterton's something else. What he did was appalling, but he sees it as the lesser evil. As a writer he's used to bending the plot, ensuring a happy ending. Maybe he believed that if he intervened there could be one.'

'Not at the beginning,' Mott declared grimly. 'What he wanted was revenge on an unfaithful wife. He's deceived himself into thinking he had a Greek god's right to manipulate his human puppets.'

'Or,' Nan Yeadings suggested gently, 'he deceived himself into thinking he wanted vengeance, and simply couldn't bear to lose her. In which case, given time, and once they're sorted, they could all survive together.'

Yeadings rose and stretched. 'Whatever,' he said. 'Apart from the paperwork, it's up to others. And right now out in the dark you can bet that the day's heat has run someone ragged. There'll be plenty more to keep us busy tomorrow.'

FOLLOW

T H E

MURDER

CATHERINE DAIN

A FAITH CASSIDY MYSTERY

Psychotherapist Faith Cassidy believes her new client Natalie is simply working through her anger when she talks about killing her husband. However, when Natalie is charged with murder, Faith is stunned, especially since she may be sued for negligence.

Faith knows the only way to save her client *and* her career is to find out who killed Natalie's husband. Ignoring threatening phone calls, the sudden demise of one of Craig's cronies and the murder of his former girlfriend, Faith tries to sort out the dirty dealings and dangerous games—where following a murder leads to a date with a killer.

**"Faith is a strong and gutsy heroine whose flaws
make her even more likeable."
—*Booklist***

Available September 2003 at your favorite retail outlet.

WORLDWIDE LIBRARY®

WCD468

DESERT

BETTY WEBB

NOIR

A LENA JONES MYSTERY

Clarice Kobe is found beaten to death and her ex-husband is the prime suspect. Lena Jones thinks there's more to the murder of her neighbor. Knowing Clarice had a darker side, Lena follows her suspicions to a deadly showdown.

Lena's search for Clarice's killer leads her into a depraved world where love and hate are interchangeable. As she closes in on a killer, she will be forced to make a final choice between acceptance and fear, between life and death, between leaving this world...or embracing it.

"A must read for any fan of the modern female PI novel."
—Publishers Weekly

Available October 2003 at your favorite retail outlet.

CROOKS, CRIMES AND CHRISTMAS

FOUR FESTIVE TALES OF FOUL PLAY...
WITH ALL THE TRIMMINGS

A WAY TO THE MANGER — SUSAN SLATER

A local teen is missing and Ben Pecos begins to piece together some disturbing facts. The girl harbors a dark and painful secret that puts her on a collision course with a ring of human predators.

THE SANTA CLAUS MURDERS — ED GORMAN

Sam McCain stumbles over a dead Santa at a Black River Falls Christmas party. Sam begins to look for answers, and finds deception, blackmail... and a second body....

WHAT CHILD IS THIS — IRENE MARCUSE

Christmas morning Anita Servi goes out to buy bagels—and comes home with a baby boy. Anita investigates the mystery of his mother's murder.

THE GOLD BAND — MICHAEL JAHN

When Bill Donovan finds a gold ring inside a Christmas goose, his investigation leads to the kind of mayhem that promises a holiday to remember.

Available November 2003 at your favorite retail outlet.

WORLDWIDE LIBRARY®

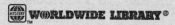

The Hydrogen Murder

Camille Minichino

A Gloria Lamerino Mystery

Gloria Lamerino is called in to investigate the murder of her former colleague, physicist Eric Bensen. Her understanding of Bensen's breakthrough research on hydrogen convinces detective and almost-beau Matt Gennaro that this is a high-stakes crime with no shortage of suspects.

Bensen's research has enormous potential for big business. Gloria is determined to expose the data tampering, deception and fraud by members of Bensen's team. When the person with the most to gain from Bensen's death is murdered, as well, it takes her most brilliant analytical skills to identify a killer.

"...a stunning debut..."
—Janet Evanovich

Available September 2003 at your favorite retail outlet.

🌐 **W(●)RLDWIDE LIBRARY** ®

WCM467